Diminished Responsibility

By Karen J. Kincy

Cheryl,
Best Wishes
KJKincy

ISBN 1448637732
EAN-13 9781448637737

For Rick, my partner in life

And Diane my partner in crime

Special thanks to Suzy, Gloria & Mary

Chapter 1

Modesto, CA 1981

When Marissa Van Horn awoke, nearly everything in her young body hurt. The ropes that bound her hands and feet were biting into her flesh. Her right hip hurt from lying too long on the hard dirt floor. Her arms were numb from her shoulders down, the result of having her hands tied behind her back. A musty smell permeated the air, adding to the already claustrophobic atmosphere. She wasn't sure where she was, but from what she could see it appeared to be an old cellar. A single bulb hanging from a frayed wire was suspended from the ceiling, giving the room an eerie yellow tint. A wooden work bench, withered from years of use, stood against the wall. Hanging above the bench was an assortment of household tools--a corroded wrench, rusted screwdrivers, a chisel set, hammers, an ax; things that had clearly been abandoned by their owner. Next to the bench, a set of metal shelves stored old paint cans, motor oil, soiled rags and several large jars of fruit preserves covered in layers of dust and cobwebs. On the opposite wall was her only escape route; stairs leading up to a point out of her line of vision, fading into darkness.

In the dark corner across the room was a girl with an all too familiar shape lying on floor, facing away from her. Marissa tried calling out to her, but her throat was dry, leaving her voice small and weak. No one answered. She struggled to get up, rolling over onto her stomach, curling her knees into herself as much as possible. She fought to gain balance as she used her head to push her torso backwards. Just as she was able to roll onto her knees, she heard a crushing sound, followed by a blinding pain in her head. Then everything went black.

Several hours later Marissa awoke, to the sounds of pleading sobs and cries of pain bleeding through her foggy consciousness. There was a dull ache in her head, her brain was fuzzy and she felt slightly nauseated. As the sobs grew louder, she forced her eyes open, but everything was a blur. Something was telling her she needed to focus, to get away and get help. She tried to get up, but found that this time he had tied her feet to one of the cellar's concrete footings. The movement of shadows across the room had her attention and yet the harder she tried to comprehend what was happening, the immense pounding of her head made it difficult to make sense of it all. There was something sharp and shiny, occasionally catching a glint of light in the dimly lit space. Then the girl turned her head towards Marissa. She could read the fear on the face that could have been her own reflection. 'I'm sorry' Jeanette mouthed to her before turning away. She could hear her sister's pleading voice ragged and fearful, "Please, no more, leave me alone, I promise, I'll do whatever you want," followed by more screams and then sobbing.

Jeanette was lying on the floor on her back. He was kneeling over her, saying things into her ear that Marissa couldn't hear. Jeannette didn't seem to be restrained in any way. Marissa wanted her to fight back, push him… kick him. Just do something. Anything. But Jeanette didn't. Marissa could see that her sister had accepted defeat. She was enraged; she needed to help Jeannette. She tried once more to pull against her restraints but to no avail.

Then there was the other voice; the one that sent a chill through to her very core. His voice was too calm and controlled. "Don't worry, we're almost done, just a little bit more," like he was trying to reassure them that what he was doing was necessary.

"Almost your turn, Marissa. Don't worry, I haven't forgotten about you," he said, never taking his eyes off his work.

"Fetch, leave her alone, you know I'm the one that you want!" Marissa called out.

"Don't you call me Fetch! I hate that name!" boomed the voice, which was now losing some of its composure.

"L-let M-marissa go," Jeanette begged.

"Let Marissa go? Jeannette, honey, you can blame this all on your bitch sister over there. She's the reason we're all here! If she'd given me what I wanted we wouldn't be here right now. She treated me like I was nothin'. Man, I'm tired of girls like you who think you're better than me."

Marissa knew she needed to get him away from her sister.

"Fe-Mitch, we don't need Jeanette here. I know you don't want to hurt her."

"Shut up! What do you know about me?"

"I know it's me you're after. C'mon Mitch. Wouldn't you rather it was just the two of us? Like the night we went out, remember?"

"What I remember is that you were a tease. Going out with me was just a joke to you. I bet you and your sister here had a good laugh."

"No, Mitch, that's not true. You were very sweet to help with all those decorations for prom, so when you asked me out I said yes." Marissa's mind was racing. If she could keep Mitch talking long enough, maybe she could figure a way out of this.

"You said you wanted to thank me."

"That's right."

"You said you owed me. But when it was time to pay up, you said no. And then you told everyone at school."

"Mitch, you told people we slept together. We didn't, but we can fix that right now if you just let Jeanette go. You win!"

"This is just another one of your tricks. As soon as I let her go, you'll just say no again."

"I won't! I promise. It'll just be you and me. Maybe I could even be your girlfriend," Marissa suggested, grasping for anything that might persuade him to stop.

"You're lying! I've seen how you flirt with the other guys at school. I know you want to go out with them. I can't let that happen! I've had my eye on you for as long as I can remember. I loved you so much that I started a 'Marissa Collection'. I kept a ribbon you lost on the playground in fourth grade. I found your I.D. bracelet on the bus in junior high; you know the one you wore every day? You dropped a lipstick out of your purse in the hall last year--pink frost. I have every picture taken of you; pictures from the yearbook and school newspaper hanging up in my room and in my locker. I even snuck into your house last year when your mom was out in the back yard. I took that worn teddy bear you had in your bed."

"If you love me, why are you doing this? Why do you want to hurt us?"

"You humiliated me. It's all I think about. It plays over and over in my mind. I need to make it stop. If I only get rid of you, she'll still be here with the same face to remind me of you. That curly flowing brown hair," he said as he brushed Jeanette's hair from her face with his free hand. "Those unforgettable green eyes that look like emeralds sparkling in the sunlight." He continued his inventory list using the knife's tip like a pointer as he slid it down the side of her face to her cheek. "And those plump lips that look so kissable," he said with a ragged voice, as he stroked them with his thumb, resting the knife and his fingers momentarily on her jawbone. Jeanette tried to turn her head away from him, but his hand held it tightly in place. Her lips quivered as he dropped his face down to hers, lightly passing over her mouth with his. "And that body…so perfectly shaped, with those round breasts." He ran the knife along the front of her blouse, effortlessly slicing the buttons off to expose her bra and chest. He grazed the knife along her breast and down the side of her rib cage. "And your long legs that go on forever."

Jeannette was starting to cry again. It was clear that Mitch was losing control and Marissa was losing his attention.

"Mitch, stop it! You can have me right here, right now. Please, just leave my sister alone!" Marissa pleaded.

"Quit telling me what I can and can't do! I'm tired of always being the one who's told what to do. Get this, don't do that. Enough! I'm in charge this time. I bet the reporters will call this the Doublemint murders… get it? Don't you just love that commercial? "Double your pleasure, double your fun…" Mitch said in a sing-song pitch, mimicking the jingle. "I bet you girls get that all the time. They say twins share everything, so you get to share me too. There's enough of me to go around…isn't there, Baby?" he said turning back to Jeanette. "I've made Jeanette wait long enough though. Let's get back to it, shall we?" That's when Jeanette let out a blood curdling scream. As much as Marissa wanted the screams to stop, she feared that when they did it would mean something much worse. She closed her eyes, not able to watch what he was doing, trying to think of something else that could shut out the horrible reality that was worse than any nightmare she had ever had. She tried to concentrate on a plan to get them out of here. She was starting to feel very tired and she felt herself drifting away.

When Marissa woke up again she looked around to see if she could see Mitch, but he didn't seem to be there. She wondered how long they had really been here. She wondered if anyone could hear them. It seemed like an eternity had passed, yet without seeing the sun rise and set, it could have been several hours or even days. One thing she knew for sure…time was running out. Although he hadn't given them any food, once in awhile he forced them to drink some water. She now realized this was how he had been keeping them drugged, more than likely to make them easier to handle.

Jeanette was quiet now. Marissa could see her twin's body lying in a heap on the floor surrounded by a pool of blood. There was a lifeless, blank stare in her eyes. She heard a noise from a dark corner. Then Fetch was there, behind her, slowly walking towards her, then kneeling over her. He brought his face down to her head, drawing in the smell of her hair as he ran a finger along her arm. "I saved the best for last," he whispered, allowing his lips to graze her ear lobe as if trying to seduce her. She could feel the heat of his breath on her face, causing an involuntary shudder of fear. "You want me, don't you baby? It's just you and me now." His own excitement sent a ripple through his body causing a slight jerking motion, sending droplets of sweat from his forehead and hair raining onto her skin. "I'm going to get rid of these ropes so you can really enjoy this. Don't get any ideas about trying anything though, because if you do I won't be able to keep you awake for the festivities, and you wouldn't want to miss the best part."

She knew that she would only have a small window of opportunity to fight him off, because once he was on top of her she doubted she would have enough strength to get away. As soon as he freed one ankle, she sent her best ballet kick straight to his groin. Fetch let out a surprised gasp. The knife fell from his hands as they quickly moved to defend the ailing body part. He backed away, cursing at her. She tried to kick him again, but only caught wind. Fetch bent down and picked up the knife. He threw all 180 pounds of himself down on top of her, his crushing weight squeezing the air from her lungs as his body made contact. His left hand went straight for her throat as the other clutched the knife that he held to her right cheek.

"Damn it! You bitch! I told you not to try anything!" His stranglehold tightened. Mitch's voice was shaking, as his rage rose up to meet his face. Tears were forming in his eyes. He used the back of his right hand to wipe them away. As he did a red smear appeared on his face, as Jeanette's blood that had dried on the back of his hand mixed with his salty tears. "I didn't want it to be like this. I wanted you to want me. You were the one."

Suddenly, there was a loud bang as the cellar door splintered open. An almost blinding light flooded the dark space. Footsteps were hitting hard and fast against the wooden stairway down into the cellar, followed by a commotion. Marissa could feel Mitch's body weight being pulled off of her, but he tightened his vise-grip around her throat and pulled her with him. Finally his choke hold released. Marissa was sent crashing to the ground, sputtering and coughing as she inhaled the rush of oxygen.

Several police officers stood at the ready, guns drawn while another officer had Fetch face down on the dirt floor, placing him in cuffs. "Modesto Police Department, stay down! Mitchell Olsen, you are under arrest. You have the right to remain silent…" they recited as they dragged him up the stairs.

"Marissa! Marissa, this isn't over. Don't forget you are mine! We will finish this later!" Mitch yelled above the fray.

"Miss, I'm Officer Brown with the Modesto Police Department. I'm going to get you out of here. Joe, how's the other one?" Marissa looked at the other officer. When he sadly shook his head she knew they had arrived too late. She could no longer hold back the tears and the flood of emotion that she had held at bay. A tremendous sense of loss overcame her. She no longer cared about what was going on around her. Once again there was a fog forming, clouding her thoughts. This time, the sobs she could hear in the distance were her own. "Miss, don't leave me! You hang on. Medic! I need a Medic down here! She's going into shock," Officer Brown shouted into his walkie talkie as he took his jacket off and threw it over Marissa.

Marissa spent the next three days in Memorial Hospital. The injury to her head where Fetch had decided to plant his blinding blow with what had turned out to be a wrench was severe enough to need stitches and observation. Her neck and throat had suffered severe trauma, leaving her neck bruised and her voice raspy. Although the drug he had used on her was finally out of her system, she still felt its lingering effects. Her remaining physical injuries, some minor cuts and bruises, paled in comparison to her overwhelming sense of loss and guilt.

Her parents refused to leave her side, her mom trying to put up a strong front for her. As much as she needed them there, the evident grief expressed on their faces was almost as unbearable as the nightmares that continually replayed in her mind. Each time she managed to fall asleep she would wake up screaming, to see her mother's face tormented by things she could only imagine her daughters had suffered. Eventually her father sent her mom home with a family friend for some needed rest. The doctors sedated Marissa to dull both the physical pain and the mental agony she was experiencing.

Officer Brown stopped by the second day for a quick visit to check on her, but said the police could wait for Marissa to get home before they came by to talk to her about what had happened since they had already made an arrest. One or two friends from school came by, but their visits were kept pretty short when they realized they couldn't think of what to say. This too served as yet another reminder of the depth of her loss. Jeannette and Marissa had always been more than sisters, they were best friends. They were often accused of excluding other kids because they were so close. They had an almost unspoken language for just the two of them. When they began high school they each followed separate interests, Marissa's being academics and tennis, Jeannette's being dance and music. Even still they shared in each other's achievements and heartbreaks alike. They would giggle over the silliest things late into the night, raid the refrigerator together, or cry over their breakups. But most importantly they were always there for each other. Marissa felt that this time she had failed her sister. She knew if Jeanette were here now she would have climbed in bed with her, snuck in some junk food and they would have watched "General Hospital" to see what Luke and Laura were up to, or played along with "The Price Is Right". She already missed her so much, she couldn't imagine how anything else in her life would ever hurt this much or how she would ever feel happy again.

Officer Brown came by on Marissa's first day home. While he didn't want to intrude, it was now necessary for her to share with him as many details as she could remember. She told him how she and Jeannette had gone to the annual harvest festival at the Baker Ranch out on Claus Road. After a couple of hours she went to look for her sister and caught a glimpse of Jeanette leaving through the back door with Fetch Olsen.

"Do you remember what time that was?"

"I think it was around 9:00. The band was just starting to play, most of the other kids were standing around listening to them."

"Okay, and 'Fetch' as you call him, that's Mitchell Olsen?" the officer had asked, more for confirmation than a question.

"Yeah, Fetch is his nickname. He's on Downey High's football team, but everyone knows the coach doesn't play him because he isn't good enough. The coach never allows him to wear the whole uniform. It's obvious to everyone he's never going in. The players nicknamed him Fetch his freshman year because the coach used him to help track the stats, haul equipment and get him coffee. The name stuck and everyone calls him that now, including his family."

"Tell me what happened after you saw Jeanette and Mitchell."

"I followed them. I could see that Jeanette was leaning on Fetch like she was being carried to his truck. I called out to them as he was putting her into the cab. I tried to get Jeanette's attention. I yelled for her to wait up. When I caught up with them I asked Fetch what was going on. He said that Jeanette wasn't feeling well and wanted to go home, so he was going to drive her. I told him, thanks, but that I would call my folks to pick us up. That was when Jeanette said she was going to be sick and needed to get right home. She asked me if Fetch could please take her home. I didn't think it was a good idea. Fetch was kind of between us, and I couldn't really see her very well, so I pushed past Fetch. I started to pull Jeanette out of the truck, but she looked like she would pass out if she was made to stand up and walk back inside. So I said it was okay, but that I was coming along, too. Fetch just said, 'That's cool. The more the merrier.' I reached in and pushed Jeanette into the middle of the bench. As I started to get in I felt a little prick on my arm, kind of like a sharp bee sting. I remember trying to brush it off and then feeling like I was falling backwards. As I started to lose my balance, Fetch was right there and put his hands on my hips, to kind of boost me into the seat. The last thing I remember hearing was Fetch saying, 'I've got you.' I don't remember anything else after that until I woke up in that cellar."

"How well did you know Mitchell?" Officer Brown inquired.

"Last year, one day after school, he was nice enough to stay and help me decorate for a dance at school when the rest of the dance committee bailed to go home and get ready. I thought it was sweet, so when he asked me out I said yes. Apparently Fetch thought I owed him more than just a date. When he tried to go too far I made him take me home. The next day at school, he told all the guys that I was all over him and how we had gone all the way. One of my friends knew better. It wasn't long before everyone knew he was lying. The girls started calling him 'Fetch the letch' after that, but we really haven't talked since then. He always stares at me when we are in class at school or I pass him in the halls. Sometimes I see his truck driving past our house or I catch him waiting outside my class when I come out. Once he followed me and my friends around the mall. Another time he followed me on a date to McHenry Bowl. When we came out, my date's car antennae was tied in a knot. Fetch was parked a few stalls over, watching us when we came out. I knew he had a crush on me, but I thought that if I just ignored him, he would eventually go away."

"Okay, now the hard part. I need you to tell me everything you remember about what happened in the cellar. Please give me as much detail as you can."

Marissa took the next three hours to tell the story of what had happened in the cellar. They took a few breaks when it got too intense, but she was determined to make it through. She knew that for now the only revenge she would have against Fetch was seeing that he never got out of jail.

Later that evening, Marissa was watching television when the local news came on, headlining with an update on the brutal rape and murder of a beloved local teen. The newscaster, a perky blonde, was standing in front of a farmhouse, the cameras following her around as she spoke.

"Most of you already know the story of the twins that went missing almost a week ago Friday, October 30. They were found in the cellar of this unoccupied farmhouse on Parker Rd. This tragic story has rocked the town of Modesto, where most people greet even strangers with a smile. The teenage girls, barely sixteen, were abducted from a home on Claus Road just a few miles from here. They were attending a harvest festival that has been an annual tradition at the nearby ranch. The girls' parents, William and Marianne Van Horn, reported their missing daughters to the police department after they missed their curfew, something they had never done before. The authorities tried not to assume the worst, suggesting that perhaps they had gone to another friends' house for the night, but by noon on Saturday it was apparent this was not the case. The police caught a break Sunday morning. They received an anonymous tip from a neighbor who said he thought he saw a young man at the vacant property while they were repairing a fence at their bordering property line. During the preliminary search of the property, officers found the suspect's Chevy pick up parked around the backside of that barn across the driveway." As the reporter kept walking she came to an officer and introduced him to the viewing audience. "Chief of Police Keller, what details can you tell us about what went on here?"

"On Saturday, it was suspected that we might a kidnapping. A special team trained for hostage negotiation was deployed. On Sunday when we got the tip, we confirmed that it was good and sent in our men. When we arrived at the scene, we secured the exterior of the property. We searched the pickup and found a syringe and a girl's shoe on the floor board. We ran the plates on the truck to identify the owner. When we called the suspect's home, we were told he wasn't there. We were able to determine that the suspect had the girls in the cellar, when we heard screams coming from below the house. We knew we had to move quickly and immediately sent the team into the house. We were able to apprehend the suspect before he could kill his second victim. Unfortunately, a few hours prior to our arrival, Jeanette Van Horn was murdered. Miss Van Horn had been stabbed multiple times. According to the coroner, the cause of death was excessive blood loss and shock."

"Thank you, Chief." The perky blonde appeared on the screen, continuing with her story, "The police have told us that they are continuing their investigation here at the murder scene as well as questioning witnesses. If you have any information please call the number at the bottom of the screen. Although we can't release his name as he is a minor, we can tell you that the suspect is being held in protective custody at the Stanislaus County Jail. ."

Marissa couldn't believe her ears. "Protective custody?! He raped and killed my sister! Why should they give him any protective custody? He deserves whatever he gets!"

The reporter finished up by explaining that the California penal code provides a mandatory death sentence when a murder is committed during the commissioning of kidnapping or rape. However, since 1967 there have been no executions and 177 death row inmates have had their death sentences commuted to life in prison without parole. "Since the suspect is a minor, the prosecution has their work cut out for them. It will prove difficult to impose the death penalty on one so young. The surviving twin was released from the hospital today, and the funeral for her sister will be held at the end of the week. For Channel 3 news, I'm Marsha Gibbons reporting live from Modesto. Back to you, Bob."

Marissa could feel every muscle in her body tense with anger. One way or another she would be sure Mitchell Olsen would pay for what he had done. "Well Fetch, you were right about one thing. This isn't over."

The first week at home Marissa's classmates sent get well cards and teachers sent thoughtful notes, telling her to take her time and they would look forward to seeing her return to school when she was ready. Her parents only left the house for short periods of time, and never together. At night when she went to bed, the nightmares continued, although they were becoming less frequent. Each time she woke up in a cold sweat with her heart racing. Her parents would rush into the room because she had called out in her sleep. Later, she could hear the muffled sounds of her father consoling her mother through the wall between their bedrooms.

Flowers arrived daily from friends, families and even strangers who wanted the express their sorrow for their loss. A private graveside service was held for family and close friends, followed by a candlelight memorial service at the Covenant Church where they attended regular church services.

Marissa's parents looked shell-shocked. She felt so guilty. It was her fault. Fetch had killed her sister because of his obsession with her. Why couldn't he have started with her instead of Jeanette? Then Jeanette would still be here. The look in her parent's eyes told her that her presence was a continuous reminder of the tragic situation at hand. When she looked in the mirror she saw what they saw…a ghost. Fetch's words echoed in her mind.

"She will still be there to remind me of you," and she wondered if her parents would also feel this way for the rest of their lives.

Chapter 2

Marissa had a tough time returning to school after the funeral. Mrs. Miller the school principal, had personally taken Marissa under her wing. She promised Marissa she would do everything in her power to help her through the transition. Mrs. Miller encouraged her to go forward with her academic plans, even though Marissa felt that pursuing a future was a betrayal to Jeannette. Mrs. Miller also helped the Van Horns find a family crisis counselor that could help them deal with their situation.

A year later, when the trial started, it was nearly impossible to attend class. A media frenzy had ensued, and reporters were everywhere. Marissa was forced to do home study until it was over. Listening to his attorney's opening arguments, twisting the facts into a fabrication to support a story of Mitch's innocence was more than unnerving. Seeing Mitch in the courtroom and listening to witnesses and police reports was like reliving the tragedy daily.

Marissa took the stand for two days, the first day recounting every detail of that weekend. When asked to identify the attacker, Marissa looked directly at Mitch, pointing him out to the courtroom. When their eyes met, she could see with frightening clarity his satisfaction and lack of remorse. Although she searched the sea of faces before her for comfort and support, she found none. Her parents were too emotional to offer her strength. Marissa addressed the jurors, trying to connect with each one as an individual, as she forced herself to remember things she wanted desperately to forget.

The trial affected Marissa's home life as well. Mrs. Van Horn had to take sleeping pills now to sleep at night and Mr. Van Horn started leaving the house after dinner and not returning until late at night. Most nights Marissa would fight sleep for as long as she could to avoid the nightmares that had returned full throttle. The Van Horns went around their home as if on autopilot. What had once been a wonderfully happy home, full of life and bustling with activity, was now a mere empty shell of itself.

Mitch's parents looked worse than the Van Horns did, if that was possible. It was obvious that Mrs. Olsen was on some sort of drugs to calm her nerves, evidenced by her face, void of expression. Mr. Olsen looked like a man who had taken to self-medication, the kind one gets at the local bars. The papers had reported that he had been involved in a few bar room brawls in South Modesto, where mostly drug dealers and prostitutes frequent.

The constant publicity of the trial seemed to draw out the whole town, with everyone on the side of justice for the Van Horns. It was rumored that a few locals occasionally tried to exact their own justice on the Olsen family, sending threatening messages through the family's living room window by way of rocks, or publicly humiliating them whenever they were seen in public, yelling and jeering at them.

Mitch's family was absent from the courtroom on most days. Mrs. Olsen had a younger, impressionable teenager at home that she preferred didn't hear the details of his older brother's deeds first hand. Mrs. Olsen also didn't want him to be the target of reporters snapping family photos as they entered and exited the courtroom, or hounded at home if an adult wasn't there to protect him. Mr. Olsen came on days when he wasn't working his shift at the Gallo Winery glass plant. There were many days when the only support that Mitchell had was his lawyer. Marissa wished she could feel some compassion for him, but all she had was loathing and hatred for this young man who had robbed her of not just her sister, but her family. He had robbed them both of their families, but she doubted he recognized that.

Jeffrey Kenneth was the newest attorney at the public defender's office. He had been court appointed to take on monumental task of representing Mitchell Olsen. He knew that the possibility of proving Olsen's innocence was rare, since he himself believed that Olsen was guilty as charged. However, the law said he had a right to a fair trial, so Mr. Kenneth would do his duty and see that he was given a proper defense. He had advised Mitch that a plea bargain would be in his best interest. He strongly believed that with a sincere show of remorse and acceptance of punishment they would sit better during the sentencing phase and possibly avoid the death penalty.

Mitch would have none of it. He declared his innocence regardless of the overwhelming evidence stacked against him. If it hadn't been for the police storming in and catching him in the act, Kenneth may have believed Mitch. He could be very persuasive when presenting his side of the story. And since this was all he really had in the bank, he decided he would run with it, hoping that during the prosecutions presentation a loop hole would present itself. Of course he gave the obligatory objections where he could. He tried to redirect when possible and made every appropriate motion to suppress circumstantial evidence. He took copious notes through out each testimony offered up by the lead prosecutor, hoping that he might find the smallest crack in the case. Nevertheless, at the end of the day when the prosecution rested its airtight case he was still left with nothing but the testimony of his guilty client.

On the first day of presentations for the defense, Mr. Kenneth explained to Mitch that the case wasn't going well. He was concerned about putting Mitch on the stand. He knew that no matter how well the testimony went, the prosecution would be given the chance to redirect. Even though Mr. Kenneth was more than a little concerned as to whether Mitch would be able to pull off a testimony that would convince a jury that he was remorseful, he once again suggested that his client change his plea a throw himself at the mercy of the court. Mitch refused him yet again, but told him he wanted to take the stand and tell his side of the story. Left with no other options, Mr. Kenneth called his first and only witness to the stand.

"Mitchell, do you understand why you are here today?" asked Mr. Kenneth in a soft voice.

"Yes, sir," Mitch replied.

"Mitch I'm going to ask you to take us through the night in question. Are you prepared to discuss the events of that night?"

"Yes, Sir"

"Mitchell, let's go through the night in question. Where were you on the night of October 30th, 1981?"

"I went to a party at the Baker Ranch."

"Did you see either of the Van Horn sisters at that party?"

"Yes, sir."

"Did you speak to either one of the sisters?"

"Yes."

"Tell us what you remember about that night."

"I went to the party and was there for about an hour when I saw Jeanette Van Horn in the kitchen. I wanted to talk to her so I thought I would take her a soda. I walked over to her and asked her if she wanted a drink, she took it from me and said 'Thanks'. We talked for a while and then she said she wanted to find her sister because she was feeling sick. I looked around but didn't see Marissa, so I offered to take her home and she said yes."

"What happened next?"

"I took her out to my truck and was helping her get in when Marissa came out and saw us. She said she was concerned about Jeannette, and then she said she didn't want Jeannette riding with me. I think she was jealous."

"Objection!" shouted the prosecution. "He has no knowledge of Marissa Van Horn's state of mind!"

"You Honor, my client is presenting his point of view."

"Overruled. However, Mr. Kenneth, I will allow the prosecution the same consideration when it is her turn to rebut.

"Thank you, your honor." Mr. Kenneth returned to his client. "You were saying that you thought Marissa Van Horn was jealous?"

"Yeah, it was like she didn't want me to be alone with her sister. She even insisted that she come with us. I said sure, and we all got in the truck. Then the girls started arguing over who got to sit next to me. Jeanette ended up in the middle. When I started driving she even leaned against me. I suggested that we go somewhere together. I'm a guy after all. Who would turn down a night spent with twins? I took them to the farmhouse that was up the street. I had heard the guys talk about this place at football practice. Everyone was at the Baker Ranch so I knew no one would be there. The girls never said to take them home, so I thought they were cool with it."

Marissa was horrified by Mitch's testimony. She couldn't believe what she was hearing. She hoped that the jury could tell he was lying, but as she searched their faces she really couldn't tell. Her mom who had been sitting next to her, reached over, took her hand and squeezed it. Then she leaned in and whispered, "Do you want to leave?" Marissa shook her head. She wanted to hear what Mitch thought happened that night. Mrs. Van Horn put an arm around her daughter, as if to shield her from Mitch's words.

"Then what happened?" asked Mr. Kenneth.

Mitch sat there and looked at the floor for a minute. His face grew red and tears were forming in his eyes when he looked up at the jury. Mitch was shaking as he continued. "We went inside, and I took them down to the basement. I'm not sure exactly how the next part happened because I was looking for a blanket, but all of a sudden I heard the two of them going at it again. Marissa had found a knife and had started stabbing Jeanette."

Mr. Kenneth paused for dramatic effect. The courtroom erupted in a dull roar. Marissa felt as if the air had been sucked out of the room. She looked at Mitch and found him staring at her with a smug look on his face. The judge banged the gavel against the bench.

"Order! Order in the court. Mr. Kenneth, please continue your line of questioning."

"Yes your honor. For clarification, you are testifying that it was Marissa Van Horn who killed her sister, not you."

"Yes sir."

"Tell us what happened next."

"There was blood everywhere. By the time I got over to them, they were on the ground and Marissa was on top of Jeannette. She kept stabbing her. I pulled her off, and got the knife away from her. I quickly tied her up to restrain her so she couldn't stab Jeannette anymore. I finally got her to calm down. I knew I needed to get help, but I was afraid to leave them, and I was also afraid to take them back to the truck. Then Marissa started crying. She said I had to help her so she wouldn't get in trouble."

Mr. Kenneth couldn't believe what he was hearing. More importantly, it was obvious that the jury was hanging on every word. He let the words linger, while he glanced around the packed courtroom. Behind the prosecution bench, Marissa Van Horn appeared mortified by the story that Mitch was proposing. Mr. Kenneth went back to the stand where his client was waiting. "Mitch I can see this is very hard for you. Do you need a break?"

"Yes sir. A break would be good."

"Your honor, I would like to request a 30 minute break?"

The judge clanged his gavel, "Court will take a 30 minute recess. We will resume at 10:00 a.m." Mitch and his attorney left through the side door. The judge and jury filed out through doors in the front. Marissa and her parents stood as the prosecution's lead attorney, Suzanne Lynch, approached them. "Marissa how are you holding up? You don't have to stay here. We can call you if we need you," she offered.

"I'm fine. I'm just really mad. How can you let him say those things? How can you sit there and let him lie?"

"Marissa, I know it's hard, but he is guaranteed a fair trial under the law. His side must be heard before justice can be served. I don't want you to worry about this though. I will get my turn to ask him questions about his testimony. I will expose him for the liar he is. I promise," she said reaching over to give Marissa's elbow a reassuring squeeze. "We will win this."

Thirty minutes later court resumed, and Mitch was back in the witnesses' chair. His attorney, anxious to leave his testimony as is and keep his client from saying the wrong thing announced that he had no further questions.

Suzanne Lynch made her way to the front of the courtroom, carrying her notepad with her.

"Good morning, Mr. Olsen"

"Good morning."

"Mr. Olsen, how long have you known the plaintiff?"

"Since grade school."

"How many years would you say?"

"About ten. I'm two years ahead of her."

"How would you describe the relationship you have had with her over that 10 year period?"

"I don't know what you mean?"

"Did you speak to her, did you see her outside of school…that sort of thing."

"I'd see her on the way home from school, and I'd see her playing on the playground, but we didn't really talk that much."

Ms. Lynch walked over to the evidence table and retrieved a plastic bag from the table.

"Do you recognize the items in this bag?"

"Yes, that's my Marissa collection."

"How did you come to collect these items? Did you steal them?"

"Not exactly, most of them I found."

"You found them?"

"Yeah, on the playground and stuff. She dropped them."

"Correct me if I'm wrong, but isn't keeping something that doesn't belong to you stealing?" Mitch shrugged his shoulders. "Mr. Olsen, for what purpose did you keep Marissa's things?"

"I liked having them. They made me feel good. I planned on giving them back to her someday when she was my girlfriend, but that never happened."

"Mr. Olsen, isn't it true that you have be obsessed with Marissa Van Horn for many years? And isn't it also true that at least one of these items was taken from Marissa's bedroom by you?"

"Objection your Honor. 'Obsessed' is vague wording.

"I withdraw the question your Honor."

"Mr. Olsen, did you ever go on a date with Miss Van Horn?"

"Once, in high school. She was working on the decorations for the senior prom and I helped her when everyone else left. She said she wanted to thank me, so we went out on a date."

"What did you do on your date?"

"First we went to dinner. Then after that we went to the back of the high school to park."

"When you say you went to 'park', does that mean have sex?"

"Hopefully."

"And did you and Marissa Van Horn have sex that night?"

"No. I wanted to and she knew it. She had told me that she wanted to thank me. But when the time came she backed out."

"How did that make you feel?"

"Mad at first. I mean she was such a tease!"

"What happened next?"

"I took her home."

"How did you feel about her after that?"

"I was hurt. She humiliated me at school."

"Were you mad?"

"Hell yes! She made a fool of me!"

"Mad enough to get even with her, maybe get a little revenge even?"

Mr. Kenneth was on his feet again, "Objection! Your honor, counsel is leading the witness!"

"I withdraw the question, your Honor."

Ms. Lynch went back to the evidence table again. This time holding up a men's shirt, covered in blood. "Mr. Olsen, does this shirt belong to you?"

"Yes, that's the shirt I wore to the Baker Ranch Fall Festival."

"The evidence states that the stains on this shirt are blood stains from Jeannette Van Horn. Can you explain how these got on your shirt?"

"I tried to give her CPR."

"Where was Marissa Van Horn while you were administering CPR to her sister?"

"I had tied her up, so she couldn't hurt Jeannette or me."

"I see." Ms. Lynch walked over to the evidence table. She walked back over to the witness box. She held up the bag. "Mr. Olsen, do you recognize this item?"

"That looks like the knife that Marissa Van Horn used to murder her sister."

"If that's the case, how can you explain that the only fingerprints found on the murder weapon are yours?"

Mitch shrugged his shoulders. "I wiped off her fingerprints and replaced them with mine."

"Just to make sure I understand, that we all understand." Ms. Lynch started, motioning to the everyone in the courtroom, "you watched Marissa Van Horn murder her sister, you cleaned off the murder weapon, then put your own prints on it. Why would you do such a thing?"

"Marissa was really upset and scared. She begged me to help her. I thought if I did maybe she would want me."

"Mr. Olsen, the evidence does not support the story you have told. Isn't it true that you drugged Marissa and Jeannette Van Horn? That you took them to that farmhouse against their will, you raped and murdered Jeanette Van Horn! Furthermore, isn't also true that the only reason Marissa is still here is because the police arrived?"

The courtroom was silent. Everyone waited for a response. Mitch looked directly at Marissa. He had tears in his eyes, "I didn't mean to do it. It just happened. Something inside me had snapped. I had wanted her for so long. I couldn't take it anymore. Every time I saw one of them brought back the humiliation that I felt. At the fall festival I saw Jeannette by herself. I saw an opportunity to have what I wanted with Jeannette. It was almost like having Marissa. But she turned me down." Mitch's gaze started to drift as he entered into a trancelike state. "The drugs worked quickly and I was able to persuade her to go outside for some fresh air. I knew I had to get her alone. I wasn't going to hurt her. I was just going to take her to a quiet place where we could be alone for awhile. Then Marissa showed up and tried to take her away from me." The pitch in Mitch's voice went up, it was apparent he was becoming angry. "I got mad. She was ruining my plans, so then I had to take them both. I knew Marissa would make me take them home. I had some vet tranqs that I had taken from my Ag class, so when Marissa was trying to talk to Jeannette, I grabbed one from the truck. She was occupied with Jeannette, so it was easy to walk up behind her, inject the drugs and wait for her to fall into my arms. I took them to the farmhouse. I wasn't going to hurt anyone but Jeannette kept screaming I had to make her stop. I felt so powerful with that knife in my hand." Mitch clinched his fist like he was holding the knife in his hand again. He started shaking and kept talking. It was as if he were back in that farmhouse. "They were paying attention when I had the knife. It felt really good. All of sudden I was the one in charge. But they both kept telling me to let the other one go. I knew I couldn't do that. I had to finish it, and I would have if the police hadn't come." Suddenly he stared at Marissa. "It isn't over, it'll never be over."

For a minute everyone froze as if they hadn't quite processed that Mitch Olsen had just confessed. His attorney had wanted him to confess, but not like this. There would be no plea bargain now.

"No further questions," Ms. Lynch said.

"Did you want to redirect?" the judge asked

Mr. Kenneth shook his head, "No your Honor."

"The witness may step down, and will be remanded to custody. I want to see both counsels in chambers in 30 minutes. Court is adjourned until 8:00a.m. tomorrow morning.

The attorneys met with the judge and since Mitch had confessed they needed to decide how the sentencing phase would work. The district attorney was still seeking the death penalty. The jury would be assigned the task of determining the sentence. They would begin the following morning.

The prosecution went first. "Ladies and Gentlemen, Your Honor. This is a case of premeditated murder. Mitchell Olsen took two young girls against their will to a deserted farmhouse. By his own admission he raped and brutally murdered Jeanette Van Horn. He did this of his own accord because by his own words, 'it felt good.' He intended to do the same to Marissa Van Horn and again by his own confession only stopped because he was interrupted by the police. He intended to harm. And he did. He intended to kill. And he did. The defense is going to tell you that he was just a boy when this happened. He's going to suggest that Mitchell Olsen feels remorse for his actions. But let me remind you that he has testified in this very courtroom, and lied under oath just to continue tormenting Marissa Van Horn. The state of California mandates a death penalty for people who kill someone they have abducted. It is your job as the jury to make sure that Mitchell Olsen is punished for his crimes. It's your job to be sure he can never do this again. In his own words, 'this isn't over.' I'm asking you to return a death sentence. I'm asking you to show Mitchell Olsen that it is over."

Mitchell's attorney stood and took a drink of water from the glass on the table. He straightened his tie and walked over to the jury box. "Men and women of the jury, the prosecutor just gave a very eloquent speech. However, she didn't mention the two words that require your careful consideration in this matter. Diminished Responsibility. Yes, Mitchell Olsen has admitted his guilt to what in my opinion is a heinous crime. He tortured two women, then raping and killing one of them. It is highly likely he would have done the same to the second one. He has perjured himself on this very stand. All malicious deeds and unforgivable actions. He has admitted guilt. The burden of determining guilt or innocence no longer rests on your shoulders. Instead, you have been charged with the overwhelming task of sifting through the facts and exacting the appropriate punishment for these offenses.

Appropriate punishment. What is appropriate punishment in this case? In order to determine that you have to consider the person who committed the crimes. What was their state of mind at the time it was carried out? What were their intentions? Was it premeditated? Were they completely cognoscente of the ramifications of their actions? Mitchell Olsen was a minor when he committed these crimes. I won't say he was a child, he wasn't. However, he was merely a teenager on the cusp of manhood, hormones coursing through his body, coupled with anger and rage from personal humiliation. Humiliation that Marissa Van Horn had played a part in as far as he was concerned. Teenagers by nature are confused, impulsive, irresponsible, and at times selfish. Think for a moment about your own adolescence. About the things that you were sure to be true. How many of those assumptions were an error in judgment? Maybe you even acted upon some of them and regretted it later. This is where Mitchell Olsen is finding himself. Caught up in an error of judgment of magnanimous proportions, from an obsession that he couldn't control. An imbalance of the mind, if you will. And that folks is where you have to decide if there were mitigating circumstances. He was incapable of the reasoning. Obviously, we can't go around killing people just because we have a crush on them that doesn't turn out the way we want it to. But Mitchell wasn't thinking rational. He wasn't capable of reasoning out as an adult would. Can you find it within yourselves to look beyond the crime and see a confused young man unable to reign in his anger brought on by public humiliation? A young man with diminished responsibility.

When you are considering whether this young man should face the death penalty you need to consider that he wasn't an adult at the time he committed these crimes. He did not have the self control that society would expect of a mature adult. I have confidence that this jury can understand that this young man should not be held accountable to the same degree as an adult. Diminished Responsibility. Give him a life sentence. Show him the mercy you have within you for the tormented soul that he lives with each day."

With a guilty plea before them and the compelling closing arguments presented by the attorneys, the jury entered into deliberation of the penalty phase of the trial. The words, 'diminished responsibility' weighed heavily in their discussions and cast an imposing influence on the final decision. When court resumed, the jury filed in. Not one member made eye contact with the prosecution or the Van Horns. When the foreman stood to read the verdict, he looked nervously around the room and cleared his throat. He looked down and read from the slip of paper in his trembling hands. The jury's recommendation was for a life sentence. The judge issued a sentence of life in prison with possibility of parole in 25 years. The judge remanded the defendant into the custody of the county jail; announced court adjourned and banged his gavel. The case was closed.

The sentencing did little to ease the pain the Van Horns had endured. Nothing could bring Jeanette back or restore their family and make it whole again. Marissa still felt the guilt that survivors often experience. Her parents would always look at her and be reminded of the other daughter they lost and therefore would never again see Marissa for herself. She knew they didn't intend for it to be this way, but the burden of their loss was too great for them to give her what she needed. This knowledge left a vacancy within her; one that she was afraid could easily be filled with bitterness if she wasn't careful. This tragedy had markedly changed her life course.

Now, as Marissa had sat waiting for her turn to cross the stage, she reflected on the events since coming home without her sister. She had overcome her tremendous grief. She had managed to make some new friends; she had even gone to her senior prom. She received honors for academic achievement and as a result had been accepted to U C Berkeley. Most importantly she had survived.

"Marissa Van Horn," the Downey High principal called out, as she walked across the stage to receive her high school diploma. The past two years had been difficult, but there was something electric in the air today. A cheer went up from the crowds as Mrs. Miller handed her her diploma. Mrs. Miller took an extra moment and drew her into a hug. "It's a new start Marissa. You are a unique and strong young woman. Don't ever let anyone tell you differently," she said for only Marissa to hear.

True to her promise, Mrs. Miller came through, with support, encouragement and friendship. She was able to offer Marissa something that no one else had thought to give her…hope for a future.

Mitch's last year and a half had been very different. Due to the severity of his crime, the district attorney had made a successful motion keeping him out of juvenile detention, saying the facility wasn't designed for securing murderers. The judge had agreed and held him without bail through the trial in the Stanislaus County Jail. His attorney had at least been able to persuade them to hold him in his a private cell, concerned that with the notoriety of the trial and civil outcry for justice, it was not safe for him to be mixed in with the general population.

Once the sentencing was complete, Mitch was escorted to a conference room in the courthouse. His attorney and family met with a representative from the prison to explain what Mitch and his family could expect while being housed at San Quentin. He did not sugarcoat the news. Inmates in the cell block to which Mitch had been assigned were lifers; men convicted of murder carrying a life sentence with possibility of parole. Visits were allowed only once a week by anyone other than his attorney; even then it would take place in a partitioned room, no physical contact allowed. Because Mitch was only nineteen with a conviction of rape, they were placing him in a single cell, since even among convicts, raping a young girl was seen as the lowest of crimes. Mitch's case had received statewide media coverage, so there would be no mercy shown to him. The odds of survival would depend on keeping him alive the first year he was in, if he made it that long, perhaps newer inmates would take the attention, allowing the threat to decline over time. He would be allowed one hour a day to be outdoors. His meals would be served in his cell. The only contact with he would have with the other inmates would be through the iron grates of the cells in his block. The guard recommended that Mitch be very careful, avoid conversations with inmates and treat guards with the utmost respect as they would be his lifeline.

The time had come for his family to say good-bye, as first thing in the morning he would be transported to San Quentin. His younger brother, Alan, offered a quick, 'See you' like he was going off to summer camp, but Mitch knew he didn't yet understand what was happening. His father simply said, "You're a man now, so do your time like one. We'll see you when you get out," making it clear he had no intention of visiting him.

His mother gave him a hug, the last he would have for years. It was obvious she was struggling to say some encouraging words as she sent him off to face his punishment but it was difficult to offer consolation when she knew in her heart that the sentence was deserved. In the end, she could only say, "I love you son. Do what they tell you, I'll visit when I can." Mitch was painfully aware of the disappointment his parents had in him and the fact they had accepted his verdict as just. There would not be an appeal.

His last night spent in the county jail was anything but peaceful. Men in other cells yelled out to him, things they would do to him if given half a chance, things they thought others would do to torture him later on and how he better hope he was never left alone. He put the pillow over his head, trying to muffle their words, but their voices penetrated none the less. Finally, a guard came through and told them all to quiet down. Even after they were quiet the words continued to ring in his ears. For the first time since this started, Mitchell Olsen was afraid.

Mitch wasn't sure what to expect when he arrived at San Quentin State Prison, but one thing was for sure, his time spent in the county jail did not prepare him for his new lifestyle. The prison's location sat on what could be considered a piece of prime California real estate. The San Francisco Bay lay in its forefront, while rolling hills dotted with evergreens provided a picturesque backdrop. As the transport bus pulled onto the prison access road, he could see the stone façade of the fortress. A turret looming over the entry served as a tower for posted armed guards. Had he not known this was a prison, the building could have easily been mistaken for a European medieval castle. The prison gates clanged closed once they were inside, locking in the finality of his circumstances.

Mitch was escorted in shackles to the main entry for inmates. The guards made quick work processing his paperwork and issuing his prison standard clothing; denim jeans, light denim shirt, black work shoes, underwear, a booklet outlining prison rules and schedules, and a bible. These would be the only items he was allowed in his cell for the time being. Depending on his behavior he could eventually earn the right to other privileges, such as visits from their rolling library, work detail within the prison and possibly co-mingling with other inmates in the dayroom.

Mitch was taken to his cell on D-Block, flanked by two uniformed prison guards, passing through a series of doors, each unlocked and locked as they went. The only noises on the block were the footsteps of the three men echoing off the concrete walls. The gauntlet of cells along the way housed other lifers. Many were perched on bunks, looking out with mild curiosity, while others leaned against the concrete wall, staring him down as he passed by, daring him to make eye contact.

"Here we are, home sweet home," the guard announced when they had arrived at Mitch's cell. It was a small 8' X 6' room, three concrete walls, one barred with a sliding door. A single metal bunk bed stood against a cinderblock wall with a pillow and a neatly folded wool blanket in the center of the thin mattress. A small booklet and a bible rested atop the blanket. A stainless steel toilet to the right of the bed, close enough to double as a night stand if it had a lid. A single roll of toilet paper balanced on the plumbing protruding from the wall. Mitch was freed of his hand cuffs just before stepping inside.

"The chaplain will be by in awhile. He makes a habit of personally welcoming each inmate. You can refuse to see him, but that would be unwise, as he will most likely be the only friend you will have in here. Meals are brought daily per the schedule in your handbook." The door clamored as it slid into place, the guard throwing the lock before turning to walk away.

When the main door to the block slammed shut behind the officers, a few of the inmates shouted out their own colorful greetings and offers to give Mitch a replay of his crimes, where he played the role of Jeanette Van Horn. These would be mild by comparison, to the threats made to him when the lights went out that night.

Mitch sat on the edge of his bunk, head resting in his hands. His only thought was that he didn't belong here. No one understood how Marissa Van Horn had humiliated him publicly, had pushed him too far and left him with no other recourse. Her testimony in court had portrayed her as the victim, innocent of any accountability. She acted as if she hadn't done anything wrong, that she hadn't been a tease, hadn't spread rumors about him and hadn't pushed him to punish her. Someday he would make sure she understood just what she had done to him.

The Sangre Brotherhood came about nearly twenty years ago, when the Chaplain himself was an inmate at San Quentin. The gang grew, both inside the prison and out on the streets, financing their operations with numerous crimes from drug trafficking, pornography and racketeering, just to name a few. After his own parole, the Minister elevated him to Chaplain status. Eventually, they were able to place him back in San Quentin, to help lost souls within the prison system find their way to greater meaning in life.

The Chaplain had worked for the prison for going on ten years and was well respected. The warden saw him as a trusted employee and an important liaison to soften the hardship of prison life for the inmates, helping to maintain a little balance in the day to day drudgery. The guards protected him while on his personal visits unless he requested to be left alone for quiet confession or study. He was a confidante to many an inmate, offering a nurturing comfort, fatherly advice or spiritual counseling. This was especially true for the new arrivals.

He had viewed Mitchell Olsen's entry into the prison from behind the veiled one-way glass window in the Warden's office. He could see the defiance already present in Mitchell's demeanor, in his walk and stature that tried to carry a 'don't touch me' attitude. He had seen it in others before. They always took a little longer to come around. So he decided to wait until today to make his initial visit, giving Mitch a night of cat calls to fully realize his vulnerability. If Mitch needed further proof of his defenselessness, the chaplain had no doubt he would get it soon enough.

At 10:00 a.m., the chaplain made his way to D-Block. Officer Baldwin led him to Mitch's cell, and introduced them before letting him in. Mitch agreed to a private meeting, so the guard took his leave with a warning directed at Mitch that he would be just down the hall. Mitch nodded an acknowledgement and the two men were locked in together. He had never been religious; in fact he had only been to one church service in his entire life--his grandmother's funeral. He wasn't sure how to act around a member of the clergy. He found himself suddenly uncomfortable. The chaplain took a seat on one end of the bunk, so Mitch took up the other end.

"Mitchell, I make it my practice to make a stop in the first day or two while new inmates are getting acclimated. The first couple of weeks in here are pretty rough and I find that many young men, such as you, find solace in our meetings."

"Uh…Father."

"Oh I'm not Catholic, so a simple Chaplain will do. That's what everyone calls me."

"Chaplain, I'm not religious, I don't really believe in God, so I'm not sure we would really have a purpose in meeting."

"I understand. But you might be surprised to know that I offer far more than just religious counseling. Think of me as a friend. Just in case you change your mind, I've taken the liberty of writing down a few scriptures for your reading pleasure, and have marked the passages in this bible. I know they gave one to you when you arrived, but we'll just trade them out. I'll use that one for the next person I need to give a reading to, if that's okay."

"You can have both of them; I don't plan to read either."

"Yes, I've heard that before as well. You'd be surprised at the number of men wishing for a bible after having 23 hours a day alone in a cell. Boredom has a tendency to set in. In the absence of other things to entertain the mind, many an inmate has become a bible scholar. I'll just leave it anyway. If you want to get in some reading, you can. In the meantime, is there any particular concern you have so far? I'm a pretty good listener and I am received fairly well by both prisoners and guardsmen, so I can help resolve most issues you may encounter."

"I think I'm okay for now."

"Okay then, I'll just call Officer Baldwin back. If you change your mind you can request a meeting and they will bring me to you anytime. It was good to meet you."

Later that afternoon, Mitch found himself opening up the good book for a little look-see. He went through the list of suggested readings the chaplain had left for him. While paging through to the third selection, a folded scrap of paper slipped from between the pages. There was a hand written note with no name indicating to whom it was written, or whom it was from.

"When you are ready, we can help each other out. Our organization recruits men with your special abilities. Rewards can be generous. We can discuss this at our next session."

He couldn't imagine what special abilities he had. He hadn't passed a single class in school and he had already served a year and a half in the county jail, which certainly did not provide any means to learn a trade. This note was obviously meant for someone else. He folded it back on its original crease and carefully placed it where he had found it, still wondering what could have been meant by it.

Two nights later, after lights out, the taunting began again. He was amazed at how relentless the inmates were. They seemed to work as a team, taking turns throughout the night. Sometimes the threats came from someone close by, some farther down the hall or even above him a few levels. Voices carried and echoed through the chambers, loud roars or raspy whispers. Sometimes two would banter back and forth, one pretending to be the dominant one, the other subordinate calling himself Mitch, begging for mercy. It was then, that suddenly a door opened from down the hall.

A small splinter of light radiated its beam on the high sheen of the concrete floor, then it closed. The voices faded off. Two pairs of footsteps following two beams of light were coming closer. Inmates began whooping and banging on the bars. "Mitch, Mitch, Mitch, Mitch…" they chanted, then more whooping.

Mitch's pulse was quickening, as the footsteps came to a halt in front of his cell. The clinking of a key in the lock brought on an instant nausea as the chanting grew louder. The door slid open and a flashlight was pointed directly into his eyes, causing him to squint. No words were spoken, the two men jerked him to his feet, forcing him to turn around, then shoved him towards the wall. He tried to push away, but a night stick was pressed against the base of his skull as leverage was applied holding his face against the concrete. The second man quickly restrained his arms using a leather strap similar to a belt, pinning his arms down at his sides. Within second his pants fell in a heap around his ankles.

Mitch tried to think of something he could use to bargain with the two men, but he found it difficult to think with the racket of the inmates and the pain in his skull. Now he could feel the first man's hot breath on the back of his neck. The smell of soured liquor permeated the small confines of the space. "You're gonna love this, Mitch," the voice spattered in his ear. Thirty minutes later a very subdued Mitch laid on his bunk, knees brought into his chest, wrapped in a blanket. As he stared at the wall of his cell, thoughts of revenge occupied his mind. One more thing Marissa Van Horn would have to pay for.

The next day, Officer Baldwin escorted the kitchen custodian while he passed out the morning's breakfast. When they got to Mitch's cell they found him lying still on his bunk in a fetal position. The officer called out to him, but Mitch refused to answer him. Not knowing whether or not Mitch was ill or just being non-compliant, the officer called for backup. When helped arrived, they decided to take the non-responsive prisoner to the infirmary.

Once there, a doctor tried to examine him, but Mitch refused. He said he'd be fine; he just wanted to go back to his cell. They allowed him to eat his breakfast in the infirmary before returning him to his cell. A few hours later the chaplain dropped in for a visit.

"Mitchell, did you get a chance to get to any of the suggested reading I left with you?"

"Yes, Chaplain, I did."

"Did you find it of any use to you?"

"The second selection left me with some questions."

"Go on."

"There was an interesting note left inside, making mention of one's special talents."

"Yes, it is our belief that everyone has some. Was this of particular interest to you?"

"I'm not sure I have a special talent."

"Before we can go further with our discussion I have to know that we have complete trust between us."

"Absolutely. I trust you. After all you are a man of God."

"Yes, we'll see, it's more a matter of me trusting you. You'll have to provide me an assurance that you are trustworthy."

"Like what?"

"For starters, your trip to the infirmary today; was there any mention of the events that found you in their care?"

Mitch's eyes widened, realizing that the chaplain had knowledge of what had happened to him. He shook his head no.

"That's very good. Then we will consider your trust already earned. If I can guarantee that a repeat of last night will not occur again, will you continue to keep things to yourself and work hard to prove your worth?"

Mitch nodded, not exactly sure what he was agreeing to, but he knew he didn't want any more night visits.

"Very well. I represent people both within and outside of the prison. These friends can help get things done. We are always looking for new recruits. You have been on our list for quite some time."

"What will I have to do?"

"From time to time we will ask favors of you. They will be tasks that we will assist you with, but need to have someone take care of as not to create suspicion for our people on the outside. We will ask you to help keep a look out for new recruits that can be useful on the outside as well. In return you will receive both our protection and compensation."

"What kind of compensation?"

"We can handle that numerous ways. Sometimes it is in return of services. We are in the position to make things happen on the inside and the out. We will also set up an untraceable bank account for you. Each time you provide a service, a payment will be made to your account. When you get out you should have quite a nest egg to start your new life. If you serve us well, we would be able to offer you a position within our organization when you leave this place. Our investors are many and we dabble in many financial endeavors that would certainly provide you with great opportunity you would never know otherwise; and let's just say our benefits are much better than any you'll find elsewhere."

"Can you get me out of here?"

"We have access to attorneys who represent our people. Normally the brotherhood does not condone the type of crime you have committed, but we support a man evoking his right of superior status, particularly a white man's. However, I must say there really was no question as to your guilt, so our organization would not spend money on what would clearly be futile effort. We can however improve your situation while you are in house. But Mitchell, make no mistake, we can also make it much worse. I'll need your decision now."

"When you put it that way, it seems there isn't one to be made. When will you need my services?"

"Good boy. We'll let you know. Just be sure you always do your homework when I give you a reading assignment."

Chapter 3

Coming!" Marissa yelled as she grabbed her purse to pay for the pizza delivery. It was move-in day. Betsy Emery, Marissa's best friend and college roommate, had convinced Marissa they should move to Seattle, get jobs and share an apartment. It was thrilling to start a new life. After nearly six years of counseling, she was confident that she was dealing with the events of her past, and making some positive changes to look forward instead of back.

After Marissa left for college she had continued counseling in Modesto once a month. Her family had worked through her sister's death together and had found a way to become a new family without her daily presence. Her mother had always been very protective of them and since Jeannette's passing, this had only gotten worse. But, Marissa had learned to accept this as her mother's way, and tried to help by checking in with frequent calls home and visits when possible.

Her last four years were spent at U C Berkeley as a criminal justice major. Her goal was to help people like herself who had been a victim of violent crime. Rather than pursue a career as a trial lawyer, she felt compelled to be more behind the scenes. As a paralegal she would be working up the case, making sure small details weren't overlooked, so that justice would have its day in court and prevail.

During college she'd volunteered for a rape recovery clinic where women could come for both physical treatment, as well as, legal advice and counseling. She had met many young women who had found themselves defenseless. Through her work she felt that she was helping validate their pain and bring about closure.

By the time Marissa earned her degree she was ready for new challenges. Both her parents and her psychologist had been supportive of the move to Seattle, encouraging her to embrace new opportunities.

1987 was proving to be a year for change. She celebrated her decision to make a fresh start, by going for a personal make over for her new life. She bleached her brown hair blonde, and had it cut into a trendy new hairstyle with layered bangs to produce that 'big-hair' hairdo that was so popular. Marissa had landed a job as a paralegal working for the district attorney's office in downtown Seattle. As a graduation gift, her folks bought her a couple of stylish business suits for her new career, with shoulder pads in the jacket with a straight skirt that were becoming all the rage.

Betsy was hired as a staff writer for the Seattle Times, reporting for the real estate section, which is how they found the perfect apartment in the famed historical Queen Anne district. Betsy had been working with the photographer for her story about the renovations in the Queen Anne area, when the owner had walked out with the 'for rent' sign across the street from the shoot. The building had once been a stately home in the Victorian era and had been well maintained over the years to keep its vintage charm and quaint accoutrements. It had three stories and each of which had been converted into two-bedroom apartments. The girls were lucky to get the third floor apartment because it had an incredible view of the Seattle skyline.

The location was phenomenal. The Pacific Northwest Ballet, Seattle Opera and Seattle Center were all within walking distance. The monorail was also a short walk, connecting them to Westlake Park where a new shopping center was slated to open in the next year. Within a few blocks were cafes and pubs that on the weekends had live entertainment, drawing in the younger crowds.

There were only three other tenants. Mrs. Gottsfrey, the landlady, lived on the first floor. She reminded Marissa of the hippies in Berkeley. She was about 4’11’ and weighed all of 95 pounds. She always seemed to wear tie-dye or batik printed clothing, flowing skirts, and Birkenstocks. Her hair, which was light brown with natural gray highlights, was worn long and straight down her back. Her eyes were framed by rose tinted glasses that slid half way down her nose. Her apartment was decorated in ‘ode to the sixties’ motif, including the beads hanging in the doorway. There was a strong aroma of scented candles and burnt incense, with just the faintest hint of what the girls thought was marijuana. She informed the girls that ‘landlord’ was just a title, that she really wanted them to think of her as their second mom since both of their moms lived in California. Mrs. Gottsfrey seemed to be a warm and caring person, but Marissa was having a difficult time thinking of her as her mom. They seemed to be from different planets; in fact, she had to stifle a laugh just imaging her mom and Mrs. Gottsfrey having lunch together.

Ben and Jack were cute guys about their same age who lived in the second floor apartment. Betsy and Marissa met them when they managed to wedge their new couch between the wall and the boys' doorway on the second floor landing. Ben & Jack's generous offer to dislodge the sofa turned into a whole day of heavy lifting up two flights of stairs. The girls were so appreciative that they insisted the boys stay for pizza.

The doorbell rang again. Marissa opened it, surprised to see Western Union delivery man. "Oh, hello, you don't look like the pizza guy, can I help you?"

"Yes Ma'am. I'm looking for Marissa Van Horn. I have a telegram for her."

"I'm Marissa…a telegram? That's interesting."

She signed for the envelope just as the pizza arrived. Telegram and pizza in hand, Marissa went off to the kitchen where her hungry friends were now collapsed into the chairs around the dining table, laughing at one of Betsy's corny jokes.

"Dinner is served, people. Dig in I'll be right back." Marissa excused herself so she could open the telegram.

"Congrats on your new place. [stop]
I've never been to Seattle, and will look forward
to a visit someday when I get out. [stop]
I like you even better as a blonde. [stop]
I'll be watching you. [stop]
Mitch [stop]"

Suddenly the room seemed to be fading away and Marissa was finding it difficult to breathe and her heart was pounding in her chest. She leaned against the wall for support. She was feeling very light headed and slightly nauseous. She slid down the wall to the floor. How could he know where she was already? The lease wasn't in her name, it was in Betsy's. All the utilities and the phone bill were also listed under Betsy's name. How could he send her a telegram from prison?

"Marissa? Marissa, is everything ok--? Marissa! What are you doing on the floor?" Betsy noticed the goldenrod paper clenched in her hand. She bent down. "Marissa, what is it?"

"It's from him," she mumbled as she offered the telegram for Betsy to read.

Betsy quickly scanned the message. "Oh no... Marissa, it's going to be okay. We will deal with this, okay?" Marissa was looking down. "Marissa, look at me." Marissa looked up, her eyes teeming with tears. "We will handle this. We will get help, whatever help you need. We can call the police. We'll figure it out. Ben," Betsy called out, "can you bring me a glass of water please?"

"What's going on?" Ben asked as he came into the hallway, handing Betsy the water.

"Drink this," she said as she handing the glass to Marissa. "Marissa just got some news. I think we're going to have to ask you guys to leave for tonight. Thanks for everything. We'll make it up to you another night, okay?"

"Yeah, sure thing. Are you going to be all right?" Jack asked as he joined them in the hallway.

"We'll be fine. Thanks again for your help. We'd still be at it if you two hadn't pitched in."

Betsy followed them out and locked the door behind them. She turned back to Marissa who had moved to the couch.

"How could he find me? I just don't get it. We were so careful."

"I don't know, but we are going to find out. First thing tomorrow, we are going to the police. We will report this, and if they can't help us we will find a private detective who will."

"I can't afford a private detective. I used the last of my savings moving here."

"I have some money. I'll loan it to you," Betsy offered.

"Betsy, I can't ask you to do that. Furthermore, I'd understand if you want me to move out. I mean living with me, how safe can you feel?"

"First of all, you aren't going anywhere. And second, he is in prison. He isn't getting out for 19 more years. For now, I think we're safe. He can't get to you physically, so he is trying to get into your head."

"We've only been here one day. One day! If he can find me that fast while he is in prison, what chance do I have if he gets out? I've worked so hard to put this behind me. The last thing he said to me was, 'It isn't over.' It's never going to be over, is it?"

"He definitely wants you to believe that, but remember, he's in there and you're out here. A telegram is just paper. You don't have to let him win. Marissa, we are going to enjoy Seattle and everything it has to offer."

"Thanks, Bets, I hope you're right. One other thing, we cannot tell my parents about this. My mom would want me to move home or she'd move in here with us."

"No argument here, I've met Marianne Van Horn. I love your mom, but I don't want her as a roommate."

About that time there was a knock at the door.

"I'll see who that is," Betsy offered. She looked through the peep hole into the hallway. "It's Mrs. Gottsfrey," Betsy whispered and then opened the door.

"Betsy dear, are you two girls all settled in for the night? I just had a nice chat with Mrs. Van Horn. She called me to check on you since your phone isn't hooked up yet... such a sweet woman. I told her she could call me anytime. Marissa, I promised her that I'd check on you and that tomorrow you'd come down and use my phone to give her a call yourself."

"Thank you so much, Mrs. Gottsfrey, I'm sure my mother appreciated that. I don't want to impose; I can go to a pay phone."

"Now that's just nonsense. You just come down whenever it's convenient and use my phone. Mr. Gottsfrey, God rest his soul, left me with a decent retirement, and I can afford to do nice things for my family—and like I said that includes you girls. By the way, did the Western Union guy find you okay? I offered to sign for your telegram and bring it up myself, but he insisted it had to be personally signed by you, Marissa."

"Uh, yeah, he did. Thanks."

Mrs. Gottsfrey stepped further into the apartment. "Not bad news I hope? It must have been important. I've never received a telegram myself. You always see that in the movies though when someone dies or needs money. No one died, did they?"

"Uh no, no, nothing like that, it was just--"

"--Thanks again, Mrs. Gottsfrey, we are so tired though. Do you think we can invite you in another time? Marissa and I were just going to turn in" Betsy said, steering her to the door.

“Oh here, I almost forgot. Move-in brownies,” Mrs. Gottsfrey said, handing over a plate wrapped in foil. “They’re my special recipe.”

“How sweet of you,” Betsy replied taking the brownies and forcing a yawn as she opened the door to the hall. “We will really enjoy these. See you tomorrow.”

“Goodnight girls.”

“Goodnight,” they said in unison as Betsy shut the door.

“Special recipe…you don’t think..?” asked Marissa

Betsy started to giggle, “Well there’s one way to find out. I’m starving, let’s eat them!”

A few blocks away a man placed a call from a pay phone. "It's me….yeah, it's done. It was delivered about 30 minutes ago. Wire my money to the address I left with you. This was a onetime deal; I don’t need attention drawn to me, so lose that number."

Chapter 4

Detective Cordova of the Seattle Police department was understanding and sympathetic as he listened intently to Marissa explain the details of her situation. He was older and reminded her of her father. "Miss Van Horn, I'll do the best I can to help you, but I need you to answer a few questions for me. First of all is there anyone close to you that could possibly have a connection to Mitchell Olsen?"

"Please, call me Marissa. To my knowledge there's no one in my circle of friends that has any connection with Mitch. I thought about this last night after I got the telegram and I just can't think of anyone." she replied. "I even tried to think of someone that may be doing this as a joke, but no one comes to mind."

"That would be a pretty cruel joke," added Betsy.

"I agree, I don't think this is a joke. I'll work on confirming a point of origin with Western Union, but for the moment let's assume that at the very least it came from Mitchell with some help from the outside. Does Mitchell have any siblings, family members or friends that might be keeping him informed about you?"

Marissa thought for a few minutes. "He had a younger brother, but he was five years younger than Mitch. His mom kept him out of the courtroom during the trial, so I can't imagine he even understood what had happened back then. I don't remember anyone in high school really being Mitch's friend so I doubt there is anyone there who would be in touch. His folks were pretty shaken by what happened, but they never indicated any bitterness towards me. They were just relieved that he didn't get the death penalty."

Although he suspected he already knew the answer, he had to ask, "Have you had any other contact with Mitch before now?"

"Absolutely not. Most people in high school knew what college I was attending, so if he had wanted to send me something he could have done it then. But I never received anything."

"Who knows you moved to Seattle?" Detective Cordova inquired.

“It isn't like I've been living my life in secret for the past six years, but I have tried to protect my privacy as much as possible since the trial," Marissa explained. "Some of our close friends had a going away party for us in Berkeley before we left, so all of them would know, and then of course our families, but other than that I'm not sure."

"Was the party held in a public place, like a restaurant, or was it in someone's home?"

"It was at our favorite hang out, Zachary's Pizza," Betsy volunteered. "Do you think someone there might have been watching?"

"At this point, anything is possible. Do you think you can put together a list of guests that were there?"

"We can do anything if it will help," offered Betsy. "I'll call our friend Judy who organized it to make sure we don't forget anyone."

"That would be great. Now, I don't want you two to worry. I'm going to follow-up with this. I'll contact the prison in California, see what I can find out and let them know what has happened. In the meantime, I want you to live normally, but take some security precautions. Try not to go out alone whenever possible. Be sure to keep your doors locked both at home and in your vehicle. I'm going to beef up the patrol detail in your neighborhood. I don't believe you are in any immediate danger. From what you have told me about Mitchell Olsen, he's the type of guy who would want to carry out any plans he may have himself. What he's doing right now is baiting you. That's all he can do until he is out. I'll do my work and get in touch with you in the next day or two to let you know what I find out. Here's my card," he said, handing one to each of the girls, "let me know if you think of anything else or if you should hear from him again. You can call anytime, day or night. If I am not in, dispatch will contact me at home."

"Thank you, Detective Cordova. I really appreciate this. I feel better already," replied Marissa.

"We both do," Betsy added.

"I have a daughter about your age. I know how I'd feel if she were in your situation. Like I said, if either of you need anything, don't hesitate to call."

He watched the girls leave his office, hoping that he could find out the information necessary to keep them safe and give Marissa some peace of mind.

Chapter 5

A couple of days later, as promised, Detective Cordova called with an update. "Marissa? Detective John Cordova. How are you doing?"

"Hanging in there. I started my new job today. Staying busy is good, keeps my mind off other things."

"Good. Here's what I was able to find out. Mitchell Olsen is still in prison. According to the warden at San Quentin he is visited each week by his younger brother Alan. He is only allowed visits on Saturdays and other than his brother, he has only had visits from his attorney during the trial, and his mother comes once a month with his brother. There was also a rumor going around down there that Olsen has been talking about you recently, but no one is offering specifics. There was an inmate, Leo Fernandez, who was released three weeks ago. Apparently Fernandez was given a job in the prison library and delivered books to Olsen's cell block. One of the guards saw Olsen's brother give him a lift went he was released so there is a connection."

"Do you think that this Leo guy sent the telegram for him?"

"I doubt it. Leo hasn't been seen by anyone in California since his ride picked him up the day he was released. According to his parole officer, he has issued a warrant for parole violation. The telegram originated in Fairfax, barely over 7 miles from the penitentiary, Saturday morning about 30 minutes after visiting hours ended. And guess who was visiting? Alan Olsen."

"Maybe Alan sent it then?"

"I'd say that is more of a possibility than Leo. I did some checking with PacBell. It seems that Alan has received several calls from pay phones in the last couple of weeks. Locations have been in Berkeley, Modesto, one near Zachary's pizza on the day of your farewell party, and the last one was from Seattle at 8:32 on Saturday night. The call was made from the pay phone in front of the liquor store two blocks from your apartment. In his mug shot Leo has a distinctive scar on his left cheek. I went down to the liquor store and showed them his picture, and the guy said he remembered him coming in there about that time and bought some smokes, some Jack Daniels and left."

"What does all this mean?"

"My best guess right now is that this guy Leo owed Olsen a favor. He's probably been watching you for a couple of weeks and followed you to Seattle, and then reported that the telegram had been delivered. If he had wanted to hurt you he would have done it by now."

"What do we do now?"

"I can have you put into protective custody if you want, but like I said before, until Olsen's out of prison I think you are physically safe."

"No, I don't want that. He has ruined too much of my life already. There has to be another solution."

"The next thing would be to call in a security expert to make sure your home is as safe as it can be. Since there is a warrant out for Leo, I will put out an APB for him in Seattle. If he turns up we can question him and see what he knows. Then we can go from there. The Modesto police tried to question Alan, however sending a telegram isn't a crime, so they can't arrest him and he was not volunteering any information. He told them they should talk to his lawyer."

"I see. It sounds like you're telling me there is nothing more to do but wait."

"One other thing you might consider is taking this to your boss. The DA's office here may have access to some information that I don't. If something else comes up, please call me right away. If I hear anything more I will get in touch with you."

"Thank you for all your help."

"You're welcome. Stay safe."

Marissa hung up the phone. She walked over to the bay window to look up and down the street. She could see the pay phone on the corner, which stood empty at the moment. She didn't see anyone out there, but couldn't help wondering if she would spend the rest of her life looking over her shoulder for someone who might be watching her.

A sudden knock on the door startled her. She walked over and looked through the door viewer. Mrs. Gottsfrey was in the hallway. She opened the door.

"Oh, Marissa, good. I thought I saw you come in. Listen honey, I don't want to alarm you, but I'm worried that something is going on in the neighborhood. I've noticed that the police have been going up and down our street all day. I just want you girls to take precautions if you go out."

"Thank you, Mrs. Gottsfrey, we'll be careful. If my mom calls you, please don't mention this to her. She really worries and I wouldn't want her thinking we aren't safe," Marissa asked her.

"Of course dear, I wouldn't want your mom to worry either. Did you call her yet today?"

"I called today at lunch. She was happy to hear from me. She had heard that we were supposed to have some rain, and she was worried that maybe we didn't get everything moved in yet."

"Oh honey, we are almost always supposed to have rain! Surely she can't be worried about that?"

"Well, my mom tends to worry about everything. But she's my mom and I love her!"

"What a good daughter you are. Okay sweetie, I left my dinner on the stove, so I'm going to go finish making it. I have a very nice gentlemen coming over tonight. We always watch Masterpiece Theatre together. Tonight is 'Goodnight Mr. Chips'. It's a romance, and I'm kind of hoping for a little 'Goodnight with Mr. Chips' if you get my drift?" she said as she tapped Marissa's ribs with her elbow.

"Mrs. Gottsfrey, you, devil, you!"

Chapter 6

It was hard to believe that over three years had passed since Marissa and Betsy had moved to Seattle. They had adjusted nicely to their new home. Although Marissa's mom called her daily, she had come to terms with her daughter living so far from home and was thrilled that Marissa was doing so well. Mr. and Mrs. Van Horn came a few times a year to visit, and to Marissa's astonishment, Marianne had hit it off with Mrs. Gottsfrey and the two of them often corresponded. Marissa also went back home to Modesto for holidays and visits from time to time, but it was Seattle that was home to her now.

There had not been any more incidents concerning Mitchell Olsen since the day they moved in three years ago, but Marissa still kept her guard up. When she went out, she was always careful to look around for someone who might be watching her. She had taken a self defense class with a co-worker but she hoped she never had to use the skills she had learned.

Marissa had met a few guys over the past couple of years, but no one special. She dated a man from work off and on for awhile. In the end neither felt there was enough on which to build a relationship, so they parted as friends. Betsy had set her up on a few dates also. One was with a sports reporter from her office. It turned out that he liked to watch sports, talk about sports, play sports and considered dating a sport. He still referred to the stages in dating as getting to 'first base' or making a 'touch down'. He kept stats on how many times they held hands, hugged or kissed. Marissa quickly decided that losing him was her favorite sport.

Marissa loved her job with the District Attorney's office. She found the work to be both challenging and rewarding. Her boss, Mr. Rosenthal, was an accomplished trial lawyer and ran the office with the precision of a Swiss clock. He believed in representing the people and bringing criminals to justice. As a paralegal, Marissa was an integral part of his support team. She worked closely with the police and forensic labs gathering necessary reports, spent hours researching the law, and communicated directly with clients and witnesses, preparing depositions and taking statements. She followed the trial from inception to end, monitoring the progress and ensuring that everything ran smoothly.

There were always several cases going on at once, although not all of them were high profile. But there was one that tore at her heart strings. A young woman and her daughter had been abducted during a bank robbery. The men robbing the bank had felt it necessary to take hostages and assumed that police would be less likely to pursue with a woman and child at risk. They were dumped in a heavily forested area near Deception Pass, bound and gagged and left to die of starvation or be attacked by wild animals. The men were apprehended the next day and it took another 8 hours of intense questioning before one of them broke and finally told the police where to 'find the bodies'. The police were surprised to find them both alive, although severely dehydrated. The woman said her daughter still has nightmares, and her husband now does all the banking.

It was for cases like these that Marissa had decided to go into this field. She felt each time she helped one of these people find closure and a case reach justice, it was like avenging Jeanette's death. She kept her sister's picture on her desk to serve as a reminder to give each case individual attention, that victims were always someone special to someone.

She appreciated the other people in the office. They were hard working and like Mr. Rosenthal, they were there to do the people's bidding. They were a close-knit group and enjoyed sharing a pizza when they worked late, or going out for drinks to unwind after a tough day or to celebrate a big win in court. They hit it off from the start and were quick to include Marissa whenever they went out.

Ben and Jack had also been great friends to Marissa and Betsy. The foursome often went out on the weekends to pubs or restaurants in the neighborhood. They had found a comfortable ease together that made them best of friends.

Mrs. Gottsfrey had proved to be a constant source of amusement. Once, the fire department was called out because all the smoke alarms in the building went off. The fire engines came blaring down the street at 2:00 a.m. causing everyone in the neighborhood to run outside in their P.J.s. Mrs. Gottsfrey came out in hers, a leopard print midriff top with matching spandex bottoms, a hot pink satin night mask, a silky black robe, and black furry slippers with stiletto heels. The firemen rushed in the building, ready to fight a blaze. When the fire crew emerged, they announced that there was no fire, only smoke damage and they would have the building cleared within the next 30 minutes or so. The fire chief called Mrs. Gottsfrey over to discuss something privately, although the girls could overhear the conversation.

"Mrs. Gottsfrey, can I speak to you?" the chief asked.

"Certainly Chief, if this is about updating my smoke alarms, I'm all over it."

"No, Ma'am. Could we step over here please?" he said in a quieter tone, guiding Mrs. Gottsfrey to the side of the truck.

Curiosity getting the better of the girls, they tried to follow without being too obvious.

"Ma'am I'm not sure you realize, but the fire was started by a scarf smoldering over an ash tray in your bedroom."

"Oh, I'm so sorry. I just don't know where my head is sometimes."

"Yes, well the cigarette burning in the ashtray wasn't…it was… I mean.. that is to say… that it wasn't … of the normal variety of cigarette, if you are understanding what I'm getting at here."

"What?....Oh….well, yes, I guess I do. Are you going to tell on me? Please don't take me to jail…I just don't think I could handle that."

"Ma'am. Mrs. Gottsfrey."

"Call me Judy."

"Judy. No, I'm not going to tell anyone. But you really need to be more careful. Now, I'm the only one that knows. I disposed of it, but you can't count on that the next time."

"Thank you, Chief. I'll be more careful, I promise. How about you coming over and fire proofing my place sometime? I bet there are all kinds of code violations you can help me overcome."

"Call me Bill, and I'm sure we could arrange something."

"Chief, is there a Mrs. Bill?"

"Not since she ran off with her yoga instructor."

"Well Bill, then how about coming by on Friday night? We can make a little fire of our own?"

"Can I bring anything, Judy?"

"Are you allowed to bring out the hook and ladder? I've always wanted to drive one of those."

"Not really, they may need it at the station. I could give you a tour of it another time."

"In that case, how about we meet at your place so you can show me how your hose works."

"See you Friday night, Judy."

"See you Friday, Bill."

Marissa and Betsy, who now had tears running down their cheeks, quickly ducked around the backside of the fire truck and out of eye sight as they finished their conversation. Mrs. Gottsfrey came around the corner, "Now see, girls, that's how to get a date!" she said to them as she passed them by. The girls could no longer contain themselves, collapsed against the truck in a hysterical fit. Ben and Jack noticed the two laughing and came over to see what was so funny, as getting up in the middle of the night did not hold much humor for them.

"What is so funny about a fire?" Jack asked.

Of course this just made them laugh harder, "I think this is one of those 'had to be there' moments," Marissa managed to get out. Her lack of response caused Ben and Jack to become impatient.

"Fine, don't tell us. I've got an early morning, I'm going to bed!" Ben announced turning towards the house.

"Wait, I'll tell you," Betsy offered, then started laughing again.

"Never mind," Ben said, Jack following him in a huff.

Marissa looked at Betsy. "You really did have to be there," she said.

"Absolutely," Betsy replied, "Hey, you know why firemen wear red suspenders?"

"Ugh, Betsy, is this one of your corny jokes?"

"It's not like the polar bear joke."

"Okay, Betsy, why do firemen wear red suspenders?"

"To hold up their pants of course!"

"Betsy, don't quit your day job."

"Do you think Mrs. Gottsfrey's heard that one?"

"I'm pretty sure she wrote it!"

The girls giggled all the way back to their apartment.

Marissa, Betsy, Jack and Ben had a standing invitation for Sunday night dinner at Mrs. Gottsfrey's. As it turned out Mr. Gottsfrey had been a big wig at a Hollywood movie studio, and before retiring in Seattle the couple had resided in Beverly Hills. They had met several celebrities over the years, and she had kept in touch with them. Sometimes these acquaintances would be invited also, turning Sunday's with Mrs. Gottsfrey into dinner and a show. She had also worked her way into their lives as a trusted friend. If one of them was dating someone that was semi-serious, they had to bring them to Sunday night dinner to pass the Gottsfrey Test. She wasn't the best cook, but her dinners were always something they looked forward to, and they all did their best to make it a priority. They had become a family.

Mitch sat on his bunk reading his bible. It wasn't the first time a hit order had come through. He knew the drill. Tonight two men would come to him after lights out. They would present the appropriate opportunity for him to meet the target, and insure he returned to his cell and was locked in before the body was discovered.

It had been almost seven years since he had received his first assignment from the Chaplain. The target was a member of the brotherhood who was suspected of working with authorities to provide evidence against them. While waiting to see if his information was accurate, he was left at San Quentin in a protected cell.

After Mitch's hour in the yard, he came back to find that the Chaplain had left a bible on his bunk and provided Mitch with some required reading: Psalm 119:173 "May your hand be ready to help me, for I have chosen your precepts." In the margin a single name had been handwritten. Mitch knew the name. A small bookmark had been left, a picture of a clock with the hands pointing to two and twelve. He lay back on his bunk, staring at the ceiling trying to make sense of the reading and the bookmark. Two men came at 2:00 a.m. No words were spoken. They escorted him quietly to the cell of the inmate. His door was opened and Mitch was pushed inside. He wasted no time. He walked straight in, grabbed the man's throat and held on tight until the man fell limp beneath him. When he had finished, the two men opened the door and returned him to his cell.

The next morning the Chaplain had come by to commend him on a job well done. A large amount of money had been added to his bank account. Mitch decided to ask him for a name for his own use outside, as he was in need of someone with certain skills to carry out some business for him. The Chaplain provided him with Leo Fernandez's name and instructions on how to reach him. Mitch remembered meeting him once before. The Chaplain assured Mitchell that Leo could do what he needed. If additional coaxing was necessary, Mitch only needed to mention the Chaplain's name and he was confident no further questions would be asked.

Chapter 7

The weather in Seattle, though often wet and rainy, today offered a beautiful afternoon. The sun was shining brilliantly, warming the coastal breeze on Pike Street. Marissa was enjoying her Saturday morning, wandering through the markets. The square was abuzz with shoppers and merchants exchanging smiles and pleasantries. Fresh produce and fresh flowers were displayed in an array of color. Sidewalk restaurants produced an intoxicating aromatic sampling as restaurateurs and sidewalk vendors prepared a wide assortment of ethnic cuisines. Marissa strolled at a leisurely pace, taking in her surroundings. With the assistance of the fishmonger, she picked out a salmon at Pike Place Fish Market and laughed as he bantered with the other guys behind the counter, while he packed it in some ice for the ride home. She quickly picked out her produce, fresh bread and flowers. She wanted tonight to be perfect.

Betsy had gone to her folks' for the weekend, so Marissa had the apartment to herself. Last night before she left, Betsy had loaned Marissa a sexy wrap-around black dress, with soft cap sleeves, a plunging neckline, and soft romantic ruffles at the hemline that fell gracefully at her knees. A wide belt accentuated her slim waistline and the gentle curves of her hips. Low heeled strappy sandals gave the dress a relaxed elegance. She couldn't wait to see Brian's face when she met him at the door.

As she rode the monorail back to her stop, she couldn't help but smile. She had been seeing Brian for the past two months, but it felt like she had known him forever. She leaned her head back against the window, remembering the night they met. Betsy and Marissa had found Wexby's Pub a fun place to go on Saturday nights. It was always packed with people they knew from the neighborhood, teaming with energy. Jim Wexby, the owner, brought in local talent each week.

On this particular night, the entertainment was a comedian. He was going on at great lengths about his failed relationships and agonizing love life. He was talking about how confusing women are, and how men just didn't stand a chance with any of them. Betsy and Marissa were laughing hysterically. Then, right in the middle of his routine he stopped and asked, "Can you turn up the house lights please?" There was a curious lull in the audience. He repeated his request, "House lights? Please?" The lights were brought up, and he was suddenly standing next to Marissa. "Hello, can I ask your name?"

Marissa, a little surprised by the turn of events, answered, "Marissa."

"Marissa, I noticed you laughing at my helplessness when it comes to women. Perhaps you can help me figure out what I'm doing wrong. First of all, how's my appearance? Am I dressed okay?"

Marissa and Betsy had already commented to each other how good-looking he was. "You look fine."

"Okay, so I look 'fine'. Not exactly high praise, but we'll work with it. Now, could we pretend like we haven't met before?"

"We don't have to pretend, we haven't met before," replied Marissa. A few people in the audience chuckled.

"Hey-I'm the one who's making the jokes here. Okay, let's go a step further. Let's say you are dazzled by my charming wit, because unlike my usual approach, I have managed to impress you, and you have agreed to go out with me."

"We're still pretending, right?"

The audience let out an 'ooowe'.

"Marissa, you're killing me here, but yes, we are still pretending. What would be your ideal date?"

Marissa was suddenly very self conscious. She was finding herself attracted to this man. She tried to think of something witty to say, but her heart was racing and she thought even if she could get words out, her voice would probably crack. She shrugged her shoulders and gave him a smile. "Okay, I'll give you another minute to think. The last woman I asked about her ideal date told me it was any date that I wasn't on with her." The room filled with laughter. He turned his attention back to her, "Anything yet?" Marissa shook her head. "This is what I'm talking about. Men, I'm telling you, we don't stand a chance. When the most beautiful woman in the room can not answer the question of what is her ideal date, where can we go for answers." He moved back to the stage, the lights were dimmed again. "Dating is a crap shoot, if you bring her flowers, take her to a nice dinner, you're predictable. If you do something original, you're trying too hard. If you do manage to get past that awkward first date, and on to a 'relationship' it gets even trickier. They always want you to share your feelings, right, ladies? Guys, BEWARE. Do not under any circumstance show emotion while sharing *your* feelings. They say they want a guy who isn't 'afraid to cry', but in truth, they don't want you to actually cry. There is a catch though, because when she is sharing her feelings you had better exhibit some emotion!" He went on for another ten minutes before completing his act.

When Brian emerged from back stage he immediately went to find Marissa. He walked over to where Marissa and Betsy were finishing up their drinks. "Excuse me, Marissa; I would truly like to apologize if I made you feel uncomfortable in any way."

"Well, you did put her on the spot," Betsy chimed in.

"I realize that," Brian said. "It's just that I could see you when I was on stage. Something came over me, and I knew I had to talk to you right then. I just couldn't wait and take the chance that when I finished you might have left and I would never have spoken a word to you."

"That's so sweet! Isn't that sweet, Marissa?" Betsy cooed, as if talking to a small child.

Marissa kicked her under the table, and offered up a friendly glare at her friend before returning her attention to the matter at hand.

"Does this pick up line work for you, Mr. uh…?" Marissa asked.

Brian chuckled, "Brian, Brian Benton. It's not a line. Usually I don't even leave the stage. Please, will you at least let me buy you a drink and you can decide for yourself if you think I'm sincere?" He was slowly breaking down Marissa's defenses.

She glanced over at Betsy who gave her a slight nod. She turned back towards Brian, "Marissa Van Horn and you may buy me a cup of coffee. It's chilly out, and we need to be leaving soon."

"Yes!" he exclaimed, loud enough to get the attention of the neighboring tables. She liked the way his deep blue eyes crinkled at the corners as a disarming smile spread across his face. When their eyes met, she read in them genuineness and felt safe. That was all she needed. "Stay right here, I'll be back."

"Marissa, he seems nice. I see Ben and Jack over there. I'm going to go join them." Betsy said as Brian walked away.

"Bets, don't go," pleaded Marissa, clutching Betsy's sleeve, "I need you here!"

"No, you don't. What you need is to give this guy a real chance. You deserve a love life. I'll be right over there if it doesn't work out, but I doubt you'll need me." She watched Betsy pick up her coat and purse and walk over to Ben and Jack, who turned to wave at Marissa as Brian returned with two steaming cups of coffee.

He was easy to talk to and they found out they had a lot in common. They enjoyed the same music, read many of the same books; they had both grown up in California and were trying to start a new life in Seattle. Brian was a couple of years older than Marissa. He told her how his folks had been killed in a car accident when he was very young. His only living relative, his grandmother, had raised him in Sausalito. Financially, she was very well off and had been able to send him to private schools. He had been exposed to the arts all through his childhood. He too had attended Berkeley and they seemed to have just missed meeting on a number of occasions. His major had been psychology, but on the weekends he had started going to open mike nights at comedy clubs. During his second year at school, his grandmother passed away, leaving him everything in her estate. He enjoyed making people laugh, so after he graduated he decided to pursue a career as a comedian.

Marissa felt an immediate connection to Brian. There was a safety with him she had not felt in years. He wanted to know everything about her and he patiently listened as she shared her story. She told him her sister had been killed when they were in high school, how devastating that had been to her family. She told him how protective her parents had been of her ever since, and that her move to Seattle had been a way to find her independence. She knew the day would come when she would tell him everything, but for now this enough.

The similar challenges they had overcome, each losing family at a young age, growing up in California and attending Berkeley seemed to cement the bond they had formed. They spent the evening walking and talking.

When he left her at her door, several hours later, he held her gaze again as he traced her cheek with his thumb. "Miss Van Horn, it's been a pleasure," he said, as he bent down and lightly kissed her goodnight. "I can hardly wait to see you again. Can I pick you up tomorrow morning say around 11:00? We could go to Sunday brunch at the Space Needle."

"Sounds good. I'll see you then." He kissed her once more, then turned and walked down the street. She watched him as he passed the liquor store a few blocks away and turned the corner. She turned and went inside. That was the first date.

In the past two months they were growing closer every day. They met downtown for lunch when she could get away from the office, they met at one or the other's apartment to cook dinner together a few nights a week, visited museums on the weekends, took walks in the evenings to get exercise. They went to ball games and music concerts. They enjoyed each other's company in a way that felt as if they had always known each other. A few weeks ago Marissa had finally shared the details of her sister's death and everything since then. He listened intently as she relayed the details, stroking her hand gently for encouragement, offering support. When she finished Brian's eyes had been wet when they met hers. He had taken her hand and pulled it towards him, covering it within his own. He had thanked her for trusting him with such a confidence. It was at that moment she knew she was falling in love with him.

As the monorail pulled into the station, she was pulled back to present. She gathered her shopping bags. Today was Brian's birthday; she was determined to make it his best. She was lost in thought as she walked down the street to her apartment. She never saw the stranger who followed her off the train and kept a close pace on the opposite side of the street. She didn't see him step into the shadow of a covered porch across the street and light up a cigarette as she opened the door to the apartment. And she wouldn't see him later when he set in motion events which would once again turn her world upside down.

Leo Fernandez was a tall man with a lean but rock hard body, a feature that had served him well over the years. In his line of work it was often necessary to blend into the scenery and blending is what Leo did best. If he needed to be a business man he was able to sport a tailored suit. If the occasion called for less formal attire, such as presenting himself as a homeless man, he could easily make the transition to a starving street dweller. He could be anybody's banker, grocer, dry-cleaner or drug dealer.

Leo's slight build afforded him a disarming quality which worked to his advantage. Not only did he often go unnoticed, but even when he was seen, it was never as a threat. This was a serious mistake many had made in the past, and he knew more would make in the future. He had spent time honing his skills in martial arts and hand to hand combat; skills he had put to use on many an occasion without leaving a trace of his existence.

Four years ago, when the San Francisco police had arrived at his door, Leo was confident they had the wrong man. When they presented the charges against him, he knew they couldn't possibly have evidence of his crime. Nonetheless a jury had found him guilty of murder in the first degree, and sentenced him to life in prison without parole in San Quentin State Prison. It was during his stay while awaiting his appeal that he had met Mitchell Olsen, the young man from Modesto, also sentenced to life without parole. He had remembered the Chronicle carrying news of the violent crime that shook one of California's quiet little towns.

The kid had told him he was innocent, but then that's what they all say. Leo couldn't help feeling sorry for him just the same. He was so young to spend so much of his life incarcerated.

After Leo's appeal came through, the kid's brother came around and offered him a ride and some much needed cash. Leo didn't turn it down, assuming it was a onetime deal.

Yet here he was three years later, once again doing Mitchell Olsen's bidding. He had tried to refuse but this time the request was backed up by the Chaplain. Furthermore the state of California had Leo listed as a wanted man, and it was becoming necessary to have some cash to support his increasingly difficult lifestyle. He needed cash to get some papers so he could hide. When the call came through he was desperate. It was more than just an errand this time. The amount they were paying this time would go a long way towards helping his current situation. The money and the fact that no one denied the Chaplain's requests became the driving motive for his willing assistance.

He'd been following her for weeks. When he first started she was very careful, always looking around before she stepped out on the sidewalk or looking back over her shoulder and she was seldom alone. Since meeting the comedian she had been more carefree. Just goes to show you how blind love really is. Over the past few weeks she had really relaxed and he had been able to follow her more closely without being seen.

He watched her as she walked through the market place. She was indeed a beautiful woman. Her long, blonde hair was pulled back in a French braid with a few wisps hanging loose around her face. Her jeans accented her figure in all the right places. He knew he wasn't supposed to do anything to her, but he couldn't help wonder what she would feel like next to him. He would execute the plan when the time was just right in the next few days. He knew patience would present the prime opportunity he was looking for.

Chapter 8

Brian arrived right on time. Marissa met him at the door, handing him a glass of chardonnay as she reached up to offer him a kiss. "Happy Birthday, get ready to be wowed." He followed her into the kitchen where she was poaching the salmon. He could see the dining table set for a romantic dinner for two.

He came up behind her and slid his hands around her waist, nuzzling his face near to her ear. "I'm always wowed by you." He planted soft kisses along her neck. "You look fabulous, and dinner smells fantastic."

"If you don't go away, I'm not going to be able to finish making it. Why don't you go put on some music for us."

"Are you sure?" Brian asked as he teasingly reached to untie her apron. "We could start with dessert instead," he suggested as he made another pass at her neck.

"Brian Benton!" She exclaimed, pushing him away. "I have been working on this dinner all day. Besides you wouldn't want to ruin your birthday surprise now would you?"

"Hmmm, let me think," pulling her back towards him. The look on her face told him that skipping dinner was not a possibility. "Okay," he said releasing her, "you win, for now, but remember I am the birthday boy!"

"I know, that's why you get to pick the music. Now scoot!" she replied as she swatted him with a kitchen towel.

By the time she had dinner ready, Kenny G was playing on the stereo. Brian had lit the candles and poured more wine for dinner. She took off her apron and joined him in the dining room. "Everything looks amazing. I can't believe you did all this for me," he said.

"I love you, Brian. Here's to you," she said, raising her glass.

"I love you, too. Here's to us," he replied, raising his glass to meet hers.

After dinner he offered to help with the dishes. "Absolutely not, Birthday Boy! But I will allow you to go in the living room and light the fireplace. There really isn't that much to clean up and I'll be there in less than five minutes."

As she finished up the dishes, she couldn't help think how lucky she was to have found Brian. Even though they had been dating for a relatively short time, she felt that they had known each other for years. They had such an ease between them. She knew he was her soul mate.

When she came into the room, she found Brian leaning against some cushions on the floor in front of an inviting fire. She slipped out of her shoes and lowered herself next to him. He put his arm around her, pulling her into a long kiss. "Hello."

"Hello."

"Have I told you how beautiful you look tonight?"

"I think you may have mentioned it"

"Have I told you how much I love you?"

"I never get tired of hearing it."

"Marissa," Brian said affectionately, "I know it's my birthday, but we can just sit by this fire, I have no expectations."

"Sh-h-h. Tonight is perfect Brian. It's your night, and this is what I want to do," Marissa replied. She reached over and pulled his face close to hers. "I want you, Brian." She kissed him softly and wrapped her arms around his neck. He pulled her into his lap, facing him, drawing her closer until their lips met in a deepening kiss. He untied her belt, allowing her dress to fall open. He let out a slow breath as he slipped his hands under the fabric and down her spine. Marissa slowly stood and took his hand, pulling him up, and then led him to her bedroom.

Leo could see the flickering firelight through the bay window sheers. He had found a porch of a vacant house across the street that was well hidden in the shadows. He would sit and wait. After a couple of hours he saw silhouettes walk past the window and the bedroom light come on, then go off. He pulled out the duffle he had hidden behind the planter box earlier and took out a blanket and wrapped it around himself. He lit up a cigarette and leaned back against the porch wall, settling in for a long night. Several hours later, when the sun had come up, Leo watched Brian Benton emerge from the building. He decided this was opportunity presenting itself.

Brian left the building; distracted by the wonderful woman he had left sleeping. It was overcast today, but not raining yet. If he was lucky he'd make it back before the rain started. He was thinking about how he was going to wake her up when he got back. He was thinking about what they would do after breakfast. He was thinking about the shower they were going to take...together. He was so lost in thought that he missed the 'good mornings' and smiles sent his way as he walked to the coffee shop. He didn't notice the stranger watching from across the street when he came out holding the bag of croissants. He never heard Leo step in behind him, nor did he realize that Leo was walking mere feet behind him matching him step for step.

Leo on the other hand was quite conscious of every breath that Brian took. He was quite aware that Brian was lost in thought and not paying attention. As they came upon the alley on their right, Leo decided it was now or never. He grabbed Brian from behind and pulled him into the alley, and then quickly pushed him behind a nearby dumpster. Brian was taken off guard as he unwillingly stumbled into the alley. As he felt the push from behind there was little he could do but put out his arms to break his fall as he was losing his footing. The building's concrete wall was rushing towards his face. As his head made contact with the cement, he felt a stabbing pain in his side, and then another, and still another. A sharp pain in his chest felt as if his lungs were crushing with each breath he tried to take. He felt his wallet being taken from his pocket and saw a blurry figure scoop up his paper bag. As he slid down the wall to the pavement, he heard footsteps leaving quickly. As hard as he tried he couldn't pull in a breath, and then everything went black.

Chapter 9

Marissa could hear the rain gently tapping on her window pane. The apartment was cast in shadows, but she could hear a fire sizzling in the fireplace. She awoke slowly to the realization that Brian was missing. She called out to him, but there was no answer. She got out of bed and pulled on a dressing gown as she padded out to the living room. "Brian....Brian?" No answer. Obviously he wasn't here. She followed the smell of brewing coffee into the kitchen, where a note was taped to the cupboard. "Went out for croissants, keep warm by the fire, be back in a few..."

She took down a cup and filled it with coffee. She went to the door to retrieve the morning paper before going to sit in front of the fire. Waiting for her on top of the Seattle Times was a brown bag from the new Starbuck's on the corner. When she bent down to pick it up, something fell out from underneath. It was a driver's license with a red smear on it stuck to a napkin. A hand written note scrawled in blue ink said, "Don't wait for him, he won't be back." She looked at the photo on the license; it was Brian's.

For a moment nothing registered. She looked up and down the hallway to see who could have left this for her to find. Everything was quiet. She ran down the stairs and banged on Ben and Jack's door. "Ben! Jack! Open up! It's Marissa. Hurry!"

A muffled "Coming" came from behind the door. Jack looked like he was struggling to open his eyes. Obviously she had woke them up. "What's up?"

"Jack, something's happened. Did you hear anything this morning in the hall?"

"Sorry, no. I got in late and crashed. I'm surprised I heard you. What happened?"

"I'm not sure. Brian spent the night last night. He went out for croissants, but I don't know how long ago. I went to get the paper while I waited for him, and found this on the door mat." She showed him the license and the note.

"Okay, let's not panic. You go back to your apartment and wait for him in case you get a call. I'll go down the street and see if I can find him anywhere."

"All right, but hurry."

"And Marissa, while I'm gone you might want to put on something else, just in case."

Marissa looked down, now remembering she had her robe on. "Good idea."

"I'll be back as soon as I can."

Marissa ran back up the stairs and quickly put on some jeans, a sweatshirt and sneakers. Then she heard the sirens go racing past her building. There was an abrupt stop. It sounded close. From the window she could see a commotion just about a block away. Her heart started beating faster. Something inside her told her it was Brian. She ran out the door, down the two flights of stairs and out the main door to the sidewalk. By the time she reached the alley a crowd had formed blocking the entrance. She fought her way through them, pushing to the front of the group. She found Jack standing there trying to get the attention of a police officer. “Marissa, I can’t see what’s going on. No one seems to know anything,” he said to her.

There were two police officers standing behind a section of police tape. They were keeping people away from the paramedics who could be seen crouching down behind a gurney.

"Excuse me, sir; I think that might be my boyfriend in the alley. Can I please see him?" Marissa anxiously asked one of the officers.

"Hold on, let me check," he replied.

He walked over to ask one of the men tending to the patient. She could see them talking but couldn't hear what they were saying. When he returned he lifted the tape up, "I'm sorry miss, this is considered a crime scene. We need to keep all unnecessary foot traffic out. You can however, wait over near the coroner's van. You can see him when they load him in."

"C-c-coroner? Does that mean he is dead?" she asked, already knowing the answer.

"Yes, Ma'am, I'm afraid so. Miss, do you need to sit down? You aren't looking too good. Miss…" his words were now trailing off in her mind. She had to think. Maybe it wasn't Brian. Maybe this was someone else and Brian was going to walk up any minute wondering what was going on.

“Marissa, you go sit down over there. I’m going walk up the street and see if I can find him, okay?” Jack said.

"Yeah, okay," Marissa said, lost in her own thoughts. Her mind was still racing with possibilities, when she felt someone take her arm and put another one around her. They were walking her towards an ambulance. She turned to look. Was it Brian? She was met with a familiar face.

"Detective Cordova? My boyfriend, Brian Benton. I think it might be him in the alley" Marissa said. She handed him the blood smeared driver's license.

He glanced down at the picture. He pulled out a handkerchief and took the license from her. He then turned and carefully handed it to another officer. "See if this matches the vic over there, and then put that into our evidence."

"Yes, sir."

"Miss Van Horn. Why don't you come with me. I think we need to have you looked at first, and then we can talk."

He led Marissa to the open ambulance. He had her sit down on the bumper and put a blanket around her. He motioned to a paramedic and asked him to take a look at her. "Wait here. I'll be right back," he instructed her. "Don't leave her alone, okay?" he ordered the paramedic.

She watched him walk over to the scene. He stood there for a few minutes, and then slowly walked back towards her. The dampness from the drizzling rain was beginning to soak through her sweatshirt. A shiver ran through her, but she knew it wasn't from the cold. "Marissa, we've made a positive I.D. based on the photo. I'm so sorry, it's Brian."

Marissa dropped her face into her hands and began to sob. Detective Cordova pulled her into a fatherly hug for a moment. "Marissa, I know you need some time to take in this news, but I'm going to need you to hold it together for a while longer," he said as he pulled away from her. He reached down and pulled her face up so she would look into his eyes. "As soon as you're ready, I'm going to need you to tell me everything that happened. I don't want to rush you, but the sooner we know what happened, the sooner we can find who did this."

She nodded. She felt as if things were moving in slow motion around her. The words she had heard were echoing in her head, their meaning lost to her for the moment. For the time being shock and disbelief seemed to be keeping her emotions at bay. "I'm not sure what happened. But I'll tell you what I do know…."

Leo was watching from just behind the police tape. He watched as they covered the body and placed it onto the gurney. He was amused watching the police dumpster dive looking for a weapon. They would eventually find it, but he would be long gone by then. But, of course, there wouldn't be anything to tie it to him.

He glanced over in Marissa's direction. She was sitting alone on the bumper of the ambulance. She seemed to be staring off into the distance. It was a shame that he had needed the money so bad, because he really hated doing this to such a striking girl. In another place and time, he might have taken it upon himself to try and cheer her up. Even in her sadness there was beauty. He had done what he needed to do here. One more thing left and he could call and collect his pay.

Chapter 10

Marissa could hear the rain gutter outside gurgling. It was pitch black in her room. She was curled into a fetal position with the covers billowing around her. She pulled the pillow to her chest, breathing in the lingering scent of Brian's aftershave lotion. She buried her face in it, wishing she could suffocate herself in its smell.

There was a soft knock at the door. "Marissa?" No answer. "Marissa?" Betsy called again opening the door. She walked over to the bed and sat down. She reached over and placed a hand on Marissa's shoulder. "Marissa, I came as soon as Ben called me. I'm so sorry. Please talk to me."

"There's nothing to talk about. Brian is gone," Marissa responded, without turning over. Her voice was low and stilted.

Betsy laid down next to her, putting her arms around Marissa. "I'm so sorry."

"He's gone. It took so long to find him. I loved him so much. I can't believe he's gone." Marissa broke down, her body shaking as the flood of emotions overtook her. "Bets, what am I going to do without him? I don't think I can go through this again. I barely made it through the last time."

"Sh-sh, it's going to be okay. You didn't have me the last time," she whispered, holding her in a protective cocoon. Betsy pulled back the hair that had fallen in Marissa's face and laid her cheek against Marissa's. "I'm here. I'm staying right here."

It was Monday morning. Marissa was still sleeping. Betsy got up and called both of their employers to say they would not be coming in today. She made some coffee and then called Marissa's parents to let them know what had happened. They offered to come right away and asked Betsy to make reservations for them to stay at a nearby hotel. She said she would also make arrangements for a car to pick them up at the airport when they called her with their flight information. She took her shower and dressed. When she finished, the apartment was still quiet. She looked in on Marissa who was still in bed.

At noon, when Marissa still had not come out, Betsy decided it was time to go in and speak to her. "Marissa, you need to eat something. Can I bring you a tray?"

"No, thank you. I just want to be left alone," she responded.

"Okay, but I'm leaving a glass of water on your night stand. You at least need to drink something or you'll get dehydrated. I called your folks. They'll be here by this evening."

"You shouldn't have done that. They don't need to come."

"Marissa, your folks want to be here to support you. Now is the time you need your family. I'm putting them up at the Sorrento downtown. We can pick them up for the service and then go out for a bite afterwards. "

"What service? Brian didn't have any relatives. There won't be a service."

"We are planning a service for him,' Betsy replied.

"We? Who is 'we'?" Marissa asked.

"'We' is you and me. We are planning a memorial. Don't you think it's the right thing to do? Don't you think there are people who would want to come and remember him? He had people he went to school with, people who were fans of his, and we have all become his friends. We need to mourn him as well. What about you? Don't you need some closure to this?" Betsy was trying to be as gentle as she could, but Marissa needed to hear that she wasn't alone grieving Brian's death. "Now, I really need your help if I'm going to do a good job with the service, but I will understand if you aren't up to it."

"Fine. What do we need to do?" Marissa asked.

"We will need to decide on a location, but you should know the police will not release the body until an autopsy has been done. We may want to have a memorial service for friends and then you can decide what we should do about a burial service. I think since he didn't have any living relatives to make this decision, you should be the one to decide. Maybe you can talk to Detective Cordova about it and see if he can help you figure out who to talk to about all of that."

"Actually Brian and I discussed this once when we were talking about his family. He told me that he wanted to be cremated. His grandmother is in a mausoleum in Sausalito, so I think we should send his remains there," said Marissa. "As for a memorial service, could you talk to Jim about using Wexby's?"

"Sure I'll take care of that. Now go take a shower and get ready to meet your folks," Betsy said, turning Marissa towards the shower. The door bell rang. Marissa glanced at Betsy with a look that said I don't want to see anyone. "I'll get that, you go!"

Marissa turned back towards Betsy, "Thanks, Bets. You're a good friend."

Marissa came out of the bathroom in her robe and slippers and her wet hair wrapped in a towel. Everything was quiet. She walked out to the living room to see if anyone was around. She saw some roses on the kitchen counter and a note: "Mar, went to Ben & Jack's to talk about the service. Roses came for you as I was leaving. Be back soon, Bets."

Marissa wondered who would be sending her roses. She removed the card and opened the small envelope. "Never forget, you will always be mine. M.O." Marissa's lungs could hardly keep pace with her sharp intakes and rapid heart beat. Her mind was racing as the last 24 hours replayed in her head, tying together the loose ends. The cryptic note left on her door, the assault on Brian, and now the flowers. She picked up the flowers and threw the vase against the wall. "Damn it! Why did you have to kill him? Why can't you leave me alone?!" she screamed at the empty room. Hot, angry tears were running down her face as she collapsed on the kitchen floor and leaned back against the refrigerator, burying her face in her hands. A few minutes later Betsy came rushing in with the guys.

"Mari-!" Ben started to yell, then saw her in the kitchen and rushed to her side. "Marissa? Are you okay?"

"He did it! He did it!" was all she could say, choking through the tears as she rocked herself back and forth, "He did it! He did it!"

"Marissa, you aren't making any sense. What are you talking about?" Jack asked.

Marissa's trembling hand reached up to give him the note that was wadded up in her palm.

"What's this?" Jack looked down, "I'm sorry Marissa, I still don't understand. What does this mean?"

"R-r-oses. Mitchell Olsen. He sent me flowers from jail. He k-killed Brian," Marissa managed to get out between sobs.

Jack gave a quizzical glance towards Betsy. Betsy grabbed the card from Jack and read it to herself. Jack sat down next to Marissa and put his arm around her, pulling her towards him. "Sh-sh-sh, it's going to be alright."

"I'm calling Detective Cordova," Betsy announced, picking up the phone.

Jack helped Marissa up and led her to the sofa. Ben brought her a glass of some amber liquid. "Here, drink this. It will help calm your nerves a bit."

Betsy entered the room. "Detective Cordova is on his way. He should be here within the hour. He said not to touch anything in the meantime, and he's also sending over a unit to watch our house for the next 24 hours."

Chapter 11

Several hours later Detective Cordova had given assignments to his teams and convinced Marissa and Betsy to check into a hotel for the night. The police had taken over the apartment and were dusting for prints in the event that someone had been in the apartment or left any trace of evidence. Betsy told the police they would be staying at the Sorrento with Marissa's parents who were coming in for the memorial service, so if they needed anything they knew where to find them.

Detective Cordova assigned a young police officer to the girls. He was to sit outside their hotel room and escort them anywhere they went for at least the next 24 hours. He was very concerned that the murder of Brian Benton marked a turning point in a new series of events that were escalating. Keeping Marissa safe was his primary concern, and until they had more answers this was going to be a challenge.

The department had two men working their way through Marissa's apartment building, collecting fibers, papers, fingerprints and such, while others were commissioned to the streets. The instructions to the men were to question neighbors, merchants and anyone they found on the street. They were to search in every trash can, every alley, manhole, crack or crevice for clues. He had pulled the photo of Leo Fernandez out of his file and circulated it to the officers with instructions to show it to everyone and see if anyone recognized him.

Leo Fernandez had become a master of disguise. A couple of years ago, he had found a plastic surgeon who had a need for some 'surveillance' and as a bonus for a job well done he had removed the scar from Leo's face. For the past couple of weeks he had dressed up as a homeless person, in a torn overcoat, ripped gloves, a stocking hat and hadn't showered in weeks. This morning he had gone home, showered, shaved his face and head, put on clean camouflage pants, black boots, a green work jacket and an army hat. He had applied a temporary tattoo to the back of his neck, an emblem which was associated with a white supremacist group. He knew he would be mistaken for one of those loonies from the woods by anyone passing by, and they wouldn't bother him.

Leo sat on the bench waiting for the bus to arrive, guaranteeing him a front row seat for the unfolding drama taking place down the street. He'd seen the girls leave with the young officer about thirty minutes ago. Now several officers emerged from the building fanning out with their notebooks and showing a photo as they went door to door. He sat calmly as an officer approached him and showed him the photo.

"Hello sir, Officer Johnson with the Seattle Police Department," he said as he showed Leo his badge. "There has been a recent crime in the area, and I was wondering if you might take a look and see if you recognize this man?"

Leo looked at the photo of himself taken over five years ago. He hardly recognized himself. The man in the photo was thirty pounds heavier; he had a full head of red hair, a mustache and a scar on his left cheek.

"I don't mind at all, Officer, but I must tell you I'm not from around here. I'm actually from up north, just in town for some supplies. I haven't seen anyone looking like this around here, I'm pretty sure I'd remember someone with a scar like that."

Officer Johnson was looking into his Leo's eyes with a penetrating stare. "You look really familiar to me." For a moment, Leo thought he had been caught, and then the officer said, "You kind of look like that guy from that movie from a few years ago, that one where the guy gets the girl in the end…'An Officer and A Gentleman" with Richard Gere…you know, his buddy. I can't think of his name."

"Oh, you mean David Keith? I get that sometimes, but that's not me."

"I guess that's his name. Thanks anyway. Here's my card. If you happen to see this guy when you're around today, maybe you can give us a call."

"Sure, be happy to. Hey, what did this guy do, do I need to worry?"

"He's a suspect in a murder case, so I wouldn't approach him if you see him."

The bus pulled up. "This is me," Leo said as he handed the photo back to the officer, "I hope you find your man." He turned and boarded the bus.

"Yeah, thanks," the police officer replied and turned to walk into the store on the corner.

Back at the apartment another officer walked in with an evidence bag. "Detective Cordova, we found this in a dumpster out back. It looks like it could be the murder weapon."

The detective carefully removed the knife from the bag. It was a Henkel kitchen utility knife with a five inch blade and a wooden handle. Not exactly the type of knife a person would use on the street in a robbery. There was blood on the blade and handle. "Okay, type-check the blood against that of our victim and dust it for any prints."

"One more thing, it matches the set on the counter in the kitchen," the officer reported.

"Kitchen? You mean this kitchen?" Detective Cordova asked.

"Yes, sir. There is a knife block on the counter with an open slot. The handle on the murder weapon matches the handle on the kitchen knives, and the branding is the same."

"Okay, make sure the forensics team gets photos for our files, and run those tests. Also make sure to check the kitchen knives against prints of the girls, and identify any others. We also need to check alibis for both girls just to cover our bases."

"Yes sir, I'm on it."

Detective Cordova was certain neither girl had anything to do with the murder, but he still needed to eliminate them as suspects. So far, he didn't have any other prints or evidence linking anyone to the crime. Unless they came up with something soon, finding the killer would prove an impossible task.

About that time Officer Johnson walked in. "Sir, we may have a lead. Mr. Morrison, store keeper across the street remembers seeing a bum hanging around this week. He said he didn't get a real good look at his face, but he thought that it could be this guy. He said the hair color was close, but the guy that came into his store had a beard. He saw him duck into that doorway across the street a couple of times. It's been kind of cold at night so he didn't want to run him off since he thought the guy was just trying to stay warm."

"Has he seen him today?" Detective Cordova asked.

"No, the last time Mr. Morrison saw him was yesterday morning, about an hour before the body was found in the alley. He said he thought he saw the guy in the crowd too, but he didn't have his hat and coat on, so he couldn't be sure it was the same guy. If he was in the crowd, maybe one of our officers got a picture of him in the background or something."

"Good work, Officer Johnson. Give Jimmy a call and see if he has the crime scene photos developed already and then see if you can take them over to the shopkeeper and have him take a look to see if he can identify him in the crowd." Officer Johnson turned to leave as another officer was coming in.

"Sir, I just spoke with a woman who got off the bus from downtown. She said she is almost certain that this guy was getting off the bus when she got on. She said he looked different. The man she saw was clean shaven, had a bald head, and was wearing army type clothing, but she said the eyes were a dead ringer. She said no one forgets eyes that cold."

Officer Johnson looked down at the photo in his hand again. He tried to imagine this guy without hair. Maybe if he were a little thinner. All of a sudden the recognition dawned on him.

"I saw this guy too. He was at the bus stop across the street. I talked to him, but he has lost weight, he didn't have a scar and he really didn't look like the photo."

Detective Cordova asked, "Did the woman remember what stop that was?"

"She said she caught it on Madison. She works in that area."

"Sorrento Hotel is on Madison. Get an APB out on Leo Fernandez right away, and call the hotel and be sure Marissa and Betsy are safe. I want you to increase security detail over there. Officer Johnson, we will discuss your lack of observation later on."

"Yes, sir."

Leo purposely got off at the Madison Street bus stop, just in case someone happened to recognize him. He knew the police would concentrate their efforts on protecting Marissa and draw the attention away from him. As soon as he got off there, he caught a taxi and went back to his own hotel. He changed into a business suit, removed the tattoo, and put on a hat and rain coat. He stepped off the elevator and into the lobby, carrying a leather duffle and a briefcase. At the front desk he asked about the envelope that he had expected which they gave him, and he checked out. He walked outside and ordered a taxi to the airport. He wasn't getting on a flight, but he could create the illusion that he was leaving town on a plane. Then they might not check the bus stations. Once at the airport, he would change clothes one more time before he went back to the bus station to get out of town.

Chapter 12

Leo's taxi pulled up in the passenger drop off/pick up zone of the Alaska Airlines terminal at SeaTac Airport. The curb was bustling with travelers coming and going. Business men toting small wheeled bags, families with small children and luggage carts pushed by dad, loaded down with excessive amounts of baggage, strollers and car seats. An older couple was standing off to the side, trying to avoid the fray of hectic traffic. Leo paid the taxi driver and pulled his duffle and brief case from the back seat.

He entered the terminal, mixing in with the throng of people moving through the lines and finding departure gates. He found his way into the nearest restroom, but before stepping into a stall he noticed a limousine driver dressed in a dark suit and chauffeur's cap at a sink, pouring over a map. He had set his sign down on the mirror ledge, and Leo was intrigued to read the name "Van Horn" neatly printed on white poster board. The driver looked up for a minute, and said to Leo, "Hey, are you from Seattle?"

Leo was caught a little off guard as he was still lost in thought over the name on the sign. "Uh...yeah. You need some help with directions?"

"Actually, yeah. I'm new to the area, this is my second job and I'm still getting used to the freeways. I'm looking for the Sorrento Hotel on Madison Avenue. Do you know the best way to get there?"

"Yeah, sure, let me show you on your map," Leo offered, looking around to see that for the moment the restroom was empty.

The driver moved toward him as he unfolded the map. Leo reached over with one hand taking hold of one side of the map as if preparing to take a closer look. With his other hand he quickly whipped up and backhanded the guy across the Adam's apple then sucker punched him in the gut, taking him by surprise. Once he was gasping for air, Leo quickly rendered him unconscious with a strangle hold and pulled him into the handicapped stall. He made quick work of putting on the limo driver's clothes. The pants were a little large around the waist so he stuffed in some wadded up toilet seat covers and cinched up the belt to keep them up. He buttoned the jacket up the front to hide the stuffing. He pulled the fake mustache out of his duffle and quickly glued it to his upper lip.

He put his own pants onto the driver's legs, leaving them hanging at his ankles, and then hoisted him onto the john. Leo stuffed his clothes and some paper into the duffle bag, filling it as full as possible. He placed the bag on the driver's lap and folded his dangling arms, criss-crossing them across his stomach. He folded the man's torso forward, using the driver's own body weight to pin his arms inward, preventing them from dangling on the floor. He used the duffle bag as leverage to hold up the upper body so it couldn't completely slump over. Leaving the latch on the stall in place, he crawled under the stall wall into the neighboring stall where he stood and brushed off the dirt, just as he heard someone entering the restroom. He walked out, washed his hands, and adjusted his tie and hat in the mirror. He retrieved the map from the floor and the sign from the shelf and walked out in search of the Van Horns.

He went out to the curb where other drivers awaited arrivals and held up his sign. Leo watched as the couple he had seen earlier met his sign with dawning recognition. He made his way towards them, "Mr. and Mrs. Van Horn?"

"Yes, that would be us," Mr. Van Horn answered. "Do you know where you are taking us?"

"Yes sir, the Sorrento Hotel on Madison. It's a beautiful hotel, one of the oldest in Seattle. Have you stayed there before?"

"No, we haven't."

"You are in for a treat. They pride themselves on old world charm with superior service. It has an awesome location. Are you here for business or pleasure?" Leo inquired, making small talk as he imagined a limo driver would do to put his clients at ease.

"Sadly, we are in town for a memorial service. We are meeting our daughter at the hotel tonight and then going to dinner."

"I'm sorry for your loss, folks. Perhaps I can be of further assistance and take you to your restaurant as well?"

"We aren't sure yet of the arrangements she has already made, but if we need further transportation we'll let you know."

"Glad to be of service, sir." Leo said as he finished putting the luggage in the front seat. He opened the back doors for his passengers, "You two sit back and relax, and let me take care of the driving. There's a phone in the back seat if you'd like to give your daughter a call and let her know you're on your way. No charge."

"Thank you, that is most kind," Mrs. Van Horn said as they got into the back seat.

Leo got in front and raised the glass between them to give the clients some privacy for their call. He also turned on the speaker to the back so he could overhear their conversation.

"Hi honey, it's Mom.... Yes, we landed just fine and found our driver. We are en route to the hotel. Oh dear, are you sure you're safe? We don't need to go out to dinner tonight if it isn't safe. Your father and I are fine staying in with room service. Well, if you're positive. Our driver has offered to stay with us if you don't want to drive your car tonight...okay dear, we'll tell him to wait when we arrive. See you soon."

Leo couldn't help but smile. He knew he wouldn't get paid for this, but it was just too good to pass up this kind of opportunity. The Olsen brothers had their own plans, but that didn't mean that Leo couldn't have a little fun of his own.

Chapter 13

Marissa and Betsy were in the lobby downstairs when the Van Horns arrived. They walked over to the girls and greeted them with a round of hugs. When Mr. Van Horn pulled Marissa into his warm bear hug embrace, Marissa couldn't fight the stinging tears as they rolled down her face.

"It's going to be okay, sweetheart. We're here. We love you and we'll stay however long you need us," he said into her ear as he held her close.

"Thanks, Daddy. That means more than you know."

"Now, let me go get checked in. I know your Mom wants to freshen up a little before we take off for dinner. The limo driver said he would take a smoke break while we got settled. Is that okay?"

"Sure. I'm going to let the police officer know what our plans are so they can follow. We'll wait down here until you come back down."

Thirty minutes later they were on their way. The driver took them to the restaurant and promised to return in an hour. They made small talk during the meal, everyone trying to avoid the subject that weighed so heavily on all of their minds. They tried to not think about the officer that was sitting two tables over for their protection. They tried not to talk about Brian's attack, and they tried to find other things to discuss besides the service being held tomorrow for the man that had taken Marissa's heart with him to an untimely grave, leaving her struggling to be strong to face a future without him.

Leo used the time wisely while the Van Horns dined. He took the car and refilled the gas tank. He reviewed the map for the quickest route out of town. He had less than an hour to put an escape plan in place. He had probably already risked more than he should have for a cheap thrill. He had initially thought about taking advantage of this situation and taking Marissa out for a little test drive in the limo after dinner if he could get her away from the group somehow. But after rethinking the plan, he decided that the Olsens were not someone he wanted to mess with, especially now that Mitch was connected to the Chaplain. No need to have the police and the Brotherhood after him.

When the Van Horn party emerged from the restaurant, Leo was leaning against the hood of the car. He dropped his cigarette to the ground and extinguished the stub with his shoe. He moved quickly to the passenger door, opening it, and helped each of the women inside. As Marissa took his hand, he could feel a pulse of excitement race through him like an electrical current. He caught her gaze briefly. Her green eyes were hypnotic and he had to force himself to look away as to not arouse suspicion.

Once at the hotel, Marissa thanked Leo after everyone was out of the car. She walked over to him and asked what she owed him. "Actually, my fee has already been taken care of, so you don't owe me anything."

Puzzled by the response, Marissa said, "Do you mind my asking by whom?"

"Let's just say a mutual friend and leave it at that, shall we?" he replied.

"Well, thank you for all your help, Mister.... you know I didn't catch your name. I'm sorry, I'm a little preoccupied."

"Totally understandable, Marissa, I'm sorry for your loss." He stepped in close to her to shake her hand. "Leo Fernandez, at your service," he said at a whisper so only she could hear. He held her hand tightly, pulling her towards him, leaning in closer as he spoke. "Marissa, I have a gun in my pants. If you say one word before I leave, I will pull it out and aim for your mother. Now, unless you want to be grieving for 'mommy' too, you will say thank you to me one more time, and not say another word until you no longer see my tail lights leaving this driveway. If we are clear, say thank you."

Marissa was breathing hard. She looked around for a moment to see if the police officer was watching, trying to think if she could get his attention faster than Leo could pull a gun. She thought about her self defense class and wondered if she could place a kick to his groin and disable him. As if reading her thoughts, Leo squeezed her hand and gave her a hard stare. "Don't think about it, Marissa. I've got nothing to lose here. I've already killed once this week, and I can easily do it again if it means I'm going to jail anyway."

Marissa shook his hand and said, 'Thank you."

"Good girl," Leo mouthed to her. "You're welcome, Miss Van Horn. I hope to see you soon." He turned, got behind the wheel of the car and slammed the door.

Marissa caught the eye of the police officer. She looked at her folks as the car left the parking lot, then yelled, "It's him! It's Leo Fernandez. He's driving the limo!"

The police officer drew his weapon and took a firing stance, but it was too late. Leo burned rubber as he squealed out of the lot, putting enough distance between him and the officer that the policeman couldn't get a clear shot. "Is everyone okay?" he yelled over to the group. After they all nodded affirmatively, the officer used his walkie-talkie and called in the APB and license number of the limousine before approaching the Van Horns and Betsy, now huddling around Marissa.

"Okay, folks, I think everyone needs to get inside right away." He immediately called in the description of the limo as he escorted them to Marissa's room. Once the room was secure, he questioned Marissa on what Leo had said to her, called in the details and then posted himself outside the door. An hour later the officer knocked on the door and came in.

"Here's what we know. The original limo driver was found in the restroom at the airport. He will be fine, but Leo attacked him and left him unconscious. He is getting medical attention at a hospital and a full recovery is expected. We found the limo abandoned about 3 blocks away from here. Witnesses in the area saw the driver leave the vehicle and flag down a taxi. No one thought it was unusual enough to note a license plate; they just thought the driver was having car trouble. Our trail is cold. We don't think he'll be back. Sometimes these guys like the chase. We think that he was probably just trying to play a mind game of sorts. Had he wanted to hurt any of you, he had plenty of opportunity to do so, and didn't. To be on the safe side we have team of officers covering the hotel for the night. The hotel brought in extra security as well, and tomorrow we will cover the memorial service with both uniformed and undercover policemen. Mr. and Mrs. Van Horn, there is an officer outside waiting to escort you to your room so you can all get some rest before tomorrow."

"Well, I don't know if we should leave the girls--," Mrs. Van Horn started in.

"Mom, we'll be fine. I think the officer is right. We all need to get some rest," Marissa replied.

"Come on Marianne, they have protection and so do we. Let's let the girls try to sleep and we'll try to do the same," Mr. Van Horn added, "Goodnight girls."

"Okay William. But I doubt anyone is going to sleep much tonight…," she trailed off as her husband led her into the hallway.

The officer turned to the girls and said, "Ladies, if you need anything, I'm right outside the door all night long. I know it will be difficult, but try and get some sleep," he said as he stepped out and shut the door.

Marissa and Betsy each collapsed on their beds. "Are you going to be okay?" Betsy asked her.

"I'm too exhausted to think about anything right now. Let's try to get some sleep."

They got ready for bed, but they both listened to each other toss and turn all night waiting for dawn to break.

Chapter 14

The Van Horns and Betsy were escorted to Wexby's with motorcycle cops flanking a limousine, not driven by Leo Fernandez. When they arrived they were greeted by Jack, Ben and Mrs. Gottsfrey. When they told them of the trouble the night before, it was Mrs. Gottsfrey that said, "If he has the nerve to show up here today, we will all kick his ass!" Marissa had to laugh at the thought of little Mrs. Gottsfrey, in her 70's retro polyester pant suit taking on Leo Fernandez, a 20-something hard-bodied killer. As preposterous as the idea was, she had to wonder who would really win. She had seen Mrs. Gottsfrey take on some pretty relentless door-to-door solicitors, chasing them down the street with Mr. Gottsfrey's shotgun, calling them an assortment of colorful names as they ran for cover. Of course everyone in the neighborhood knew it was a prop gun from a John Wayne movie that had been given to Mr. Gottsfrey as a gift, but the solicitors didn't know it.

Jim Wexby had gone all out. There were trays of appetizers at each table and a food buffet to feed half of Seattle. Jack and Ben had found a few posters of Brian that had been used to advertise his show times and had them displayed on easels. Friends and neighbors sent floral arrangements that Jim had placed around the restaurant, and a table with a basket for cards and a guest book was set up near the door. A podium was placed on the stage for the service, and Julia, a performer that played piano during the dinner hour, had offered to play soft music as guests were arriving.

Within thirty minutes the restaurant was packed. Jim Wexby opened the service by welcoming everyone. He continued by talking about what a remarkable young man Brian Benton had been, the first time that he had met Brian, and his accomplishments as a young comedian. When he finished, Jim opened up the service to anyone who wanted to share a memory or say some fond words about Brian.

Marissa stood up and walked to the microphone. "For those of you that may not know me, I am Marissa Van Horn. Brian and I only met two months ago, but it was love at first sight. Anyone that knew him knows he was a charming, warm, intelligent and witty man. The people in his life were important to him and he would do anything for them. He taught me what it means to love someone with all your heart and I will miss the future that we may have had together. He will be a tough act to follow and will always have a special place in my heart."

When she finished there wasn't a dry eye in the place. One of Brian's friends was quick to step in, sharing heartwarming stories as well as funny anecdotes about Brian. By late afternoon, only Betsy, Marissa and their family were left. They helped Jim clean up, even though he insisted it wasn't necessary.

Officer Cordova returned to the hotel to explain that the girls apartment had been cleared and to give them an update.

"I can't give you all the details as our investigation is still in progress. We ran all the prints we were able to lift from the apartment and building. We found two prints that place Leo Fernandez in the building. A single fingerprint was found on the back door jamb and a partial print in your kitchen. We found a torn latex glove in the trash, so we think that he may have torn or cut a glove without realizing it, which would explain how the partial prints were left behind. The knife found in the dumpster behind your apartment is a match to the one missing from your set of kitchen knives and is consistent with what could be the murder weapon.

"He was in our apartment?" Marissa said with disbelief. "Betsy could have walked in on him! Betsy, he could have hurt you too!"

Betsy took one of Marissa's hands and held it tightly, "But he didn't, I'm fine."

"Do you have any leads on his whereabouts yet?" inquired Mr. Van Horn.

"Not specifically, but we found an apartment in downtown Seattle that had been leased to him. We were able to confiscate several 'costumes' from his closet. He has probably been following Marissa for a very long time, and because he changes his appearance often, no one noticed him. His phone records show where he accepted a collect call from the pay phone at San Quentin. This is the first real lead we have that proves a link between him and Mitchell Olsen. Of course Mitchell can still deny it, as any inmate with phone privileges could have placed the call, but we suspect it was him."

"How are you going to keep these girls safe with this lunatic running around?" Mrs. Van Horn asked, desperation apparent in her voice.

"Our plan is to watch both the girls' and Leo's apartment for any signs of activity. However, I don't think he is around anymore. You girls might consider relocating to a new apartment if you don't feel comfortable in your own any more. That would certainly be understandable, but I don't think he will risk being seen in this area again. Our precinct artist has drawn several sketches of possible appearances for Leo. We have distributed them throughout the city as well as implemented a statewide man hunt for him. We plan to provide around the clock surveillance for at least the next two weeks, and we will let you know when we plan to pull the detail."

"Maybe you need to move back home," suggested Mrs. Van Horn.

"You know you're welcome if that is what you want to do," Mr. Van Horn said, "but we also know you have built a life here with a career and friends. If you feel that you just want to move to a new apartment, your mother and I will stay and help you find one and help you move."

"Thank you, Daddy. I will think about it, but I still need some time before I make any decisions about moving," Marissa answered, "Betsy and I need to discuss it together, as it's a decision that affects both of us."

Detective Cordova stood up to leave, "It's time I got home to my family. I'm sure my wife already has supper on the table and is wondering if I'm going to make it home or not. She usually understands, but I try not to push the envelope too often. Do you girls plan to stay here tonight or go back to your place?"

Betsy answered with, "I think we'll stay here one more night and return home tomorrow. The Van Horns are scheduled to return to California tomorrow, and I think it would be nice for us to spend their last night all together in the same place. What do you think, Marissa?"

"I think that sounds like a good plan. I'm too exhausted to pack up tonight anyway."

"We don't have to go tomorrow if you want us to stay," Marianne reminded her.

"Mom, I really appreciate you and Dad coming and being here for the service today. I still don't know what I'm going to do but I know that at least the next couple of weeks we will stay put. I don't think there's anything more you can do for us now. If we decide to move, maybe you could both come back in a few weeks when we know what we are doing? I have to get back to work anyway, so I won't really be home much. I have a lot of catching up to do there. You might as well go home for now."

"That's sounds like a good idea. We'll leave in the morning, and give you girls time to make some decisions. We can come back like you said, Sweetheart, just as soon as you need us to," Mr. Van Horn said more as a statement of fact rather than an offer of help. He knew how his wife operated and could tell that unless he was firm, she would not be coming home with him on the plane. He also knew that Marissa needed time alone to deal with everything that had happened.

The next morning they had breakfast together and then said their goodbyes before the Van Horns left for the airport. As the girls each went off to their jobs, they agreed to meet at Wexby's after work and go home together so neither of them would return to the apartment alone.

Chapter 15

It was visitation day at San Quentin. Alan waited in line to go through the security check as he did every week. His mom had stayed home today again, and he knew that he was running out of excuses to give Mitch.

Ever since Alan had told Mitch about Marissa's new boyfriend he couldn't stop talking about her. At first, Mitch just talked to Alan about her, but his obsession was growing and he found that he couldn't control the thoughts that had become all consuming. He mentioned her when his mom was visiting one day, saying how he had heard she had a boyfriend. Mrs. Olsen had been shocked that he knew anything about Marissa, and expressed her concern that perhaps it wasn't a good idea for Mitch to be trying to keep tabs on her.

He turned on his mom with a voice so chilling that she didn't recognize her oldest son. "She is mine, mother. And everyone just needs to remember that." Later she told Alan that she was relieved that Mitchell was in a prison and not able to hurt anyone. She said she didn't think she could keep visiting Mitchell and listening to him obsess over Marissa. She hoped perhaps Alan might be able to talk some sense into him before it was too late. It was the first time she recalled being afraid of one of her children. It would not, however, be the last time she would fear for her own safety or Marissa Van Horn's.

Alan made it through security and was waiting for Mitch to come into the visitation room. He had brought him the usual smokes, bar of soap, and some cookies from their mom. Sometimes Mitch got those and sometimes the guards kept them for themselves. Alan never mentioned it to Mitch, no sense borrowing trouble over some cookies.

Mitch picked up the phone on his side and Alan picked up the handset on his. "It's done," were Alan's first words.

"Really? That's great, man. Thanks," Mitchell responded. "Okay so next we have to—"

"Whoa, Mitch. We need to wait awhile. Our man is really hot right now, and we need to let some time pass here or we are going to blow it."

"Alan, don't forget what she has done to our family. If it wasn't for her, you wouldn't be spending your Saturdays visiting your big brother in jail!"

"I know, I know, but listen, Mitch. We have to lie low for awhile. Give it some time. According to our guy, she is under constant watch right now. The police follow her around like she's got them on a leash."

"Okay, Alan, but not too long. We have a lot of work to do still."

"Bro, you are in here for awhile yet. We have plenty of time. She's not going anywhere with anyone."

"I guess you're right. Hey, where's mom?" Mitch asked.

"You know, our old man's got her working a second job. He's such a bum. He can't even hold down one job, and Mom's workin' two! He says it's her fault you're in here cuz she coddled you too much, made you soft and that's why you fell for Marissa. If you were out you'd be helping to bring in some money so she needed to make up for her mistake."

"He can be glad I'm in here, because if I was out there, there's no way I'd let him treat mom like that, and you shouldn't either!" Mitch exclaimed, admonishing his younger brother.

"Whatever, Mitch. You're not there man, I don't think it's fair for you to be judging me," Alan argued.

"Yeah, you poor thing. I'll trade you places!" Mitchell said a little too loudly as a guard walked over as if to cut their time short. Inmates that got excited during visitation quickly lost the privilege. Mitchell waved him off, indicating he knew and wouldn't do it again.

"Sorry, Mitch, I wasn't thinking. I'll have a talk with dad," Alan replied, trying to appease his brother.

"That's better." The bell sounded that time was up. "Tell Mom I love her and I would like to see her next week, okay?" Mitch requested as he got up to return to his cell.

"Yeah, okay, Mitch, I'll do that," Alan promised. "We'll see you next week."

Alan left feeling the same as always--frustrated that he had to spend his Saturdays visiting Mitch and making excuses why Mom couldn't come. He'd been doing this so long he couldn't remember what it was like before Mitch went to prison. Sometimes he felt confused and guilty that he was helping Mitch in his revenge against Marissa Van Horn. But a large part of him held an inexplicable resentment towards her that left him following

Mitch's requests even when he questioned his reasoning. His need to try to hold what little sense of family he had always overrode his conscience.

Chapter 16

Marissa and Betsy decided that they weren't ready to move from their apartment. For better or worse it was home. They couldn't imagine daily life without Jack and Ben around or Mrs. Gottsfrey looking in. Of course Marianne wasn't pleased with this decision, feeling that recent events were too close for comfort. She kept after the girls until William finally stepped in and promised to install a new security system for them, one that would directly dial the police if there was a break in. Mrs. Gottsfrey, so relieved that they were staying, insisted on paying for the system, saying that it would be a good selling point for future tenants.

Two months had passed since Brian's funeral. The police had not been successful in locating Leo Fernandez, and although Detective Cordova was not pleased, he took this as a sign that he had left town. He wished he could keep a detail on Marissa's apartment, but he was reminded by the chief that the department didn't have funds for individual citizen protection.

Marissa decided the best way to get through her grief was to throw herself into her work. She went in early and stayed late, insisting that it kept her mind off things. Although her work was impeccable, Mr. Rosenthal started noticing Marissa was pale and seemed tired most of the time. He told her he wanted her to take a long weekend, refusing to take no for an answer. When she tried to pack up some files to take home, he caught her at the door and took them from her, insisting she needed rest or she wouldn't be allowed back in the office on Monday.

Friday morning, instead of going into the office, Marissa stayed home. She lay in bed and realized how exhausted she felt. She finally got up, went to the bathroom to shower and took a long, hard look at herself in the mirror. Her eyes had dark circles under them; her face had the pallor of someone in a hospital. Her hair looked dingy, and unkempt. She hardly recognized the face staring back at her. She decided to take a hot bubble bath, and depending on how she felt she might make an appointment with her hair salon for that afternoon.

When she emerged from her bath, instead of feeling better, she felt more tired. She wondered if she was coming down with something. She felt flushed and slightly nauseated and decided maybe she needed to eat something. She wandered out to the kitchen and found some blueberry muffins Mrs. Gottsfrey had left for them. She made herself a cup of tea and sat down in the chair propping her feet up on the ottoman.

She looked out the window, thinking about Brian. She missed him, but more than that she missed their future she had already started to envision; the wedding they would one day have had, the children and grand children they would have shared, the life they would have made together. Through the window she saw Mrs. Gottsfrey outside, sweeping the front sidewalk. A man across the street was weeding his flowerbeds, and a young mother was pushing a stroller. An occasional car drove past on the street below, and once in awhile she could hear Mrs. Gottsfrey call out a greeting to a passerby. Life was moving forward, and she knew she had to move on with it.

Marissa walked in ten minutes early for her appointment with Henri. The receptionist led her to a changing room and gave her a spa robe and slippers, along with a key to a locker in which she should put her belongings. She was still feeling tired and a little nauseated, but had decided that if she forced herself to get out, perhaps she would feel better. She was seated in a waiting room, looking through some magazines of hair styles, contemplating a change when Henri came for her.

"Darling, how are you?" he said, kissing her cheek. "I'm so sorry to hear about Brian."

"Thanks," Marissa said, hoping to quickly change the subject. "Henri, I need your help. I need a little pick me up."

Henri didn't miss a beat, "Sweetheart, you have come to the right place. Let's go over to my station so we can discuss some ideas, okay?" Marissa followed him over. He was dressed in some very tight fitting slacks, black loafers and a black and silver smock. He wore black framed glasses and had one pierced ear adorned by a silver stud. "You know, darling, it has been awhile since we have changed your hair style. It isn't looking very healthy right now." He ran his fingers through her hair before picking up a brush to detangle it.

"Henri, surprise me. I really just need something new. I give you my permission to make a dramatic change."

"Wow... Honey, as much as that would make my day, I don't think you should be making any radical decisions right now, forgive me for reminding you."

"Henri, I promise I won't be upset. Quit arguing and just give me a new look."

"Okay, but you have to promise you won't be mad later on. No buyer's remorse allowed!"

Two hours later, Marissa looked into the mirror. She saw before her a transformed face. Henri had taken her back to her natural color, a dark brown. He had left her hair just past shoulder length without bangs, parted on the side, leaving her hair with soft natural curls. It looked a little like Julia Robert's hairdo in "Pretty Woman."

"Now, Darling. This hairdo will be so easy. You just wash it, and spray some of this in it, and crunch it a little like this," demonstrating the technique as he spoke, "it is perfect for our Seattle weather and your beautiful curl. It is a win-win. We need to let your hair take a break from bleaching it blonde, so let's let keep your natural color for a bit. Okay?"

"Sure, Henri." Marissa stared back at her reflection. "I really like it a lot. Thanks" She left the salon feeling a little better than she had in awhile. Even if this feeling was just temporary, it felt good to feel like she was in control of something.

When she arrived home, she had that nauseous feeling again. Betsy had just got home from work. "Hi---Oh, Wow! You look fabulous. I just love it!" she said, as Marissa ran for the bathroom. Betsy could hear her throwing up. "Hey, are you okay? This isn't about your hair is it?"

Marissa called through the door. "I haven't felt real good all week. My boss thought I looked tired and made me stay home today, so I went to get my hair done. I feel like I have the stomach flu, but it seems to come and go."

"Really? Has someone at work had this too? I haven't heard of this going around. Flu season hasn't really started yet."

"Only Dana, but she's pregnant so that hardly counts. Bets, I need a few minutes, okay?"

"Yeah, sure. Sorry, I was just worried. Your hair looks really cute though, if that makes you feel better…" she trailed off.

Awhile later Marissa emerged from the bathroom. "Feeling better?" Betsy asked.

"Much, but Bets, I think I need to run out to the drug store."

"I can go for you. Do you need some something to settle your stomach?"

"Not exactly. I think I might need a home pregnancy kit."

Betsy stared at her friend for a few minutes, not quite registering what Marissa was saying. When it finally sunk in, she said, "Okay, so you're saying you think you might be…Okay, you stay here, I'll be right back. Or should I stay here and you'll be back? No, you don't feel good. Are you okay to stay alone for now? Of course you are. Okay, I'll be back, you stay here…" She was still talking to herself when she grabbed her purse and went out the door.

Marissa already knew the answer. She realized it was true the moment she told Betsy about Dana. She was about five weeks late but hadn't thought about it with all the stress. If it was true, she would be about 2 months along. She sat down on the couch, thinking about how this would change her life; a baby…Brian's baby. She knew it would be hard to be a single mom, but she knew without a doubt it was what she wanted more than anything in the world.

She was still thinking about it when Betsy came back in, somewhat out of breath, carrying the Bartel's Drug Store bag. "Here, I can't stand the anticipation! Hurry up!" she ordered.

"Betsy, I know it is true. I don't need the test, but I'll take it just the same."

"Really? Oh Marissa, are you sure? Are you okay?"

"I'm fine. I'm happy. It's what I want. Of course I wish Brian was here to share in our lives, but if I can't have him, at least I can have a part of him."

Ten minutes later, the indicator on the test stick confirmed Marissa's suspicions. "It's positive!" She sat down on the couch again with Betsy. "What are you thinking?" she asked Betsy.

"I'm thinking that this is exciting. I'm going to be an aunt! That's okay isn't it—if the baby thinks of me as an aunt?"

"I wouldn't have it any other way" Marissa said.

"You're going to be a Mommy!" Betsy said grabbing Marissa's hands as the two of them smiled at each other. "We have to tell Mrs. Gottsfrey!"

"Okay, but not tonight. Can we just keep this between us tonight? I'd like to tell my folks first, and then Sunday at dinner we can tell Mrs. Gottsfrey and the boys."

"I hope I don't burst before then. The reporter in me just wants to report!"

"Try hard, Lois Lane. I need to have a day or two to get used to the idea."

"Tomorrow we go shopping for maternity clothes!" Betsy exclaimed.

"Am I showing already?"

"Not yet, but why wait? Please, can we go shopping tomorrow?"

"Sure, why not."

Marissa's parents took the news better than she thought. She was a little concerned about how they would feel about their unwed daughter having a baby. Their reaction couldn't have been more caring. They asked her how she felt about it, if she had been to a doctor yet, if she had thought about what she was going to do about a place to live once the baby came, because their apartment was too small for a baby too. She assured them she was happy, she would schedule an appointment on Monday, and the rest would fall into place in time.

At dinner on Sunday the rest of Marissa's family was supportive as well. Mrs. Gottsfrey was already offering her babysitting services, the boys were immediately ordering her to stay seated and helping her with her chair, not letting her clear the table or do the dishes. During dessert however, there was more shocking news that Marissa had not anticipated.

Ben said he had an announcement. He had found a job on Whidbey Island and would be relocating there in a month or so because the commute each day would be too much. He glanced at Betsy who exchanged a quizzical look with him. As if this news wasn't enough to absorb, Betsy cleared her throat and announced that she would be moving with Ben.

Marissa looked at Jack who looked away from her. Then she looked at Betsy and Ben who were smiling. Betsy put out her left hand which had a beautiful diamond on it. "We're engaged!"

Marissa, more than a little confused, again looked at Jack and Mrs. Gottsfrey, who didn't seem surprised at all by this news.

"How long has this been going on?" Marissa asked. There was a dead silence in the room for a minute.

Then Betsy told her, "Ben and I have been seeing each other off and on for a year. At first, we didn't say anything because we wanted to be sure before we told anyone, and then we were going to say something, but the whole thing with Brian happened and the timing just wasn't right. I'm sorry Marissa, I didn't want to keep a secret like this from you, but I just couldn't bring myself to tell you when you were so sad."

"I'm glad for you, for both of you." Marissa said. "I'm sorry you had to keep this to yourselves, but I understand why you didn't want to say anything. And you!" she looked at Jack, "You knew all this time didn't you? You didn't say anything? I can't believe you kept this a secret all this time."

"Ben blackmailed me with a secret, so I had to keep quiet"

"A secret, huh? Okay Ben, what's the secret?" Marissa asked.

"Nope, can't tell you. Jack kept mine, so I can't tell on him."

"Do you know Jack's secret?" Marissa asked Betsy.

"Sorry, they are too tight lipped. Changing the subject though, I think that I will stay with you for a few more months and then we can turn my room into a nursery for the baby. That way you don't have to worry about moving. What do you think?" Betsy said.

"I think Whidbey Island is too far for you to be when I need a Lamaze coach! What am I going to do without you?"

"Hey, how about me?" Jack piped in. "I'll be your Lamaze coach. I'm convenient, I live just below you, and I am already an uncle so I think it will be fun."

"Thank you, Jack. That's very generous." Turning her attention to Betsy "Let me get a better look at that ring! And you can't get married until I've had the baby I can't possibly be the maid of honor if I'm pregnant!"

"Don't worry. We're planning a long engagement."

The group chatted late into the evening. Mrs. Gottsfrey enjoyed listening to the kids planning their futures and seeing them all so happy. It had been too long since she had seen Marissa smiling like she was tonight. She was absolutely radiant.

Chapter 17

"Yes, Mom, I'm fine. The doctor said everything is fine with the baby. Now that we're past the first trimester, he wants to do an ultrasound on my next appointment. For now he has me continuing prenatal vitamins, regular exercise, a good diet, and moderate work schedule…… No…no, Mom…really…you don't need to come…Mom, I'm fine. Betsy is still in the apartment. If you wait until she moves out with Ben, then I will have a room for you…..Mr. Rosenthal has been very understanding about my workload, but seriously, Mom, I'm fine…." Marissa rolled her eyes at Linda, her assistant who just stuck her head in her office. She listened to her mom express her concerns for a few more seconds before interrupting her, "Listen, Mom, I just got word my next client's waiting for me, so I have to run. I'll call you tomorrow….Love you, too. Give Dad my love….bye."

"Linda, what's up?" Marissa asked.

"I was just checking on you, but I can see you don't need me for that."

"Thanks, but you're right, I feel as if I have more than enough people checking on me. Since you're here, can you follow up and make sure Wilson filed that motion for the Richardson case?"

"Yes. Don't forget you have a meeting with Bonnie this afternoon to go over the deposition schedule for the Blackwood litigation."

"I have that down." About that time Marissa's intercom buzzed. "Yes," she answered.

"Marissa, I have a Jack Reed holding on line one. Do you want me to take a message?"

"No, I'll take it. Thanks, Joan."

"I'll check on that motion and check back with you in awhile" Linda said as she turned to leave.

"Thanks, Linda." Marissa picked up the handset. "Jack? What's going on?"

"I have an appointment downtown this afternoon, and I was wondering if you wanted to grab some lunch?"

"I'm not sure I should be allowed to eat in public anymore. Since I'm eating for two, I've really started pigging out! Are you sure I won't be an embarrassment to you?"

"Very funny. I'll just be sure to keep my hands away from your food and we'll warn the hostess to put us in the back away from the other customers. It should be fine."

"Sounds reasonable. Where do you want to go?"

"How about I meet you at your office and we'll decide when I get there. Say around 11:30, if you can take off a little early?"

"That's great, I have a full afternoon, so that will get me back in time to finish up a few things. Hey there's a new Gourmet Deli that opened up down the street. I haven't been there yet, but everyone says they are great. I have a craving for pastrami on rye."

"Far be it from me to interfere with a pregnant woman's cravings! See you at 11:30."

"See you then."

The morning passed quickly for Marissa, as she worked on updating her files, making lists for Bonnie of people they would need to schedule for depositions in the next couple of weeks, as well as the witnesses in the Blackwood litigation. They were still in the process of working another high profile murder investigation, but the details on that were still coming out, and the new prosecutor assigned to the case wasn't sure if they could make the charges stick. As if on cue, Linda buzzed in at 11:30 telling her Jack was waiting in reception for her. Marissa tidied up her desk and grabbed her purse and jacket to head out to lunch.

As she walked toward him, Jack noticed that Marissa's gait had started to change, and she was starting to show a little. He smiled at her as she approached. "How's the little Mommy doing?"

"Sh-sh—not everyone here knows yet!" Marissa whispered as she pulled Jack away from Linda's desk and then hid behind him so she could sneak a peek to see if Joan was listening. She knew if Joan found out it was only a matter of time before everyone in the office knew.

"Sorry, Mar, didn't know you were keeping it quiet."

"It's okay, but Joan the receptionist is a bit of a gossipmonger. People in the office have nicknamed her Joan Rivers. She even uses the phrase, 'Can we talk?' If she finds out I'm pregnant, she'll probably have you pegged as the father and the baby named before we get back from lunch."

"We have one of those in our office too. Here, let me help you with your coat. It's chilly outside."

"Thank you, sir. So what kind of business do you have downtown today? Is Boeing sending their engineers out shopping for parts or something?"

Jack chuckled. "You don't have a clue what I do, do you? No shopping. We're having a big meeting with Air Force and DOD officials regarding equipment revisions we are doing on aircraft they are using in the Gulf War."

"Wow, that means you are a lot smarter than I give you credit for. I'm seeing a very different side of you, Jack Reed. And I thought you were just another pretty face for all your female acquaintances to admire."

"So, you think I have a pretty face?" Jack asked raising his eyebrows a little.

"Jack, are you flirting with me?"

"What kind of guy would that make me? Flirting with a pregnant woman? By the way did you know that your cute little wiggle is turning into a cute little waddle?"

"Jack! You're terrible! That's just downright mean!"

"You love it and you know it, so don't act defensive. You've never looked happier, and that is the truth. It's good to see, Marissa." He held the door to the deli open for her, "After you."

"Thank you, but if you're going to watch me 'waddle' maybe you should go first."

"Shut up and just go in already."

After they ordered, Jack ushered Marissa to a corner table looking out over the street. "Don't you just love to people watch?" she said as she gazed out the window.

"Sometimes," he replied, watching her, not the people outside.

"Marissa, I've been thinking," he started. "I'd like to help you with the baby. Not just the Lamaze coaching, but you know if you need some help during the night, feeding, all of it. I know I may not seem like father material, and I'm not out to be a father figure, but I am just downstairs and if you needed help with anything I'd be right there."

"Jack, that is the kindest, most generous offer anyone has ever given me. And I will take you up on some help, but honestly my life is going to go through a major change. I won't be dating for a long time; you need to think of settling down yourself with a nice woman someday soon. You don't need to saddle yourself down with a single mom. You should be getting married and starting a family of your own."

"That will happen in time, but lately the women I have been dating are not the type of woman I want to settle down with. I think I need to take a break from my typical dating pool and focus on my career for the time being. In the meantime, I can help you out. I worry about you all alone, especially with that nut job still out there somewhere."

"Well, okay then, but only if you promise that if a potential Mrs. Jack Right Reed comes along, you will run out on me to pursue her."

"It's a deal. Can I come with you to your next check up? I know it seems a little weird maybe, but if I am going to be your coach, I would like to know everything about this pregnancy."

Marissa stared at him for a moment. "Yes, absolutely, I'd love the company. But are you sure you are comfortable with this?"

“Positive. Besides, it will be good practice for when there is finally a Mrs. Jack Reed. I’ll be ready.”

They spent the rest of lunch watching people dodging the puddles forming outside, talking about movies they wanted to see, and Betsy and Ben’s move to the island.

Chapter 18

February, 1991

Mitchell Olsen lay on the thin mattress in his cell contemplating what his next move should be. His last visit with Alan had not gone well. Alan was beginning to show signs of weakness. He wasn't sure what was making Alan change his mind. Maybe he was just going soft because of the recent news they received from Seattle.

Leo had told Alan that Marissa was pregnant and due in July. Alan expressed his concern for her unborn child but Mitch didn't care. It was just another reminder of how she gave herself to someone else. Leo also reported that she was seen with another guy. So far there seemed to be nothing physical going on, but Leo was keeping an eye out for any changes.

Mitch had chosen not to tell Alan about his membership into the Sangre Brotherhood. Alan believed the Chaplain was only a contact person, nothing more. He had no idea the things Mitch was doing within the prison walls to keep Leo on their payroll and the Chaplain on their side. He knew Alan wouldn't approve, and worried that in a weak moment he might tell someone, which would prove to be a fatal mistake.

Alan had suggested that maybe they should leave Marissa alone. He kept saying that he didn't want Mitch to get in trouble and have to spend more time in prison. But Alan didn't understand that Mitch couldn't do that. He didn't understand that she still occupied Mitch's thoughts. He still woke up in cold sweats at night thinking of her body, dreaming of finally taking her for his own. He didn't understand the intense humiliation he still felt from the memory of her rejection, the ultimate reason for him being where he was today. For that he could never forgive her. He would never forget and would make sure she would pay a price. Marissa Van Horn would forever be bound to him. It wasn't over.

Mitch had thought long and hard about his next move. Valentine's Day was coming up. It was time to once again remind Marissa whose 'Be Mine' she needed to be answering to. So far all they knew was that she was pregnant. Although she didn't appear to be taking any lovers, there was no sense in sitting back and waiting for that to happen. She needed to be reminded why she shouldn't be getting involved with anyone.

Alan took a little more coaxing, but eventually he agreed to call Leo.

Chapter 19

"Jack, I'm Dr. Mahoney. Pleased to meet you," she said after Marissa introduced them. "Okay, let's see…" she said as she reviewed the chart, "Your blood pressure is fine, your urine tests are normal…Marissa, how's the morning sickness? The last time we spoke you were having quite a time with it."

"She's been really sick, and not just in the morning. Are you sure this is normal?" Jack asked.

"I've been better this week, but Jack's right it was pretty bad for the last couple of months," Marissa added.

"You're at about four and a half months now, and while some women do experience morning sickness throughout their pregnancy, you should be seeing some relief."

"I still can't stand the smell of fish, but I haven't had to throw up for the last two weeks, so I think it is getting a lot better."

"Sounds like it's subsiding, but if you need a refill on the anti-nausea medication let me know. Your weight's a little higher than I would expect given how sick you have been, but within normal boundaries. Are you still taking your vitamins and eating smaller meals throughout the day?"

"Yes."

"How about exercise? I'd like you to be getting a moderate amount."

"We go to the gym every other night together. She has been working with a personal trainer who specializes in pregnant women."

"Jack wouldn't agree to go with me unless I asked for professional help!" Marissa exclaimed.

"Jack is a smart man. It seems like you are in good hands. How about sleep and work. Are you doing okay with your schedule?"

"My boss has been wonderful. I've been able to leave early and a couple days a week I work from home, bringing home some files to make calls on when I don't have to be in the office. He's giving me time to train my assistant to take up the slack while I'm gone on maternity leave. I'm sleeping fine. On days when I work from home, I take a nap at lunch time, and during my lunch break I usually find a quiet place to put my feet up for 30 minutes or so."

"Everything is coming along nicely. I want to do an ultrasound today, just to take a little look-see to be sure we are on track with your due date. We can usually tell the sex of the baby at this point. If you don't want to know, let me know now, and we can turn the monitor away and I'll be sure not to tell you."

Marissa looked at Jack, "What do you think, do we want to know?"

Jack chuckled, "It's whatever you want. We can be surprised if you want to keep the suspense going."

"I'm not sure. I think I want to know. I'm really not one who likes surprises much."

"You heard the lady, we want to know if you can tell."

"This is going to be a little cold." Dr. Mahoney raised Marissa's gown and squirted the cold gel onto her stomach. "Look at the monitor, there she is…"

"She? It's a girl…" Marissa looked at Jack, "she said 'she'!"

Jack held Marissa's hand as her doctor adjusted the probe of the ultrasound machine to bring the picture into better focus. They stared at the screen as she explained what they were viewing. Jack squeezed Marissa's hand when Dr. Mahoney pointed to the baby's heartbeat. Then she highlighted a point on the monitor and froze the screen.

"See here, these are the hands."

Jack stepped in for a better look. "Excuse me, doc, but am I just seeing something wrong, or are there three hands instead of two?"

"Ah, I was wondering when one of you would to notice."

"Notice? Is there something wrong?" Marissa asked, alarm present in her voice.

"No, no, nothing is wrong. I told you everything is fine. However, you should know that you are having twins."

"Twins? Really? Jack, did you hear her? I'm having twins!" Marissa smiled up at him.

"Yes, I heard. That is amazing. Are they both girls?" Jack said, looking a little stunned.

"Best I can tell from what we see, yes," Dr. Mahoney replied. "Now I know this is a bit of a surprise, someone might say we should have seen this as a possibility; however identical twins aren't hereditary, so despite Marissa being an identical twin herself, this really was just a fluke. This will change your due date a bit. We usually deliver twins up to five weeks earlier than full term, and we usually schedule them c-section to prevent any problems. But we can discuss this after you get dressed. You can meet me in my office. Jack, if you'd like, my nurse can show you where that is and Marissa can get dressed and meet you there."

"Uh..sure." He released Marissa's hand, and obediently followed the nurse out the door.

The doctor turned her attention back to Marissa, "He seems like a great guy. Having one baby as a single mom is a lot of work, but having two can prove to be next to impossible. You really are going to need someone to be there to help you out."

"I'm still reeling from the news myself. It's definitely a surprise, and not what we had discussed, so Jack and I will have to have a talk about this."

"As your doctor I would encourage you to give this a lot of thought. Once the babies are here, you will find it can be very overwhelming, so you need to have your support system in place. If Jack isn't in this for the long haul, you may need to reevaluate his role in all of this. I'm not trying to be negative, but I have seen this before when there was only one baby involved."

"No, no, it makes sense. We will talk about it this week. I definitely will have some decisions to make."

"If you need other resources, let me know. My nurse can provide you with a list of parent support groups. There are a couple that are for single moms with twins, and they may be able to help you network for services you will need; childcare, breastfeeding, things like that. It is more than just providing for two. Managing feeding schedules, naps, all of that changes when there are two crying babies. She also will give you a list of books you can read on your own that may help you plan better."

"Thanks, I appreciate your candor."

"Go ahead and get dressed. Let's not keep Jack waiting. I'm going to check in real quick with the patient next door while you get dressed, and I'll meet you in my office in 10 minutes," she said as she got to the door she turned to Marissa, "By the way, congratulations. You'll be fine, you know. We are here to help you through this. I want you to know you can always call my office for anything you need. We'll help you find the answers."

"Thank you, doctor."

The car ride home was really quiet, with Jack and Marissa both lost in their individual thoughts. It was Marissa who broke the silence. "I'm having twins. Can you believe it?"

"You're having twin girls! How great is that? How are you feeling about all this?"

"It's a little overwhelming. Jack, listen, I know this is more than you bargained for. This changes everything so if you don't want to go forward with helping me out, I would totally understand—"

"Marissa, I've been meaning to talk to you about something. You made me promise to tell you if I found Mrs. Jack Right Reed. Do you remember?"

"Yes, I remember. Of course Jack, you don't need to say another word; I can find a new coach."

"Marissa will you marry me?" Jack blurted out. He quickly pulled the car over to the curb. Then he turned to her. "I'm sorry this isn't the way I meant to ask you. Before you answer me, hear me out okay?"

Marissa was speechless but found herself nodding in agreement.

"Marissa, you are going to need help. You heard the doctor, around the clock help. You are going to need more time off from work than just a few weeks, and two babies are going to be a lot of work."

"But Jack, that isn't a reason for you to marry me."

"Okay, how about this one. I'm crazy about you. I can't get you off my mind. I love that we are friends first. These last few weeks we have spent a lot of time together shopping for the nursery and picking out baby things. I enjoy your company. I love the look you get when you are concentrating on something, the grin you get when you are being mischievous, the way you cry at chick-flicks and the person you make me want to be with I'm with you. Marissa, I'm in love with you. I'm pretty sure that is a reason for me to marry you."

"Jack, you've never even hinted to me that you felt this way, or if you have I've totally missed it. We've never even kissed, other than under Mrs. Gottsfrey's mistletoe two years ago, and you could hardly call that a kiss since I'm not even sure it was on the lips." Marissa's eyes were focusing at an imaginary point in her lap.

He reached over with one hand and turned her face to his, forcing her eyes to meet his. She saw tears forming in his eyes. "I love you, and I think if you give it some thought you will realize I have for awhile." He bent his head down to meet hers, then kissed her ever so lightly. She could feel his emotions in her soul. "This isn't as spontaneous as it seems. I've been thinking about it for months. Remember the secret that Ben used to blackmail me? It was that I had feelings for you, even when you were dating Brian. The last couple of weeks I've even been looking at engagement rings; I just didn't want to pressure you when I know your life has been in precarious balance the past few months. It just felt selfish, like I was being pushy. I didn't want you to think I was expecting something for offering to help you. I don't need an answer right now. Think about it for a few days. I'm not going anywhere. No matter what you say, there is no wrong answer."

He let her go and then pulled back into traffic. They were silent the rest of the ride home. He saw her safely to her apartment door, and pulled her into an embrace. "Marissa, I will be here for you no matter what your decision is, but I couldn't let you make this type of decision without all the facts. This wasn't the way I had wanted to propose to you, but I got caught up in the news we got today. It seemed to make things more urgent."

"Jack, I do love you. I'd be lying if I said I hadn't thought of you in a romantic sense. I definitely feel an attraction to you, and it would be so easy to just say yes. But I don't want to make a mistake by locking you into a future raising two children that aren't yours. Marriage is such a big commitment without there being children involved. We haven't even dated. So I think I'd like to maybe take this one step at a time. Can we take things slow? Nothing says we have to be married when the babies are born. Maybe we could start dating for awhile first, and see where it goes from there?"

He put his arms around her, pulling him towards him. "Just how slow did you have in mind? I've already been feeling like a heel for the things I've wanted to do with you. I've taken so many cold showers lately that Mrs. Gottsfrey actually commended me for the savings on the gas bill." He kissed her again, this time with a toe curling fervor that sent a chill down her spine.

"Cold showers, huh? We can't have my Lamaze coach catching pneumonia. I think we will need to work out another solution."

"What do you recommend?"

"Why don't you give me an hour to get changed, and we can maybe go out to dinner to discuss your problem."

"You're on. See you in an hour." He kissed her once more before turning to go downstairs. She watched him go, taking the stairs taking two at a time.

"Be careful! You're no good to me with a broken leg!" she called after him.

"See, that's why you're going to be a great mom, always thinking safety!" he shouted back up.

She turned to go into her apartment, feeling better than she had in months.

An hour later, Jack arrived at Marissa's door, wearing a dark, tailored blue suit and holding a bouquet of flowers and a box of candy in a red velvet heart. "Wow, I feel a little underdressed. My maternity wardrobe is a bit limited. Are you sure I look okay?" She was wearing a black knit dress with a matching full length jacket and some low heeled pumps. She had swept her hair up into a French twist.

"Are you kidding? You take my breath away," Jack said as he handed her the flowers.

"Thank you, they're beautiful. I'll just put them in some water before we leave."

"Sure. I'm going to set the candy over here on the counter."

"Jack, you really didn't need to go to all this trouble."

"No trouble, besides the candy is really for me. You haven't had any junk food around since you got pregnant, so I wanted to have something to eat when I come over. Besides, Valentine's Day is tomorrow. It seemed appropriate."

"Okay, flowers are in water. We can go."

Chapter 20

"Hey, Marco, can you grab that order and take it over to table four?"

"Sure, Sam, on my way."

Sam had been in business for thirty-five years in this location. Sam's Café served up what he called 'home-cookin' which meant a menu of fried food. He offered three meals a day and kept his prices reasonable. He had developed a regular customer base of older patrons from the neighborhood and seemed to know just about everyone who came in. Lately he hadn't been attracting new business. His usual morning rush was dwindling since the younger crowd flocked to the newer trendy cafes, as Starbucks was taking over every corner in Seattle. The traditional coffee shops were having problems keeping up with the times.

Two months ago, Marco showed up on his doorstep asking about the studio apartment he had for rent above the shop. His overall appearance was neat and clean, despite his slightly rugged good looks. He told Sam that he had been working as a barista at the Starbuck's downtown. Marco told Sam his hard luck story. His mother had been ill and he had quit college a several years ago to care for her. Sadly, his mother had passed away last year. Now that he had settled all her affairs he wanted to go back to school in the fall. He needed to find a place closer to campus. Sam hired Marco on the spot, gave him the apartment upstairs rent free on the condition that he worked the weekends so Sam could go to his kids' soccer games, and help with the late night bakery deliveries so Sam could stay home with his family.

To sweeten the deal, Marco promised Sam that if he bought one of those fancy espresso machines that he could whip up his customers some of those mocha frappe whatcha-ma-thingies that were currently drawing younger customers to the competition. Within the first week of hiring Marco business had picked up, especially the twenties to thirties female clientele. Marco had an easy disposition and was attentive to the customers. He was what the women referred to as 'a hottie' or 'fine'. Admittedly, Marco was a looker. He had a deep tan, dark thick hair and a chiseled jaw line that gave way to a killer smile when he laughed. Sam was very pleased with his new growing client base, as women of all ages were coming in to take advantage of Marco's hospitality, and Sam was the beneficiary. Sam's business was booming once again.

As Marco delivered the order to table four, he noticed the attractive couple sitting at table six. He had seen them in here before, usually on the weekends, sharing a newspaper in what seemed to be a comfortable silence, once in awhile pointing out something they were reading. He had noticed that she was pregnant but wasn't wearing a ring. "Be right with you folks," he said as he passed their table. There was something different about them today. They seemed to be looking at each other the way lovers look when they gaze into each other's eyes. He quickly bussed a couple of tables, checked out the group of women at table two, and proceeded to take the couple's order. "How are you doing today?" he asked.

"Wonderful, thanks. I'll have the special with a house coffee. Hon, what did you want?" Jack asked.

"I'd like the fresh fruit platter with a poppy seed muffin and some orange juice please," Marissa said.

"Sure. When are you due?" Marco asked.

"June 20th, a little over four more months to go." Marissa answered.

"My sister just found out she's pregnant. They've been trying for awhile so she's really excited. Do you know what it is yet?"

"Twin girls," Jack volunteered, looking at Marissa with that same look they had shared earlier, "and we can't wait."

"Happy for you. Hey, I'm gonna get your order right in for you, should be ready pretty quick." A man came and sat down at the table next to them, "Be right with you sir," Marco called out as he sped off to the kitchen.

Jack leaned across the table and took Marissa's hand. "You make me so happy. I had such a nice time at dinner last night. What do you say we go out tonight again? It's Valentines' Day, we should celebrate."

"That's great, but do you think there will be a table anywhere around here?"

"Let me worry about that. Can you be ready to go at 6:00?"

"Sure, I have a light load today, and I am working from home."

"Okay, I had already planned to take today off."

"Hmmm, you have my curiosity peaked, Mr. Reed. Why would you have planned to take today off? Were you expecting something?" Marissa asked, handing him her section of the paper.

"Nope, just hoping."

"And if I had said no?"

"I can tell you work for the DA's office. Is this an interrogation Miss Van Horn? Because if it is, I'd like to have my attorney present."

"No further questions....for now, but I'd like to reserve the option to pick up this line of questioning at another time."

"Marco, there was a call for you. I left the number on the board. If you want to take a break and call them back, I can have Joe wait on the customers."

Marco looked at the note, "It's nothing urgent. My break is coming up in twenty. I'll call them back then."

"Suit yourself. Table three's orders up."

Twenty minutes later, Marco took the number and went upstairs for some privacy. He dialed the number with some trepidation. Things were going pretty good right now, and although this could mean some more money on the way, he wasn't sure he wanted to move on just yet.

"Hello," answered a familiar voice.

"It's me. You called?"

"We got something for you."

"First of all, I thought I told you this number is just for emergencies."

"You didn't answer your regular number, so that made it an emergency."

"Whatever. What do you want?" Marco replied, becoming impatient with the situation.

"It's time for you to make the delivery we discussed."

"When?"

"Tonight."

"When do I get my money?"

"I wired half this morning, you'll get the other half when the package is delivered. You just keep watching her. I'll be in touch with more instructions soon."

"I need more money if I'm gonna to keep up this surveillance, and it'll be extra if you want more than just watching done the next time."

"Don't get greedy on me, Leo. The Brotherhood takes care of its own, remember?"

"It's Marco now, remember?"

"Whatever."

"Just be sure to keep sending your monthly installments."

"Later."

"Later."

Leo hung up the phone. He wasn't sure how much longer he wanted to play along with Mitch, but 'blood in, blood out' was the Brotherhood's code, so they owned him. At least his new identity was working nicely for him. There were a lot of police that came into Sam's shop and he hadn't been recognized, so he was pretty sure he was safe. He was actually enjoying working for Sam and for once he was feeling like he didn't always have to be on the move. He didn't like having to keep up the tanning appointments and coloring his hair and eyebrows every few weeks, but he was finding that honest work did have some rewards. Maybe someday he'd open his own coffee shop.

Chapter 21

Promptly at 6:00 Marissa met Jack at the door wearing a stunning red silk dress. It fell gracefully down the front, with a plunging v-neck line. Her brown hair, pulled up on one side revealed small diamond earrings. “Marissa Van Horn, you take my breath away,” Jack said. Jack was wearing a black tuxedo, carrying a bottle of bubbly and more flowers.

“Same to you, sir. Won’t you come in?”

“We have a few minutes so I brought us some bubbly, I thought we should make a pre-dinner toast….and these are for you.”

“Thank you, you’re going to spoil me,” taking the flowers and smelling in their fragrance, “But Jack, I can’t have any alcohol, remember?”

“I do remember, that’s why I bought some sparkling cider. I hear 1991 is a very good year for the Martinellis’”

“Perfect. There are some glasses in the cabinet on the right.”

Jack filled their glasses, and handed one to Marissa. "To you, sweetheart, and to the first of many Valentine's Days together. My heart is full for the first time in my life because of you." They clinked glasses and sipped from the flutes.

"Okay my turn. To you Jack, thank you for giving me your love and hope for the future."

He reached over and took her glass from her, setting them both down on the counter. He gently ran his hand down her arm, taking her hand in his. He brought it up to his lips and gently kissed it, then kissed her lightly on the cheek. Marissa briefly closed her eyes, drinking in his aftershave. He took her hand and put it under his arm, "Shall we?" He let go of her hand just long enough to help her with her wrap. "I have a car waiting downstairs to take us to dinner." He opened the door for her. Sitting on the door mat was another heart shaped candy box.

Marissa looked at Jack, "What have you done now? You brought me a box of candy last night." She was bending down to pick it up when Jack stopped her.

"Marissa, it's not from me. Maybe we shouldn't touch it."

"Well if it's not from you, then--" she trailed off.

"Do you have Detective Cordova's number handy?"

"I've got it on speed dial," she said moving towards the phone.

"You lock the door behind me, call Cordova. He can't be far, I'm going to go out and see if I can find him!"

"Jack, no! You are coming in with me. If it is from him, he's already taken two people from me, I'm not making it three!"

Jack thought about this for a split second. He couldn't stand the thought of this guy getting away again, and he would love to get his hands on him, but at the same time he didn't want to upset Marissa.

"Okay, I won't go, but I am going to go check on Mrs. Gottsfrey, so do what I said. I'll be right back. Do not open this door to anyone but me or the police."

"Just hurry, Jack."

About five minutes after he returned, Jack opened the door to Detectives Cordova and Anderson. Detective Anderson was already scanning the box with a special device. "Okay, the scan is completed there doesn't seem to be any device in it, or booby trap attached. Do you mind if I open it Miss Van Horn?"

"Not at all, I certainly don't want to open it," Marissa replied.

Detective Anderson gently lifted the box. Inside was a heart shaped note that was exactly the same size as the box, which read: "You're mine." The detective lifted the note, revealing a kitchen knife very similar to the ones in Marissa's kitchen, smeared with some red sticky substance.

"It doesn't appear to be real blood on the knife, but we can have the lab run it to see what it is."

"Do it," Detective Cordova said. "Take in the whole thing, run it for prints, specifically checking it against the ones we have on file for Leo Fernandez."

"Okay, you want me to get the team in to do the usual work up in the hall way, before I head back?"

"That'd be great, I'll get the information we need from Marissa, Jack and the landlady downstairs."

"See you back at the office."

"Thanks," Detective Cordova turned to Marissa. "You doing okay?"

"Yeah, it spooked me at first, but it's just a box. Jack is here so at least I know he's safe," she reached over and took his hand.

"You want to tell me what happened."

Jack and Marissa went over the details, including the fact that there was a very short window of time in which the box could have been left.

"Okay, well I'm going to go downstairs and talk with Mrs. Gottsfrey and see if she saw anything."

"Oh I already went down to check on her. No one answered her door, and I know she was going out for the evening."

"I think we better check anyway. She doesn't happen to leave you with a spare key does she? I wouldn't want her to be in any kind of trouble."

"Yeah, I have one. But why don't you let me go in and check. If there's anything wrong I'll let you right in," Jack offered. "Mrs. Gottsfrey is pretty private, and she might not appreciate us just letting you have access to her apartment."

"That's right. She'd probably rather we went in first," Marissa chimed in, remembering the fire incident.

"Okay, but just you Jack. Marissa doesn't need any more stress right now."

"Okay, I'll be right back."

A few minutes later Jack was back. "She isn't there; everything looks the same as always. I'm sure she is just out for the evening."

"Sir, we're all done here" an officer announced from the hallway.

"Good, we are finished as well. You two look like you were going out tonight. I wouldn't let this get in your way."

"Thanks for coming so quick," Marissa said, seeing Detective Cordova to the door.

"You're welcome. And Jack, for the record, Marissa was right in stopping you from leaving to go after Leo. Leave the apprehension to us. He will mess up, they always do. And when he does we'll nail him."

"Yes, sir. Thanks again. You have a good evening."

"You, too. Take this girl out. You two aren't going to have many more nights without kids. So go have some fun, live a little. Just be safe."

Jack closed the door, and pulled Marissa into his arms. Her eyes were already tearing up. "Sh-sh, it's okay. He isn't going to hurt you. I won't let him."

"It's really not me he's after. It's you, Jack. I can't bear it if something happens to you."

"Hey, I'm here, I'm not going anywhere. He isn't going to hurt me. We'll make sure of it. Listen, go splash some cool water on your face, powder your nose, or whatever it is you women do to your noses, I think we need to go out."

"—but Jack, I—"

"No 'but Jacks'. We're going, now get!"

Ten minutes later they were on their way to dinner.

Leo's coffee shop apartment offered a perfect view to the street below that had finally been cleared of police cars. This close proximity to Marissa had truly given him a vantage point when it came to watching her. Alan's monthly stipend wasn't much, but in reality he wasn't really doing this for the Tweedledeedum brothers anymore.

Leo still remembered the electric charge that ran through him several months ago, when the sweet Marissa had taken his hand to shake it; her soft skin, her gentle touch, and the kindness in her eyes before she knew who he was. For a small moment, that he was certain would haunt him for the rest of his life, he could almost feel what it would be like to have a woman like her want him. He also still remembered how that sweet face had turned so painfully twisted at the sound of his name. How he wished he hadn't told her.

He had stayed away for a couple of months, trying to get her out of his head, but it was next to impossible. At that point, it had been eight weeks since the day he had carried out the murder of Brian Benton. When he first returned to Seattle, he had hid in the shadows across the street from her apartment once again to get a glimpse of her. He would watch her apartment, but there wouldn't be any lights on, her curtains would be drawn. When her friends went out for the evening she seemed to stay behind. On weekdays when she would go to work, he could see how severely Brian's death had affected her; her shoulders were hunched over, she always looked down at the ground, she didn't smile. She looked tired and pale.

Two days later he had seen the sign up in Sam's coffee shop. The small diner sat on the corner at the opposite end of the block from the liquor store, but just a few doors down and across the street from Marissa's apartment. It offered a perfect view of the street, and he decided that it would allow him to keep an eye on things. He knew Mitchell Olsen wasn't through with her yet, and would send someone else to do his bidding if Leo didn't do it.

He knew Jack and Marissa had been friends for a long time, so he didn't suspect they were romantically involved until this morning when they came in for breakfast and just had a different look about them. He didn't want to cause her anymore pain, but there was a selfish side of him, that like Mitchell, didn't want her with anyone else either. So, if carrying out Mitchell's plans helped keep other men away, that was okay with him.

As he watched the street below, he saw the chauffeured limousine returning. He watched through binoculars as the couple walked out to the waiting car, and Jack helped her into the back. He hadn't planned on this. He thought for sure the message would at the very least keep them home for tonight. It was too late to rent a car, so he would have to use Sam's delivery truck that was parked in the alley out back. He ran down the stairs as quickly as he could, taking them three at a time, grabbing the keys from the hook, as he opened the back door to the shop. He ran to the truck, jumped in and turned the key. The engine had barely sputtered to life, before he threw it into gear and tore down the alley, hoping that by a stroke of luck, the limo driver got stuck at the light. He looked left down towards the intersection, and could still see the tail lights as they turned left at the next light.

He hit the gas hard, and the tires squealed a little as he rounded the corner, and ran the next two red lights. He turned left on Mercer Street. He could see them ahead about five car lengths, moving along at a leisurely pace. He followed them south on I-5, through parts of downtown.

They took the Albro Place exit, and made a right onto Albro. He had to be careful as there were fewer cars on the road here, and a delivery truck with Sam's Café logo on the side wasn't exactly easy to hide. They were on Ellis Avenue now, in what was looking like an industrial area. Where were they going? He couldn't think of any restaurants down this way. Then they turned left onto Marginal Way and drove for almost another two miles. They turned into the parking lot of the Boeing Airfield and The Flight Museum. The building looked like a red barn, complete with white trim and a gabled roof. The driver pulled up by the back door, got out and opened the door. Jack got out first, and then helped Marissa. They were met by an older gentleman, who appeared to be a security guard. Jack gave the limo driver some instructions, and then turned to follow the guard, who locked the door behind them. The driver pulled away, and Leo pulled into the lot. He could just wait for them to come out, but that wouldn't let him see what they were doing, so he would have to find a way in or at least a way to look in.

Leo drove around to the back of the building where there was a loading dock, and parked as close to the building as he could. He looked around for police or other roaming security before he hopped out. He saw a service ladder, above the truck. It looked like it went all the way to the roof. He climbed atop the truck, and pulled himself onto the ladder. He carefully climbed to the top, taking a look back down every so often to check for any unwanted company. So far no sign of anyone or anything down there, he kept going. Once at the top, he hoisted himself onto the pitched roof. Since it was dark, it was unlikely that anyone would see him there, so he army crawled to one of the skylights. He looked down and could see airplane exhibits below him. Looking off to one side, he could see a table set for six, with a linen table cloth, there was a band in one corner and he could hear music reminiscent of the 1930's. Two waitresses stood ready, dressed in thirties flight attendant uniforms.

Jack and Marissa arrived at the Boeing Red Barn a little later than Jack had planned, but when he knew they would be later than expected, he told the chauffer to call the barn and tell them to keep everything on hold a little longer. A man wearing a security uniform met them at the front door.

"Good evening Mr. Reed, Miss Van Horn. Everything is as you requested."

"Thank you, Sheldon. Shall we?" he put an arm out to Marissa.

"Sure…I think…"Marissa said, a little uncertain as to what she was agreeing to.

As they began walking through the barn, Jack explained, "I wanted to bring you to a place that held some significance to me. Red Barn used to be known as building 105, the first building William Boeing owned. He originally purchased it when he was only twenty-eight, to house the construction of a yacht he was having built. That was in 1910, six years later his focus changed to aviation, and he began a company called Pacific Aero Products, and at that time converted this building to his engineering office and manufacturing plant. In 1917, the firm changed its name to Boeing Airplane Company, after they had produced the B-1. Fifteen years ago, the building was sold to the Port of Seattle, and 7 years ago, it was restored and reopened as The Museum of Flight. I wanted to share this with you, since my work is such a big part of my life."

Marissa looked bewildered.

"How we doing…you okay so far?" Jack asked.

"I'm moved beyond words, it is all so incredible."

"Well be sure to keep up, there will be a test at the end. There's more, are you ready?"

"Sure, let's do it."

"I mainly work on government contracted aircraft. That isn't very romantic. So tonight I thought I'd take you back to the 1930's and show you the first luxury airliner." He walked her over to the table that was situated next to a fully restored Boeing 80A-1. It was a silver and hunter green biplane.

"She's beautiful" Marissa said, walking over to look inside.

"She only seated 18 passengers. She was equipped with a heated cabin, comfortable leather seats, a bathroom with hot and cold running water, and individual reading lights. It was still pretty cold and really noisy, but it was the best for the time. In 1930, a woman by the name of Miss Ellen Church, who happened to be student pilot and nurse, convinced Boeing to hire women as stewardesses to provide for the needs of the passengers and persuaded them that by hiring women it would help flight travel seem less daunting."

"Way to go, Miss Church!"

"I thought you'd like that story," Jack said, pulling Marissa towards him.

"It is amazing, thank you for sharing this with me. I feel so honored."

"Are you hungry?"

"Famished!"

"Right this way, Miss," leading her over to the waiting table.

Marissa turned her attention to the rest of the room; taking in the flowers, the band, which had begun to play 'Happy Days Are Here Again'. "Oh Jack, you're going to make me cry. This is the most romantic thing anyone has ever done for me. But how did you put this together on such short notice?"

"I've been planning to surprise you for a couple of weeks, but I had a little help from our friends." As if on cue, Betsy, Ben, Mrs. Gottsfrey and Fire chief Bill walked down the stairs to join them.

"Now I really am crying!"

"Here," Jack said, handing her a handkerchief. "No tears tonight. We are celebrating a new beginning."

As Leo kept watching he could see the couple coming into view, and walking over to look at a plane. He realized what he was seeing were not just two friends. He was watching two people in love. The band started in with "Happy Days Are Here Again"…A few minutes later, four more people joined them, greeting them with smiles and hugs. As touching a moment as this was, Leo had seen enough. "Enjoy those happy days, Jack, I have a feeling they aren't going to last long." He knew what needed to be done; the sooner the better.

Sheldon was doing a perimeter check, when he spotted a delivery truck. It had a 'Sam's Café' logo on the side. He thought it could have been part of the catering for Jack's dinner, but it wasn't parked anywhere near the work area they had set up as a make-shift kitchen and all the deliveries had come in hours ago. He used his flashlight and looked inside the cab of the truck. No one was inside. He looked around to see if the driver was anywhere around, but didn't see anyone at first. Then he heard a thud that sounded like it was on top of the truck.

"Hello?" he called out. "Museum Security, please show yourself!"

Leo quickly lay down on the top of the truck, holding his breath. He couldn't risk that the guard might mention the truck to anyone or be able to give his description to the police. He surveyed the area, and realized there was no one else around. He inched his way to the rear of the truck, listening every so often to see if the guard had changed his position.

"Come down or I'll call the police!"

"Okay, okay. I'm coming down, don't shoot." Leo could see that the guard didn't have a weapon, but by making himself sound vulnerable he would allow the guard to think he had the upper hand.

Sheldon was unarmed with the exception of the billy club that was still holstered in his belt.

"Easy fella, nice and slow," Sheldon instructed.

Leo got to the edge, "Okay, here I come." Using the gravitational force of the drop, he used his momentum to pull Sheldon down to the ground with him, pushing him face down onto the pavement. Before Sheldon could react, Leo had his billy club and was using it on Sheldon's skull.

Chapter 22

The evening had been absolutely magical. Dinner had been catered by a chef instructor from the Seattle Culinary Academy. The band had played for an hour after dessert was served so they could dance. Jack and Marissa had told the others about Marissa expecting twin girls, and everyone was thrilled for her, offering babysitting whenever she needed it. By the time the band had finished, the caterers were all packed up. While they waited for the band to load up their instruments, Jack went to find Sheldon to let him know they were close to leaving and ready to lock up. When he was unable to find him inside, he found a walkie-talkie in the security office, and tried to raise him on the radio; still no answer.

"Hey, Ben, I can't seem to find Sheldon, I'm going to have to go outside and see if maybe he's out back."

"Mr. Reed?" the band leader called out as he approached Jack.

"Yes?"

"We need you to come outside, Sir. I think it would be best if the ladies stayed inside though for the time being. We have a man down, and need some help."

"Okay, Ben you want to stay with the women? Chief, can I get you to come outside with me? Sounds like there may be a need for some first aid outside."

"Sure thing, I'll be right back, Judith. You stay here with the girls."

Jack and Bill went out the door, and followed the band leader to an area where the rest of the band was standing. "Jones found him when he went to get the truck that was parked over there."

Jack looked down and saw Sheldon laying face down, in a pool of blood, his head obviously the source. Bill quickly bent down and reached over to feel for a pulse. "There's no pulse, help me roll him over. Somebody, go inside and call 911, tell them we have a man in his early 60's bleeding from the head, no pulse and no breathing. Jack, do you know CPR?"

"Yes, you do the breathing, I'll do the compressions."

Jones ran off to place the call, while the two men turned Sheldon over and began administering CPR.

"Jack, I'm pretty sure we are too late, but we need to do this anyway. It's going to be hard with all this blood. Are you sure you're up for this."

"He was here because of me, yes I'm sure." Bill put in two breaths, and Jack started compressions, while Bill counted. "Come on Sheldon, if you can hear us, stay with us. Help is on the way."

An out of breath Jones returned a few minutes later to tell them that an ambulance and police had been dispatched. The rest of the party joined them, standing off to the side, watching Bill and Jack work. Within ten minutes emergency personnel were on scene, and took over for the men, and loaded Sheldon into the ambulance. One of the paramedics recognized the chief, "Hey Bill, do you know what happened here?"

"No, we know he was the security guard, working at the museum, and the young man over there found him about twenty minutes ago. We began CPR immediately, but we have no idea how long he had been here."

"Okay, thanks. We have your driver's car phone number; I'll call when we have news. We'll take care of him. Let's roll!" he called to his partner, and the ambulance tore off down the street, just as the police were coming into the parking lot.

It took another hour for them to go through the evening's details, giving statements to the officers as to who last saw Sheldon and when. The officers placed pylons and tape around the area Sheldon's body had been found. When the police had finished with them, Jack went back inside to secure the building. Then the shell shocked group piled into the limo for a very quiet ride home.

The driver buzzed the phone in the passenger consol, interrupting the daunting silence.

"Yes," Jack answered.

"Mr. Reed, I just heard from the ambulance driver. I'm sorry to tell you but Mr. Sheldon was pronounced dead upon arrival at the hospital."

"Thanks," Jack replied, hanging up the phone. He turned to the others, "Sheldon didn't make it" was all he could get out, his voice wavering as he said the words.

Marissa put a hand on Jack's, "I'm so sorry, Jack."

"Me too, he was a good man. Chief thanks for trying, I really appreciate it."

"I'm sorry it didn't work out," Bill said, "sometimes no matter what we do, some don't make it, despite our best efforts."

Leo was watching from his window when the limousine pulled up across the street. He watched as the somber group said goodnight. He watched as Jack gave Marissa a parting kiss, before she went in with Betsy. As the driver pulled away from the curb, he saw the others walking in the building. When Jack reached the door, he turned and looked up and down the street in each direction. As he scanned the streets, he looked straight at Leo, and for a split second Leo felt as if Jack knew he was there. Of course there was no possible way Jack could see him in the darkness of his room, but the expression on Jack's face was one of resolve. Leo knew the time was coming when they would meet, and for the first time it concerned him.

Chapter 23

Marissa was doing some research when Linda buzzed her phone, "Marissa, Detective Cordova, line three for you."

"Thank you, Linda," she replied, before switching to line three, "Detective, what can I do for you?"

"Marissa, I wanted to tell you that we were unable to find any finger prints on that box that was left on your doormat. Whoever put it there was very careful. The red substance turned out to be a gel used in theatrical productions for blood. While I do believe this was a threat to you from Mitchell Olsen, I can't link it to anyone at this time."

"Okay, so maybe it wasn't Leo then?"

That's what we thought too, but there's more. We found a fresh oil stain next to where the body was found, indicating a vehicle of some kind was parked there. Our men noticed a service ladder to the roof just overhead, and we dusted the rungs, and found a match to Leo. He must have been on the roof. We didn't find anything up there, but that just means he didn't leave anything behind. Our best guess is that Sheldon caught him doing something outside. There was one witness, a custodian working in the office building adjacent to the museum. He said he saw a white delivery truck parked where we found the oil stain. He couldn't remember what was on the side of the truck, but remembers there black or blue lettering. Does this sound like anything you've seen in your neighborhood?"

"Nothing comes to mind, but I'll try to pay closer attention to the vehicles in the neighborhood."

"Unless we catch a break on that truck, we don't really have much of a trail to follow."

"I see, so what now?"

"I'm worried for your safety, Marissa. I think I can convince the chief we need to bump up security, and have someone escort you to and from work. We can beef up our detail at the courthouse and your office as well. Maybe we'll get lucky, he's obviously watching you."

"Look, I don't want any more tax payer money spent to protect me. If anything you need to use me for bait, and lure him in. He's had numerous opportunities to kill me by now if he intended to do so, so let's concentrate on catching him instead of protecting me, before he kills someone else, especially someone I love."

"Actually, that may be something we need to consider. It certainly wouldn't be my first choice, but we are running out of options. Let me talk to my department, and see if we can come up with a plan that will protect you, as well as bring him out of hiding."

"Okay, keep me posted, thanks for calling." Marissa hung up the phone with a nagging feeling, the kind one gets when they think they have forgotten something important. She sat there for a few minutes trying to figure it out, but then decided she should call Jack and fill him in on the details.

Chapter 24

Marissa and Jack had decided to have a late Saturday morning breakfast at Sam's. It had been an emotional week for both of them, so they planned to spend a leisurely weekend close to home. They sat at their usual table near the window, with their Saturday morning paper. Marcus came over to take their order.

"Good morning, what can I get for you today? Ladies first."

"I'll have the granola and yogurt with a side of fruit. Also I'd like a cup of tea, Earl Grey, please."

"I'll take the short stack, eggs over easy, bacon and coffee."

"Okay folks, I'll get your order put in. Bonnie will be over with your beverages."

"Thanks."

Marcus went off to give Sam the order, Jack and Marissa went back to reading their paper. Bonnie came over, "How y'all doin' today," she said in her gravely Texan drawl. Bonnie had been transplanted here. She fit the stereotype of a diner waitress.

"Okay, I've got one hot tea and a coffee. Here's some creamer, honey and lemon. Let me know if y'all need anything else," her attention being drawn towards the door. "Y'all just find a seat anywhere you like, someone will be right with y'ewe," she shouted.

Jack was so distracted that he had reread the same sentence at least three times and still wasn't paying attention to the words. He sighed and looked up from his paper long enough to take a sip of his hot coffee and look out the window. There was a white delivery truck driving by, 'Sam's Café' was clearly printed on the side in bold blue lettering. Across the table, Marissa was looking at the paper, but appeared to be lost in thought, miles away. He reached over and took her hand. "You okay?" he asked.

"I'm fine. It's been a hard week. How about you? This hasn't been easy on you either."

"I'm doing okay. I didn't tell you but I went by Sheldon's house yesterday and spoke to his wife. He had two kids, both in college. His wife seemed to appreciate me dropping by. She said both kids were on their way home for Monday's service. Their church has started making arrangements for food and they were being taken care of by friends and loved ones. She said that Sheldon had told her all about what I was doing, and how much of a romantic he always was. It didn't surprise her that it was his idea and that I could take comfort in knowing that he was happy to be there."

"Everyone deals with grief differently, Jack. Paying your respects to Sheldon's family was your way of showing support. That's what they need the most right now. I know you feel responsible for this, but how could you have known? If anything it was because of me, not you. So if you are going to blame anyone, blame me!"

"Marissa, you can't possibly think I would do that. You can't control this man. It isn't your fault."

"But don't you see, anyone around me gets hurt. I am the reason that Leo was there. Detective Cordova said they've exhausted all their current leads to find him. They're trying to work on a plan now to trap him somehow. I volunteered to participate in anything they need to bring him out of hiding."

"Oh no! You are not going to be used as bait. That is not happening! No, absolutely not!"

"Jack, listen to me. We need to catch this guy. *I* need them to catch him. I've been looking over my shoulder for far too long. I have my babies to think about. I can't take the chance that they could be his next victims. I won't take that chance."

"As far as I'm concerned using yourself sets all three of you up as victims!"

"Don't you see? If he wanted to kill me, he could have done that already. He won't hurt me."

"I don't think you or anyone else can predict what he will and won't do." Jack quit talking, clearly agitated that Marissa would consider this cockamamie scheme. He stared outside.

"Jack, please don't be upset with me," Jack continued to look out the window, "Jack?"

He turned to her, his eyes staring hard at her now, "Didn't you tell me the detective said the witness reported a white delivery van with blue lettering at the scene?"

"...yes, but what does that have to do with..."

"Be right back," Jack got up from the table and walked towards the back of the café. He went down the hall where the restrooms were and the back door to the alley. He went outside and there it was-- Sam's truck, a white delivery van with bold blue lettering. He walked around it looking inside where there were windows he could see into. He went around to the driver's side. There was something red splattered on the bottom edge near the door. He bent down to take a closer look. He was still piecing together what his mind was racing to compute, when Marcus came around the back of the van.

"Looking for something?"

Taken by surprise, Jack flinched a little. He stood up and looked at Marcus. "Uh, no, I came out back, I needed some air, and then I thought I saw a coin under the truck, so I was trying to pick it up, but it turned out to be some trash….you know I think I'll go back in now." Jack turned to walk inside. Marcus remained back by the truck. Just as he reached the door Jack turned back and said, "Have a good day, Leo."

"Thanks, you too man," Leo responded without thinking. Then realizing what had just happened, he turned just in time to see Jack running full on at him. Jack sent a pounding blow to Leo's rib cage, producing a cracking sound. Leo balanced himself with one hand on the truck, and holding his other hand up, signaling for Jack to stop. It was enough for Jack to hesitate for a split second before taking aim with another punch. That second's hesitation was just enough for Leo, to use that hand to push Jack backwards, using his whole body's weight to propel them both to the ground, landing with Leo's left hand at Jack's throat.

Jack rolled over to the side, taking Leo with him, trying to reverse their positions. The two men rolled back and forth on the ground, Jack desperately trying to shake Leo off, using both hands to attempt to at least loosen Leo's grip. Leo was definitely beginning to overpower him. He was barely getting any air. He could feel Leo reaching down with his free hand for something. He used this opportunity to make a hard roll to the left. As Leo struggled to regain balance, Jack freed himself from Leo's death hold, slamming Leo into the wall next to them. Jack used this temporary reprieve to his advantage. He rolled further away from Leo, onto his hands and knees so he could push himself up. He struggled to a near standing position, feeling shaky. Leo was quicker to recover. He had already steadied himself against the wall. Jack could see Leo had a small handgun in his right hand. "Don't do it man, just turn yourself in."

"No way, I'm not going back in. It's gonna have to be you or me."

"I'm not a killer, but I'll make an exception where you're concerned."

"Really? I've got the experience, the weapon and no conscious. You are empty handed and couldn't kill if your life depended on it, and oh by the way…it does!"

A car engine backfired somewhere behind Jack, startling both men. Jack decided to use it to his advantage and lunged towards Leo, but Leo was quick to react and squeezed the trigger. Jack stumbled back in surprise; putting his hand to his ribcage, when he pulled it away it was covered in blood. Now finding it difficult to breath, he fell back first against the truck and then to the ground. Suddenly a door to the alley flew open. Leo quickly slid the gun behind a tire of the truck. He looked down at Jack who was struggling now to get a breath. Leo quickly moved to his side and put his fingers on Jack's neck, closing off what little remaining air Jack could get. Jack's eyes closed.

The footsteps were coming fast in their direction, Leo called out, "Hey over here, he shouted. Call 911!" Leo whipped off his apron and pressed it against the gaping hole in Jack's ribcage.

Sam rounded the van to see Marcus holding his apron applying pressure to a wound losing blood. "Marcus, what happened?" Sam asked.

"I came outside for my smoke break and found some guy trying to rob this man. When I shouted at him to stop, he shot him and took off running down the alley. Sam, he's not doing so good, go call 911!"

Sam ran inside and made the call. Marissa who was beginning to wonder where Jack was, had walked to the back of the shop, where she had seen Jack disappear. She overheard Sam on the phone. She went straight for the open back door. She walked out into the alley where she saw Marcus kneeling over Jack. "Jack? Jack!" She ran towards him. His face was white and pasty. She took his hand in hers, she leaned down close to Jack's face, and she could feel the slightest breath against her cheek. "Jack, can you hear me, Jack it's Marissa, I'm here, you're going to be okay." For a brief moment, she saw a flutter of an eyelid, she squeezed his hand. "Help is on the way, you hang on, do you hear me? Hang on!"

The paramedics arrived within a few minutes. He had lost a lot of blood and was still unconscious, Jack's pulse was thready, but it was there. "We need to get him to the hospital right away," the EMT announced.

"I'm going with him" Marissa said as they loaded him into the ambulance.

"Ma'am that is against company policy, I'm sor—Hey!" Marissa jumped into the back of the ambulance. "Okay Ma'am, I don't have time to argue with you, but you need to stay seated and stay out of our way. Before he slammed the door he looked at Leo, "Hey you did great, if it wasn't for you this guy might have died. Let's roll!" he called to the driver.

Sam and Marcus stood in the alley watching the ambulance pull away. Sam went inside, but Marcus told him he needed a minute. After Sam was out of sight, Leo retrieved the gun he hid under the truck. He wiped it clean with a rag from the truck, and threw it into the neighboring store's dumpster. Five minutes later when the police arrived, Marcus told them his story.

Chapter 25

Marissa, Ben and Betsy had been in the waiting room for what seemed to be an eternity. Jack had already been in surgery for four hours. The surgeon had told Marissa that Jack had lost a lot of blood already and he wasn't sure he would survive the operation. Marissa had been staring at the same abstract art piece on the sterile gray wall of the hospital waiting room for the last hour. A shiver ran through her, the temperature having been set to meat locker storage unit. Betsy and Ben were huddled together under his jacket, Ben looked like he was counting ceiling tiles and Betsy was closing her eyes to give them a rest from the glaring florescent lighting. Marissa got up and was pacing the linoleum. When the surgeon finally returned, his face was grim. Marissa braced herself for the news.

"Miss Van Horn, we were able to remove the bullet from Jack's ribcage, however his right lung has severe damage. He is in critical condition, and we are not certain that he will survive. The bullet also passed through and had lodged in his spine. We have done as much repair work as we can for now, until his condition is more stable. He lost a lot of blood, we had to give him a transfusion. He still has not regained consciousness. The next twenty four hours are crucial. Right now he's in recovery. Once we're sure he's stable, we'll move him to a room in ICU and keep him there until his condition improves. He's currently listed as critical. You may see him one at a time, after he's been moved."

"Thank you, doctor. Do you have any idea what time that'll be?"

"I think they should have him moved into ICU in a few hours. I have to warn you that once he is conscious, it's likely he may experience memory loss, due to the loss of blood and oxygen to his brain. We are uncertain as to the extent of the damage the bullet caused to his spine. In injuries like these paralysis is not uncommon. We need to keep him sedated to avoid further damage from movement, until he's had time to heal. My recommendation is that you all leave for now, go get something to eat, get a little rest and return around 7:00, if anything changes in the meantime, we'll call you."

"Thank you, we'll do that," Ben said.

The doctor turned and exited down the corridor. Betsy put her arm around Marissa, "He's going to be fine, you'll see."

Tears welled up in her eyes, "I hope you're right. I couldn't bear it if something happened to him."

"I know I'm right. Jack is a strong man, he's young and healthy. He loves you and has everything to live for. He'll fight and you need to stay strong for him. Let's go eat something. We'll get in a little sleep and have you back here by 7:00 so you can be here when they take him to his room."

"Betsy's right, Mar. Let's go. Jack wouldn't like it if we weren't taking care of you. Those babies need you to stay healthy."

"I know you're right, it's just so hard to leave him. Let me just check in with the desk and let them know how to reach me." Marissa went to the nurses' station and spoke with the attendant sitting there. Ben put a reassuring arm around Betsy.

"You okay?" he asked her.

"Yeah, but I'm worried about her. What if he doesn't make it, Ben? I don't think she can go through another loss, especially right now."

"Then we will be here, but he is my best friend. I know he's gonna pull through this."

Marissa returned. "I'm ready, let's go."

Chapter 26

"No one has figured it out yet, but I'm sure it is just a matter of time," Leo said.

"Mitch wants you to hang in there as long as you can. As long as Jack doesn't regain consciousness you're safe."

"I'm not so sure. The police were very suspicious when I was giving my statement."

"But they think you're Marcus, so you just stay in character and no one will catch on."

"That's what I'm doing, but I may need to make a speedy exit if things start falling apart."

"There's more you can be doing to insure that doesn't happen. We think that you should perhaps guarantee that Jack doesn't make a full recovery."

"You know how risky that would be? Marcus has no reason to go to the hospital, Chaplain!"

"Leo this was your assignment, it's your mess. If we send in a cleaning crew, you know how this will end for you. You're a smart guy. This is what we pay you the big bucks for. Make it happen." Click.

"Chaplain! Damn it!" He needed to think. He was looking down the street, when he saw a Ben's car pull up and park at the curb. Ben and the two girls got out and went inside. This might be the best time to carry out what he needed to do.

Chapter 27

Mrs. Gottsfrey was waiting when the kids got back from the hospital. "I'm so sorry, dear," she said as she gave Marissa a hug. "What did the doctors say?" Marissa told her the details, her face overwrought with fear and concern.

"I have a pot of chicken noodle soup on, it should be ready in a couple of hours, why don't you kids go up and get some rest, then you can come down here and have some soup before you go back to the hospital. Bill will join us after he finishes up at the station."

Ben gave Mrs. Gottsfrey a big bear hug, "Thanks, Mrs. G. What would we do without you?"

He planted a big kiss on her cheek.

"Now get! All of you go get some rest. Betsy if Marissa gives you any problems about lying down for awhile, you come get me. We'll tie her down if we have to. Do you hear me, missy?"

"Yes, Ma'am. I'll be good, I promise. I know the babies need rest."

The three departed up the stairs, and Mrs. Gottsfrey went back to her soup.

The hospital gift shop was full of people buying last minute gifts for patients they had come to visit. Get well cards, Mylar balloons, and flowers were at the ready, along with an assortment of stuffed animals, new baby gifts, and the standard assortment of reading material. Leo browsed the items along with everyone else, blending into the crowd. He waited patiently for the patrons to thin out, so he could be alone with the girl running the counter. When she finished ringing in the final sale he approached the counter.

"Can I help you with something?" she asked.

"I'm sure you can, Miss…um..?"

"Oh, Miss Nelson, but call me Paige," she replied, as she gave him a bright smile.

"Okay…Paige…I'm looking for something for a buddy of mine. He was brought in earlier today. I'm just not sure what to get him."

"Well, what's he here for? That usually helps a little?"

"He was brought in by ambulance, all I know is he was attacked. I haven't been able to get any details on his condition yet."

"I'm so sorry. If you tell me his name I'll call down to information and see what I can find out for you."

"Thanks, I'd appreciate that."

"Okay, just give me a minute." She picked up the phone and entered an extension number. "Julie? Hi, it's Paige. Hey, can you give me status on a patient please? His name is.." covering the mouth piece, she turned back to Leo, 'What's his name?' she whispered.

"Jack Reed."

"His name is Jack Reed….. no room yet…still in recovery….okay…uh-huh, okay, thanks Julie," hanging up the phone she told Leo, "Okay, they aren't allowed to release any specifics to us, but it sounds like your friend had to have surgery, he is still in recovery and won't be in a room for awhile yet. They said when he does get a room assigned it will be in ICU, so chances are you aren't going to be able to send him a gift for awhile, but you might be allowed a short visit after he is in his room."

"Hmm…not the news I was hoping for."

"I'm sorry. Is there anything I can do for you?"

"Can you tell me where recovery is? I'd like to check in with a nurse there, maybe they'll talk to me if I'm there."

"Sure, take the elevator to the second floor, turn right, it's the last door at the end of the hall on the left. They won't let you in, but you can pick up the phone at the door and they will send someone out to talk to you."

"Thanks, Paige. You've been very helpful."

Leo left the gift shop and went down the hall looking for the elevator.

Marissa lay on her bed, thinking about Jack. Although the police hadn't made a connection yet, she knew that this had something to do with Fetch. He was never going to let this go. Even from prison he was able to manipulate and ruin her life. She wished, not for the first time, that it had been her and not her sister that had died. At least if her sister had lived Mitchell Olsen would not have anyone to go after. No one else would be getting hurt or killed right now. She was anxious to talk to Detective Cordova.

They needed to come up with a plan before Leo could do anymore harm.

Leo found the staff lounge without too much trouble. He looked in through the small window in the door. Empty. He tried the door. It was locked. As a nurse walked towards him, he quickly turned his body the opposite direction and leaned against the wall. She used her pass key and opened the lounge door. He waited patiently as he watched her make her coffee. She looked down at her beeper, switched it off, leaving her coffee where it was and hurried out of the room, never seeing that the door behind her failed to close all the way, because the gentleman standing next to the door had conveniently placed is foot in the way. He looked both ways up and down the hall. No one seemed to be looking his way, so he quickly ducked inside.

The phone rang waking her up, "Hello?" she said, in a sleepy voice.

"Miss Van Horn?"

"Yes?"

"This is Marie from the recovery room at Mercy General. I just wanted you to know that Mr. Reed is ready to be moved to ICU. There is no need to rush over, he will be sedated and it will take them awhile to get him set up in his room."

"How long do you think that will be?"

"I'd still give it a couple of hours."

"Has he come out of it at all?"

"No Ma'am, I'm sorry he hasn't."

"Thanks you, Marie. I'll be there in a couple of hours."

"That'll be fine. Just check in on the third floor, ICU visitor's desk. They monitor everyone coming in and out. He will only be allowed one visitor at a time and then only brief visits."

"Thank you, I'll pass that along to the others."

Marissa hung up the phone and glanced at the clock. 6:00 p.m. She had slept longer than she thought. She got up and tiptoed out to the living room. Betsy was already up. "Hi, were you able to get any sleep?" she asked.

"A little, how about yourself?" Marissa replied.

"A little. Was that the hospital on the phone?"

"Yeah, no change, but they are moving him to his room. We can go in a couple of hours."

"Why don't you get changed before we go down for some soup with Mrs. Gottsfrey?"

"Sure, I'll be ready in about ten minutes."

Leo had found what he was looking for in an unlocked locker. He put the scrubs over his clothes, hung the I.D. card with a photo of a "Robert Pearce" and a stethoscope around his neck. He picked up the lukewarm coffee left by the nurse and left the lounge. He walked over to the nurses' station and lifted a chart from the counter. He caught a glimpse of himself in the mirror. He looked pretty legit if he did say so himself. He walked to the end of the hall with purpose and confidence. He punched the 'up' arrow on the wall, to call the elevator.

A couple of candy stripers walked by, giggling as they rounded the corner. As they passed him they stood up straight and put a solemn look on their faces, glancing sideways at him. After they passed him, they fell back into their carefree stroll. He heard one of them say, 'He's cute, have you seen him before?"

The other one said, "Yeah, I think he started last week, I'm pretty sure he's the one who was flirting with the nurses on Tuesday."

He was pleased that they though he worked there. So far, so good. He stepped into the empty elevator. He pushed the '2' button, and the car started moving. "Right here waiting' by Richard Marx was playing on Muzak. 'Wherever you go, whatever you do, I will be right here waiting for you.' Truer words had never been sung. The car stopped, second floor, Leo exited and went to find recovery.

Chapter 28

"Marissa, how is work going?" Bill asked, trying to keep dinner conversation light.

"Oh fine. Mr. Rosenthal is a great boss. My assistant, Linda is working out really well and should be ready to take over when I go on maternity leave."

"I've been following the Blackwood case in the papers. That's really something how he thought he could get the zoning changed on his property by blackmailing the mayor."

"Yeah, that didn't work out too well for him. I really recommend if you are going to commit a crime like extortion that you really get your facts straight first. I can't really comment on the case too much, but that part was already in the papers."

"I understand. Ben, how's the new job?..." and so the small talk continued, avoiding the subject on all of their minds, Jack. They all knew they were just killing time, until they could go to the hospital, hoping that when they got there, the news would positive.

Leo used the badge to gain entry to the recovery room. He grabbed a surgical mask as he walked in the door, putting it on as he scanned the beds in the room. He found the one he was looking for, but Jack was surrounded by a nurse barking out instructions to two orderlies. They were preparing to move him. He moved in closer to see if he could hear them.

A nurse working on charts at the station spied him. "Hey, you!" she called. "They have enough help over there, I need you over here." He could hear the other nurse saying something about ICU room 420.

"Yoo-hoo! Are you deaf?"

"No Ma'am. I am new here. I think I'm in the wrong place."

"You're in recovery, is that where you are supposed to be?"

"No, sorry" and he started to turn.

"Well, where are you supposed to be? I can give you directions."

"That's okay," Leo replied as he made a beeline for the door. He opened the door and rushed outside, nearly bowling over a nurse, knocking several files out of her hands.

"Hey slow down, this is a hospital, not the Indy 500!"

"Sorry," he mumbled, keeping his eyes on the floor as he bent down to help her pick them up. When they were in a neat pile he picked them up and handed them to her.

"Thanks…" she reached over and looked at his badge, "Robert."

"You're welcome" he replied, putting his hand over his badge before she could have a chance to look at the photo too close. "I'll be more careful."

"See that you are. Now, can you do me one last favor and open the door for me?"

"Sure." When he pulled open the door, he could see that Jack had already been taken in the service elevator. "There you go, have a nice night." He left again and kept walking towards the elevator.

The group arrived together at the hospital. Mrs. Gottsfrey and Bill had come along to lend support. They got on the elevator and punched in the third floor. They stopped at the second floor. The doors opened, an orderly was waiting to get on. He looked inside, "I'll take the next one folks" he said.

"Nonsense," Mrs. Gottsfrey said. There's plenty of room young man, you go ahead and get on."

"Yes Ma'am."

"Floor?" Ben asked.

"Uh, third" he replied.

"That's where we're going. Do you work in ICU?"

"No, I'm new, so they are sending me to third to pick up some paperwork."

"You know, Robert, you don't look much like your photo," Mrs. Gottsfrey said.

Leo picked up the badge and looked at it, "Oh yeah, well, you know how photo I.D.'s are, they all look like a mug shot." He turned towards the doors so they wouldn't see his face, pulling the mask back on as the elevator opened to the third floor.

They all stepped out and Leo made his exit by going directly to the double doors. He used his badge to open them, and went inside. The others stopped to check in with the pink lady at the visitor's desk.

"We're here to see Jack Reed," Marissa told her.

"Jack Reed, Jack Reed....Nope, I don't see him on the list, are you sure he's in this hospital?" she asked as she scanned a computer screen for his name.

"Yes, I'm sure. He had surgery earlier today and was to arrive in ICU by now."

"Well give me a minute let me check my clipboard, sometimes new arrivals aren't in the computer," she said scanning the pages for Jack's name. Finally, she punched some numbers on the intercom. "Hi Miranda, it's Evelyn. You got a Jack Reed in there? Uh-huh.. yeah...okie dokie." She turned back to Marissa, "They just brought him down a couple of minutes ago. They will need a couple more minutes. Have a seat and I will let you know when you can go in."

Leo waited outside the room, watching as the nurse set the monitors. She finally walked out, turning the opposite direction. He snuck in and walked over to the bed. Jack was not conscious. He reached over and shut off the monitor. Then he reached over and pulled the oxygen mask off of Jack's face. He was getting ready to grab the pillow from the chair when he heard a nurse saying, "Right this way, Miss Van Horn." He looked out the door as a nurse led Marissa towards the room. He quickly stepped into the hall and slipped into the next room. Luckily, the room was empty. He shut the door and yanked off the scrubs. Suddenly, there was a commotion out in the hallway, "Code Blue,

Code Blue, bring a crash cart!" He peeked into the hallway and could saw Marissa being pushed out of the way as the ICU staff was rushed in every direction, rolling machines into Jack's room. He took advantage of the confusion to exit the ICU, escaping into the neighboring hallway.

Chapter 29

Marissa stood in the hallway listening to the exchange between the nurse and her supervisor.

"I don't understand, I just put that mask on him, I personally turned on and checked that monitor. I don't understand how this could have happened. I left him less than five minutes ago."

"Well obviously you didn't because no one has been in here since you left this patient. This is substandard work. We can't have this happening on this floor."

"Yes Ma'am, I understand hospital procedure. I know I did everything right though."

"At least he is stable. We are going to give you another chance, but please understand I will have to write this up. You can use the proper channels to dispute it, if you feel that you have been unjustly reprimanded."

"Miss Van Horn, you can go in now. We are very sorry for the mix up. We really are a top notch facility; what occurred here is inexcusable and I assure you measures will be taken to insure against this happening again."

Marissa went into Jack's room. The machines were beeping and whirring, his breathing was ragged, and his face was so pale. She turned back towards the nurse, "Can he hear me?"

"Sometimes they can, we always encourage people to talk to their loved ones. You never know what gets through."

Marissa nodded. She swallowed hard and walked over to Jack's bed. She reached out and took his hand in hers, with her other hand she lightly touched his face. "Jack? Jack it's me, Marissa. Can you hear me?" She watched his face to see if his eyes would open, flutter, twitch anything to indicate he could hear her. She tried again, "Jack, please wake up. I need you to hear me. Everyone is waiting to see you they are all out in the waiting room, waiting their turn. We had dinner tonight at Mrs. Gottsfrey's. It isn't the same without you. We all missed you." There was still no sign that he could hear her; he didn't look like Jack, this man who looked so fragile. "They said we have to keep our visits short, so I'm going to let the others take a turn. I'll come back when they are through."

Reluctantly, she let his hand go, and went out to let the others take a turn to see him. When they were finished, Marissa returned to Jack's room. "Jack, it's me again. We are going to leave and let you get some rest tonight, but I'll be back first thing in the morning. I love you." She reached up and kissed him on his cheek. "I love you" she said again in his ear.

"Leo," Jack whispered.

"What? Jack, are you awake? Can you hear me?" She pulled back to look at his face. "Jack!"

His eyes fluttered for a moment, like he was trying to open them. "Leo did this," he whispered again, "Love you," and then he slipped back into his deep sleep.

"Jack, did you say Leo did this? Jack, please say it again, I'm not sure I heard you?"

"Nurse!" Marissa shouted down the hall.

"Yes Miss Van Horn, what is it?"

"He spoke. Just briefly, but he spoke, and he knew it was me. Is that good?"

The nurse smiled, she walked over and checked his vitals. Everything seemed okay. "He doesn't seem to be awake, so he may have been talking in his sleep, but I'll make a note of it."

"Can I please stay the night, in case he wakes up again?"

"I'm sorry, but our policy for ICU is no overnight stays for visitors. I will take your number. If he wakes up again for any length of time, I will call you and you can come back. If he's up tomorrow you can stay longer. You should go home and get some rest to keep up your strength."

"I guess you're right. I gave them my information do you still have it?"

The nurse looked at Jack's chart, "Yes, it's noted here."

"Thank you"

"Your welcome, don't worry, we'll take good care of him."

Marissa returned to the sitting area where the others were waiting. "He spoke to me" she announced.

"Really? Oh Marissa that's wonderful what did he say?" Betsy asked.

"Well not much, but he said 'Leo did this' and 'love you'; then he went back to sleep. I called the nurse to check on him, but he was out like a light. She said that he could have been talking in his sleep, but even so that was encouraging."

"He said 'Leo did this'. Do you think we should call Detective Cordova?" Ben asked.

Yes, but I'm not sure he really meant that Leo attacked him. He could still be thinking about Sheldon. Nevertheless, I plan to call him when I get home and let him know. They said that Jack needs to rest tonight, so I think we should go home. I can come back tomorrow. If there's any change in the meantime, she'll call me during the night."

"I'm so glad he spoke," Mrs. Gottsfrey said, taking Marissa's arm, "That sounds like such good news."

"I know he isn't out of the woods yet, but I am encouraged."

"I'll get the car, you guys can meet me down at the lobby entrance," Ben said.

"I'll go out with you," offered Bill, "I could use some fresh air."

Back in the safety of his hidey-hole apartment, Leo knew he hadn't been successful with his little mission, but it was obvious Jack wouldn't be talking to the police tonight. He decided to get his bags packed just in case. He'd wait until tomorrow to see what he could find out. When he went back the next time, he'd be better prepared. He placed a call to get some supplies he would need.

Chapter 30

Sunday morning Marissa was at the hospital bright and early. She had called ahead and the nurse said that Jack had had a relatively good night, but still was not awake. Betsy and Ben had stayed behind for the time being but planned to drop by that afternoon.

Last night when Marissa had called Detective Cordova, he had told her they would return to the crime scene to see if anything else turned up. In the meantime they would post a police officer at the ICU door to make sure Jack was safe. The officer was there when she arrived. A composite sketch of Leo from Marissa's description from several months ago had been circulated to all hospital employees.

Marissa walked into Jack's room. She leaned in close to his ear like she did the night before, and kissed him lightly on the cheek. "Morning, sleepyhead. Jack, it's me, I'm here, can you wake up?" She watched his face…nothing. "Jack, wake up, please," she took his hand; tears began welling up in her eyes.

"Please don't leave us, we need you Jack. I don't know where you are right now, I'm sure it's nice, but please come back." She squeezed his hand. It was almost imperceptible, but she felt a little movement in his hand, like he was trying to squeeze back.

"Jack can you hear me? If you can hear me, wiggle your fingers." Again, his fingers wiggled just a little. "Okay Jack. That's good. Can you open your eyes, honey? Please try."

She watched his face, his eyelids fluttering just a little. "That's right Jack, keep trying."

Jack's mouth tried to form words, she leaned in closer, "Jack I can't hear you, say it again."

"Sleepy."

"Sleepy?" she felt a slight touch on her fingers. "Okay Jack, I know you're sleepy, but try to wake up, please." Jack tried again to open his eyes. "Nurse," Marissa called out. "Jack, I'm going to get the nurse."

The nurse popped her head in. "Yes?"

"Jack is trying to wake up. Can you see if there's anything you can do?" Marissa asked.

The nurse walked over to him, checked his vitals, picked up his chart to read when his last medication was given. "Mr. Reed, can you hear me?" she said loudly. "Mr. Reed, can you open your eyes?"

Jack's eyes fluttered this time nearly opening. "That's good Mr. Reed, try again for me."

Jack tried again. His eyes opened for a second or two and then closed. "Good job Mr. Reed. Can you hear me?"

"Yes" he whispered.

"Okay, good. Go ahead and keep your eyes closed. I know they are very hard to open right now. Can you tell me if anything hurts?"

"Yes" he whispered again.

"What hurts Mr. Reed?"

"My head" he said.

"That's probably a side effect of the pain medication you're on. I can do something about that. You rest now. Miss Van Horn will be here when you wake up." She turned to Marissa, "This is good, but he needs his rest. If we push him coming out of this too soon, he will be in pain, and he will be using up valuable energy his body needs to recover. I know you're anxious to speak to him, but you need to be patient."

"I can do that. I'm just so glad he's okay."

"Could you please step into the hall with me for just a minute?" Marissa followed her out the door. "I don't want to say anything negative within earshot of the patient, because we know that having hope is important to recovery. However, I need you to understand that he isn't out of the woods yet, not by a long shot. He is still critical; it can still go either way."

"I understand. Thank you though for your candidness."

"You are doing all the right things. You can try to wake him up every couple of hours. It will encourage him to see you each time. It lets him know you're here. His medication is contributing to his grogginess, but without it he would be in extreme pain. We can't have him moving around, so it is best to keep him sedated for the next 24 hours. After that we will ease back a little at a time, and if everything progresses as it should, he will gradually become more alert."

"Thank you, I'll just sit here quietly. I want to be here if he wakes up."

"Yes Ma'am, that's right, Jack Reed....I'm his brother from California. I'm trying to check on his condition before I board my plane....yes I can hold." Leo tapped his fingers on the table waiting for the nurse to come back on the line.

"Okay sir, I can tell you that he is still in critical condition. He hasn't regained consciousness but he's still heavily sedated so you might want to wait until tomorrow to come for a visit," she suggested.

"Thanks, I'll do that." Leo hung up the phone, "I think I should pay Jack a visit tonight." He pulled the contents of the package out and set them on the table. Then he went to his closet and got out a box that he kept stored in the back. He pulled off the lid, found what he needed and got to work.

Mitch was somewhat pleased at the news from Washington. Things were actually going better than he had hoped. He had listened to Alan complain about working at the cannery, mom and dad arguing, and some lame excuses about why Mom hadn't come for a visit..again. Visiting hours were just about over. He could cut it short if he wanted, but since Alan was the only family he had any contact with he would endure his complaining a little longer.

"Mitch, I heard that some guys are getting released early for good behavior. Apparently there is a shortage of prison space in our golden state. The ones they think have rehabilitated are getting a get out of jail free card!"

"Where'd you hear that? Are they guys from here?"

"It was on the news and they said it's statewide. Of course they are starting with the lesser crimes, but there is a lot of controversy over it. They're trying to push appeals through faster to get prisoners released where ever they can."

"That's very interesting."

"You can apply for the rehab counseling program. If they sign off, you could be eligible for early parole!"

"I tried it when I first got here. It's all that touchy-feely remorseful stuff. I'm not sorry, so why should I pretend that I am."

"Mitch, can't you fake it to get out early. You're a smart guy, you do the math."

"I'll think about it."

"Besides, Leo isn't going to keep this up forever. He's getting harder to manage all the time. Wouldn't you like to do your own work?"

"Sh-sh…the guard's gonna hear you. We don't need anyone hearing names."

"Yeah, okay. But you know what I'm saying."

"Yeah, yeah. You just be sure our interests are being handled in Washington."

"Thanks Mitch. It'd be nice to have you out, man, and not having to come see you here on Saturdays."

"Yeah, I'll make sure to do that for *you.* After all, I'm having a ball in here, I don't ever want to leave."

"I didn't mean it that way."

"When do you think Mom's going to come see me?"

"Maybe next time."

"You've been saying that for weeks now. I miss her. Tell her that for me okay?"

The guard announced visiting hours were over.

"I'll tell her. See you next week."

Chapter 31

Marissa had gone to dinner with Ben and Betsy, she needed to get out of the hospital for awhile. Jack still hadn't regained consciousness, but she was hopeful that he would. The drugs were making him talk in his sleep and maybe even hallucinate a little. He had mumbled a bunch of names, 'Leo', 'Marcus', 'Sam', but nothing really made any sense. Marissa could only imagine he was reliving the last week in his drug-induced state; Leo killing Sheldon, then Marcus and Sam finding him in the alley.

The Mercy General ICU unit was a well oiled machine. The nurses basically worked a 12 hour shift so a patient had more consistent care with fewer staff changes. The nurse that had been in charge of setting up the monitors in Jack's room when he first arrived on the floor had been removed from his care. A new nurse, Tina, had been assigned to replace her.

Tina was a tall, large framed woman, in her early forties. She looked good for her age, having kept herself in shape, her legs and arms were well toned and her face showed minimal signs of aging. Her pony tail of black and silver strands hung half way down her back. Her perfectly applied makeup highlighted her high cheekbones and accented her electric blue eyes. Her golden tan gave her a healthy glow under the harsh florescent lights. Tina's scrubs were cleaned and meticulously pressed, something the younger nurses didn't bother to do, giving her a polished professional appearance. She was being briefed on all the patients for the night shift, when she noticed a young man walking into Mr. Reed's room.

"May I help you?" she asked.

"Yes, I'm here to visit Jack Reed. I'm Ben, we're old friends."

She verified that he was on the approved visitors' list before reminding him of the fifteen minute limit.

"No problem, I just want to let him know we're here for him."

Tina went back to the nurse's station and started going through the charts. A few minutes later, she checked in on Jack again. Ben was gone. She checked Jack's vitals, reviewed the monitors and notes on his chart. She pulled a syringe from her pocket gave him an injection. Marissa walked in just as she was leaving.

"Hello, I'm Tina, I'm Mr. Reed's nurse for the night shift tonight."

"I'm Marissa, his girl friend. How's he doing?" she asked.

"He's resting nicely. I just administered his pain meds and his vitals are within the acceptable range. His friend Ben left a few minute ago. Mr. Reed is lucky to have so many good friends."

"We're lucky to have him! Thank you, Tina."

"I'll be on all night if you need anything let me know."

Marissa turned her attention to Jack.

"Jack? Jack it's me," Marissa said gently brushing his forehead with her fingers. "Can you wake up tonight?"

Jack's eyes kind of blinked and then opened. He looked right at her. "Hey, it's you!" he said, "I know you!"

"Jack, oh Jack, you're awake, let me get the nurse," pushing the call button.

"Where am I?"

"Jack, you're in the hospital. Don't you remember what happened?"

"I'm in a hospital? Was I in an accident?" He looked around the room.

Tina came back in. "He is awake, but seems confused," Marissa told her.

"That's normal for everything he's been through. We probably need to pull back a little on the meds, I'll note it on the chart. Mr. Reed, how are you feeling?"

Jack looked at Marissa, "Whoooze Mr. Reed?" Jack slurred, "Is she talking to me? I feel gr-r-r-eat!"

"I'm sure you do," she chuckled. "Try to keep him still as much as possible. I'm not sure you can trust anything he tells you though, so I wouldn't try to ask him anything serious."

"Thanks," Marissa said. Jack had closed his eyes again. "Jack? Jack? Are you still awake?"

He opened his eyes again, "Marissa?"

"Yes, Jack, I'm here."

"Be careful, it was Leo."

"What was Leo, Jack?"

"Leo did this to me."

"Jack, are you sure it was him?"

"Marcus is Leo."

"Jack your on some pretty heavy drugs. I don't think you're thinking straight."

"Blood. Lots of it, on the truck."

"What truck Jack?"

"Marcus is Leo. I need to get out of here; I need to keep Marissa safe." He started as if he was getting up.

"No, Jack it's me, Marissa! You need to stay in bed. I'm fine, I'm right here."

"Marissa? It's you? You're here?"

"Yes, Jack. Listen go back to sleep. I'll stay right here. See, can you feel my hand?"

"Yes."

"Okay, I'm right here, you go back to sleep."

"Marissa?"

"Yes, Jack?"

"I love you."

"I love you too, Jack."

"Marissa?"

"Yes, Jack."

"I can't feel my legs." And then he fell back to sleep.

Marissa pressed the call button again. Tina returned. "Is there something else?"

"He told me he can't feel his legs and then he just sort of passed out."

"I'm sure he's just confused, like I said I'm not sure you can believe anything he says right now. But I'll have the doctor check it out when he makes rounds in awhile. By the way, visiting hours are over in ten minutes."

"Could I please stay a little longer? I'd like to make sure he is sleeping well before I leave."

"Ten minutes, I'm sorry our policies are strictly adhered to, to insure quality patient care."

"I understand."

Marissa sat there contemplating what Jack was saying earlier. Some of it made sense, but 'Leo is Marcus'? What could that mean? She thought about Marcus. She tried to picture Marcus and then the photo she had of Leo. They really didn't look alike. Marcus had dark hair and a dark complexion. Leo was fair with red hair and had a hardened appearance to him. Marcus looked like a laid back younger man, with a fresh, near flawless face. Jack's memory must be blending things together. She bent down to kiss him on the cheek and say goodnight. He stirred a little. "Good night, Jack. I'll see you in the morning." She squeezed his hand and walked out of his room.

She was nearly to the hospital parking lot when she realized she had left her purse in Jack's room. She went back inside and cued the elevator. With everyone leaving at the same time now that visiting hours were over, the elevators where taking longer than normal. She finally made it back to the ICU desk. She explained she just needed to get her purse. The pink lady, said 'Sure, no problem, honey," before buzzing her in.

Marissa walked through Jack's door just in time to see Tina with the cord of her stethoscope wrapped tightly around Jack's throat. "Stop! What are you doing?! Help! Police!"

Surprised by the intrusion, Tina turned around and walked towards Marissa, her face twisted with anger. Marissa was blocking the door, trying to stop her from leaving. Everyone on the floor was running towards Jack's room now. The police officer came dashing into the ICU. "She's trying to kill him!" Marissa yelled pointing at Tina. Tina ran hard at Marissa, slamming her back against the wall. She pushed past and ran straight at the officer who was still a little confused. She was in a dead run when she purposely crashed into him, grabbing his gun as they went down. When she came back up her neat pony tail was lying on the floor. All of a sudden her voice changed.

"Back up, everyone!" pointing the gun at the group. "Just back up and no one will get hurt."

"Leo!" Marissa shouted. "Put the gun down. You don't want to hurt anyone. Just put the gun down. We can get some help."

"I can't do that Marissa. I'm not going back."

Marissa began walking towards Leo. "Come on Leo, you don't have to do this? Aren't you tired of taking orders from Mitchell Olsen? Don't you want to stop running?"

"Don't come any closer Marissa. I don't want to shoot you!"

"Stand back lady," The police officer on the ground called out to Marissa.

"Leo, we both know if you were going to shoot me, you could have done it lots of times by now. Why don't you turn yourself in? No one else has to get hurt."

"I can't do that."

Marissa stopped having closed half the distance between her and Leo. The police officer had stayed down, not wanting to spook Leo. Leo was very focused on what Marissa was doing. The police officer decided to use the distraction Marissa was causing to his advantage. He gave Marissa a look as if to say, get ready. He swept a foot out, knocking Leo to the ground. The gun went flying out of his hand, and slid across the floor. The officer dove for the weapon. But before he could grab it, Leo recovered and ran for the door to the stairs. The officer shouted, "Stop or I'll shoot." Everyone hit the ground; everyone except Leo, who was already at the door to the stairwell. He bolted through it, taking the stairs two at a time. The officer radioed for back up and ran after him. The chase was on, as the two men ran through the maze of corridors in the hospital. Leo pushed through a door on the first floor that led to a hallway. The officer was closing the gap between them, but Leo had a good lead. As Leo stopped to push on a door, a bullet flew past his ear. He looked down the hall, the officer was standing with his gun drawn. "Keep your hands on the wall where I can see them," he shouted.

Leo placed his hands on the wall. The officer began slowly walking towards him, gun still drawn. About that time, the door swung open, momentarily blocking the officer's view. A candy-striper emerged, startling Leo, who pushed her into the hallway to further block the officer's path. He bolted through the open door, pulling it closed behind him. The young girl who had lost her balance fell into the wall, seeing the officer bearing down with his gun drawn.

"Don't shoot" she cried. The officer lowered his weapon.

When the door swung shut, Leo had escaped behind it. He quickly took in his new surroundings. There was another door at the end of the hallway, Leo bolted through it. He found himself outside. As luck would have it, the city bus was at the curb, the last few passengers filing aboard. Leo hopped on just before the driver closed the doors and drove off. Seconds later, the officer ran out from the building and looked around in time to see Leo on the bus, waving out a window at him.

Leo turned back to see a little boy staring at him. "What are you looking at?" he said.

The boy's grandmother pulled the child closer to her, "Tommy don't stare" she admonished.

"But Grammy, he has on lipstick, like you wear. And those are girl shoes!" the little boy exclaimed pointing at Leo's size 11 white rubber-soled shoes."

"Yes, well, let's not point. Here's your book, why don't you look that, okay?" She cast a scornful glance towards Leo, "You should be ashamed of yourself, dressing that way in public," she said, then turned around to face front.

Leo was out of breath. "You don't know the half of it," he muttered under his breath. He knew he would have to get off the bus sooner rather than later. The officer would take no time to call it in. They would know all the stops.

Back in ICU, Marissa got up and ran to Jack's side. "Jack? Jack! Somebody help!" Another nurse ran over, and felt for a pulse. "Miss, I need you to step out of the room. She shouted down the hall, Code Blue! Bring a crash cart! Stat!"

Marissa shrunk back, out of the way, as doctors and nurses shouted out orders and brought supplies into the room. She couldn't tear herself away, as the skillful team worked to revive Jack. An orderly who noticed her standing there, gently took her arm, leading her away. "This way, miss. Let's let them do their jobs." Marissa nodded and followed him out the door. That's when she realized she was in pain. She doubled over, from the cramping.

"Miss, are you okay?"

"I think it's my babies."

The orderly grabbed a nearby wheel chair, helping Marissa into it. "I'm going to get a doctor." He called down to labor and delivery. "Are there any doctors still making rounds on the floor? Send him up, stat! I have a pregnant woman who has just collapsed in ICU."

Chapter 32

Leo got off at the next stop, hopped into a taxi and within thirty minutes was back at his apartment. "Wait for me, I'll just be a minute," he instructed the cabbie. He quickly changed clothes and washed his face. He grabbed his gear, which consisted of a duffle, a medium sized rolling luggage piece and a long cardboard tube. Marissa was a smart girl and she'd piece it together now that she had seen him at the hospital. It was time to go. He'd wait a day or two and then he'd call Alan to see what they wanted him to do next.

"Take me to the train station," he instructed the driver.

"You make an attractive woman you know," the driver said. "You one of those cross dressers?"

"Something like that, there's an extra twenty in it if you stop asking questions, and forget you saw me."

"Make it fifty and I'll get you there, light speed."

"What are we waiting for?"

"Marissa, the babies seem to be okay, for now, the ultrasound shows they both have strong heartbeats—

must take after their mother." Dr. Mahoney explained, "I think the stress of the situation you were in brought on some premature Braxton-Hicks contractions, I still want you to stay overnight for observation. We're going to keep you hooked up to the monitors to watch for any signs of distress. By morning if nothing has changed you can go home on the condition that you have at least one more day of bed rest at home before returning to your normal schedule. And you need to avoid stress as much as possible, I can't emphasize this enough."

Betsy who was standing next to Marissa's bed chimed in, "I'll make sure she does what she is supposed to doctor."

"Get some rest, I'm ordering a mild sedative that is perfectly safe for you and the babies, so you can sleep tonight. I want to see you in my office for a follow-up next week."

"Thank you, doctor."

Marissa turned towards Betsy, "So tell me, what is the word on Jack?"

"Mar, you heard Dr. Mahoney, no stress."

"I'm going crazy here! Not knowing what's going on with Jack is causing me more stress."

"The ICU teams worked on Jack for thirty minutes. They were finally able to get a heartbeat, but they had to put him on life support. I'm sorry Marissa, but he is in a coma."

Marissa swallowed hard. "At least tell me they caught Leo."

Betsy shook her head. "I gave Detective Cordova the information about Leo posing as Marcus at Sam's Café. They went to his apartment and found the nurse's uniform he had been wearing, but everything else was cleaned out. He's gone. They have a man-hunt going on, checking airports, bus depots and train stations."

Marissa started to get up out of bed. "What are you doing?!" Betsy shrieked.

"I'm going to see Jack. He needs me."

"Jack and your babies need you to get strong. You heard the doctor. Bed rest. I intend to make sure you get it, even if that means I have to tell the nurse out there to restrain you in your bed!"

"You wouldn't!"

"Watch me!" Betsy was trying to present a stern face, but Marissa couldn't help but smile at her.

"Okay, now that is just too painful to look at, relax your face, I'll be good."

"Promise?"

"Promise." Marissa relaxed back against the bed. "Besides I'm too tired to argue.

"That's better; those nieces of mine need their beauty rest. I'm going to stay here until you go to sleep, so no funny business. And just so you don't think that tomorrow at home you're going to pull any shenanigans I've already called Mrs. Gottsfrey. She's staying with you in the afternoon, so I can check in with my office"

"Mrs. Gottsfrey! You didn't have to do that, I'll be good!"

"It was either her, or your mom."

"Mrs. Gottsfrey is great. We'll be fine. Thank you, Bets."

"I thought you'd see things my way."

A few minutes later the nurse came in with the sedative ordered by Dr. Mahoney. Five minutes later, Betsy tip-toed out of the sleeping Marissa's room. "I'll be back in the morning, but watch her; she wanted to go to ICU to see her boyfriend. Don't let her and call me if you need me to come back."

"We'll take good care of her."

Betsy met Ben in the lobby. "How is she?" he asked.

"Both Marissa and the babies are fine. She can come home tomorrow. I told her about Jack being in the coma, but I couldn't bring myself to tell her they don't expect him to make it."

"We can tell her that tomorrow. She needs to rest right now. You did the right thing."

"I guess so, but I hated lying to her."

"Maybe you didn't. We really don't know yet. I still believe Jack will pull out of this."

"Me, too. Let's go home. I want to be back here first thing tomorrow so I can take her home."

"I'll come with you, so I can check in on Jack."

Chapter 33

Mitch had been escorted to a special conference room usually used for the purpose of meeting ones attorney in privacy. Today's meeting was not with his attorney. A young, attractive woman sat quietly at the table. She was dressed in a modest navy blue dress and a pair of too sensible black pumps. Her blonde hair was styled in a French twist revealing her cerulean blue eyes and accenting her dark California tan. She sat with perfect posture; her hands folded on top of a bible. When Mitchell walked in, she stood and reached out a hand to greet him.

"Mr. Olsen, I'm Cynthia Marshall," shaking his hand. "I'm a voluntary missionary from the First Baptist Church in San Francisco. I have been assigned to be your spiritual advisor, as part of the rehab and reform program you enrolled in here at San Quentin. Please, won't you sit down?"

She moved back to her chair at the table motioning for him to take the seat opposite her. "The program is designed to make you psychologically healthy, stimulate you intellectually and prepare you spiritually. Our goal is to return you to your community, a compassionate human being and integrate you into society so you can find happiness and success. Obviously, we at the First Baptist Church believe that first and foremost your path should be one that includes God and Jesus Christ Our Lord."

"Miss Marshall, you said that so eloquently. You already make me want to be a better man. I appreciate your willingness to work with me. I'll work hard to make you proud."

"Glad to hear it, Mr. Olsen. I've brought you a bible and we're going to start with some readings in the gospels dealing with repentance. After all, you can't move forward without admission of your sin and the Lord's forgiveness…."

Mitchell hung on every word Miss Marshall said, although he could care less about finding peace of mind in the Lord's forgiveness. His motivation was more basic than that; Cynthia Marshall, had killer legs and luscious lips. Someday, when Miss Marshall was successful in 'integrating' him into his community, he'd be sure take a vacation into hers to thank her properly for her efforts.

Leo stared at the train ticket in his hand. He had already changed his clothes in the men's room, where he added a gray wig and some pale make-up base. He was using the cane that had been in the cardboard tube, just in case the cab driver gabbed to the police. The first train scheduled to leave out of the station was to Vancouver. Canada seemed as safe a place as any to hide for awhile. Senior citizens get great benefits there, so perhaps he could hide out at a senior residence home for awhile. He purchased a ticket and checked his bag.

He hated leaving Marissa behind but with any luck it would be temporary. He knew she would never love him, at least not like she did Jack, but he had hoped that at least as Marcus she might have found him attractive and a bit charming. Maybe they could have been friends. He could have stared into those eyes for the rest of his life. He was so close to turning himself in for her. He'd have to be more careful in the future. Thank God that police officer knocked him back to his senses or he would have.

Maybe he could make a little home in Canada for the four of them. He would keep her safe from those two Olsen buffoons and the brotherhood. She might not love him at first, but she'd eventually appreciate that he did all of this for her. Most women would die for this type of devotion.

The Olsen brothers were another problem he was going to have to deal with soon. He couldn't have them send someone else to Seattle. They might hurt her. Somehow he was going to have to keep them believing that he was still watching her. He could buy a little time but somehow he was going to have to find out about Jack. It would be too easy for them to check on his condition, so he couldn't lie about that part, but everything else he could make up for awhile.

He had an hour before the train would board, so he went to the snack bar to grab some food. He noticed an elderly woman sitting in the corner. He'd go sit by her and strike up a conversation. If it looked like they were traveling together he would blend in a little better. If the police came in search of Leo Fernandez or Marcus, they would have a much harder time finding him.

He picked up his coffee from the counter and using his cane he hobbled over to a woman seated at a small table for two. "Anyone sitting here?" he asked.

"No sir," she looked up at Leo. "Have a seat, I'd enjoy the company."

"Thank you kindly, ma'am. Where are you traveling to today?"

"I'm on my way to Vancouver to visit my grandkids," she reached in her bag and produced a thick brag book of photos. "Now see, this one here is Mandy, she's four and quite a pistol—they say she takes after me…."

'Shoot me now' Leo thought to himself. If he has to listen to too much of this, he may turn himself in after all.

Chapter 34

Six weeks had passed since the incident with Leo at the hospital. Marissa visited Jack every day after work. He had come out of the coma a week after Leo tried to kill him, but was still having to go through some therapy to regain full use of his legs. The bullet had caused some temporary nerve damage when it lodged in his spine, but the doctors thought he was making good progress, especially for everything that he had been through. Jack was determined that he would be completely healed by the time the babies came in June, now only two months away.

Marissa had managed to keep most of the gruesome details from her parents, not wanting to alarm them more than they already were. Betsy was staying with her for now, except on weekends when Ben came into the city and she stayed with him in Jack's apartment.

They had a break on finding Leo Fernandez, which was encouraging. A taxi driver saw a video clip they were running on the news from the hospital security cameras. He called in and said that he had picked him up at a bus stop not too far from the hospital and had taken him to his apartment and then to the train station. He gave them a full description of what he was wearing when he dropped him off, but didn't know his final destination.

The police went to the train station to investigate the lead. An elderly gentleman said he thought he had seen him board the train to Portland, but that was where the trail ended. Portland police were notified and issued an APB for Leo.

Marissa had been thinking a lot about her past, present and future. Although she had tried to leave her past behind and create a new life that was on a forward motion, Mitchell Olsen had managed to sabotage her present and seemed hell bent on destructing her future. With Leo Fernandez still at large and Mitch continually plotting against her, Marissa couldn't help but feel a sense of hopelessness and defeat.

She thought about all the people who Mitch had harmed in some way. Jack, who meant so much to her, had come so close to dying because of his involvement with her. Brian, before him had been brutally murdered and her sweet sister, Jeannette taken so violently at such a young age. Mr. Sheldon had been an innocent bystander, yet his life too had abruptly ended because of her. How many more would be taken before this could end? No matter how hard the police worked on this case, they came up empty. She needed to keep her friends and her family safe. The more she thought about this, the solution became obvious. She needed to put some geography between herself and those she loved.

She knew Jack would never stand for it if she told him the real reason she was leaving. She knew she would need to make a convincing enough argument that he wouldn't follow her. She had six weeks until the girls were born, she would make her move in the next week or two, so that she could give them legitimate birth certificates with a new name. She would go talk to Mr. Rosenthal about the steps she could take to make a new and untraceable life for her and the twins.

She was still deep in thought, making her to-do list when the door bell rang. She opened the door, and there stood Jack.

"Hello beautiful!" He was walking with a cane, his hair in much need of a haircut, had a boyish charm, but it was the perfect accessory for the impish grin on his face.

"Jack, what are you doing here? I thought you weren't getting out of the hospital for another week."

"Surprise?"

"Why didn't you call me so I could come pick you up? And how did you get up those stairs? We were making arrangements for you to use Mrs. Gottsfrey's apartment until you could manage them."

"Yes, I'd love to come in."

"I'm sorry, of course, come in; I'm just so surprised to see you." Marissa reached up to kiss him, "Welcome home, Jack."

Jack followed her inside, "My therapist actually thinks going up and downstairs is good therapy, as long as I just go up and down a few times a day. Besides, I'm afraid if I have to stay in Mrs. Gottsfrey's apartment I might lose some brain cells."

"Sit down; let me get you a drink." Jack sat down on the couch, in the same spot Marissa had been just moments before. "Would you like a soft drink or something stronger?"

"A soda sounds great, thanks," he replied picking up the papers Marissa had left on the couch, to make room for her when she came back. As he glanced down he saw a tablet with her handwriting, 'Find apartment, hire moving company, give notice, research pediatricians, research obstetricians …'

"One soda coming up."

"Hey Mar, what's this list you have going here? Are you moving?"

"What? Why would you ask that?" Marissa all of a sudden realized what Jack was looking at. Her mind began racing for an explanation that she could give him.

"This list, it looks like a moving list. Are you moving?"

She returned and handed him his drink. "Jack, I need you to listen to me."

"Sentences that start this way never end well, I'm not sure I want to listen."

"Jack, I love you, you know that." Marissa could see Jack's jaw start to clench. This was going to be harder than she thought. She decided to stay standing so she couldn't reach out and touch him. One touch and she wouldn't be able to go through with it.

"But?"

"But, people have died because of their connection to me, you were almost killed because of me, and then we weren't sure you would ever walk again, because of me, I can't live like this watching Leo or Mitch pick off the people I love one by one. I can't stay here Jack. I need to leave, and find a place where no one knows me, and no one will find me."

"Marissa, you can't. I don't care about the risk. I love you, I want to keep you safe."

"And I want to keep you safe."

Jack stood and started over to where Marissa was standing. When he got within a couple of steps, she held out a hand to stop him from coming closer.

"Running away is not the answer. What about your parents? You're all they have left. Are you going to hide from them also?"

"I haven't completely worked out the details, but obviously I may not be able to be in touch with them, at least not at first. Eventually, I'll find a way."

Jack moved in another step disregarding Marissa's protesting hand. He reached over and took it in his.

"What about me? Why can't I come with you?"

Marissa pulled her hand from him and took a few steps back.

"I can't ask you to do that. You'd have to start over, take on a new name; your career would be over. You can't come Jack, don't you see, the fewer people involved the harder it will be for them to find me."

"You've already decided haven't you? When were you going to tell me?"

Marissa looked down.

"You were going to tell me, right?"

Marissa looked up with tears brimming in her eyes. "No Jack, I wasn't. I didn't want to give you a chance to talk me out of it. I didn't think I was strong enough to say no to you." She turned away from him, not wanting to show how vulnerable she was. She hated that she couldn't be stronger, knowing that giving in to him, put him in harm's way.

Jack walked up behind her and put his arms around her. "Don't cry. You're not going anywhere, at least not alone." He turned her around to face him. "We are going to fight this together. You don't have to be alone. If you think leaving is best, I'll leave with you. I don't care about my career as much as I care about you. I can wait tables, tend bar, drive a cab, whatever, if it means being able to stay with you."

"Jack—you can't--," she started, but was stopped by Jack's hand wiping a tear from her cheek.

"What I can't do is spend the rest of my life without you. I'm not taking no for an answer this time. I've asked you once before to marry me, Marissa. I know I agreed to take it slow, but I've been painfully reminded of how short life can be. I want us to be married as soon as possible, before you give birth. I want us to start a new life with us all having the same last name."

Jack fumbled for something in his pocket. He brought out a small aqua blue box. "Keep in mind that I can't kneel yet, so I'm kneeling on the inside." He opened the box, revealing a Tiffany engagement ring. "Marissa, I love you, I will never stop loving you. I want to be your husband and the father of your children; I want to make a life with you. I think you want that too. Please say yes."

Marissa met Jack's eyes, which were now filled with tears, as one escaped, she gently reached up and brushed it away. "Jack…"

He reached up catching her hand and holding it to his face, then turning it to kiss the inside of her palm. He took her hand and placed it over his heart. "Marissa, my heart belongs to you. My mind won't stop thinking about you. I've been cooped up in that hospital bed for far too long, so believe me when I say my body wants to remind you of how it feels about you, too." He reached up and tucked a piece of her hair behind her ear, leaned over and kissed her with an intensity that demonstrated his desire for her. "Normally I'd give you time to think but under the circumstances I don't think I can do that. I need to know now. I need to know that you love me too. I need to know that you trust me to keep us safe and you believe that we can do anything together, because we can."

"Okay, Jack. But there is one condition. You need to listen, this is a deal breaker." "

Jack didn't like the sound of this, but he nodded.

"Our vows have to say 'for the rest of our lives', not 'till death do us part'."

Letting out a sigh of relief, Jack replied, "Is Friday a good day for you?"

"Friday? That's only a week away."

"Okay, Saturday. Let's call your folks and get them here."

"Jack, we can't get married that quick, can we?"

"Marissa, you work for the county, I'm sure you can get our paperwork pushed through. Don't you know a judge or two who could marry us?"

"Well sure, but I have to get a dress and there are other arrangements to make."

Jack picked up the tablet, tore the top page off and ripped it up. "Here you go, start making a new list. I'll take care of the guys, the reception and the honeymoon—you take care of the 'girl stuff' and whatever you want for the ceremony."

He picked up the phone and started dialing.

"Jack, who are you calling?"

"Your parents, I need to ask your father for your hand."

"Jack, give me that phone," she tried to grab it from him, but he put an arm out to hold her far enough away she couldn't reach it.

"Sh--It's ringing."

"Jack, you don't have to ask—"

"Hello, Mr. Van Horn? Sir, it's Jack Reed, from Seattle….. I'm just fine sir…no, no Marissa's fine; I just needed to talk to you about something…" Marissa relaxed and smiled leaning back against the couch. "Sir, I'm in love with your daughter. I've already asked her and she said yes, but I'd like to ask your permission to marry her….Yes sir, I know she has a stubborn streak…Yes Sir, I know she can be difficult to reason with…thank you, Sir, I understand….no, no, I'm sure I'll feel the same way about our daughters…I would give my own life for hers….Thank you, Sir. Would you like to talk to her? Here she is..." covering the mouth piece Jack said to Marissa, "He said I should run, however, if I felt I couldn't live without you he felt bad for me, but he'd give his blessing."

She playfully punched his arm, and gave him a scowl, "He did not," grabbing the phone, "Daddy? ... yes, Dad, I love him…."

An hour later, Marissa hung up the phone after talking to both of her parents, who were going to fly out the next morning; Jack was sound asleep on her couch with a very relaxed and content smile on his face. Marissa was still concerned about when and where Mitch or Leo would next strike. But Jack was right, together they could do anything.

Chapter 35

He had been coming here every Saturday since he was fourteen. At the age of twenty-one he had hoped he would have his own place, a girl friend maybe, but instead he had spent much of his life, taking care of his alcoholic father, consoling an abused mother and doing the bidding of an incarcerated brother.

Visitations with Mitch were never pleasant. Mitch was always complaining about this or that. He was always after Alan for information about Marissa Van Horn, or related to what the next move would be. Mitch's fixation with Marissa had grown tiring. Alan had often thought about not coming back, but Mitch was his only brother; right or wrong he was family.

Alan waited in line to clear security, thinking about how he should tell Mitchell the news. He knew he wouldn't want to hear it but he had to be told. He thought about waiting, Mitch had been doing so well with his therapy that it was hopeful for him to apply for an early parole. This news might set him back, but he would have to be told just the same.

He moved through the line, observing the other family members going through the same process. Wives visiting husbands, clergymen coming to provide counseling, children seeing a parent perhaps they had never seen outside of incarceration, parents offering support to a son. This was not the vision of a Norman Rockwell family reunion. There would be no warm hugs, no picnics in the sunshine, or family dinners around a kitchen table. Today's visit would take place at a small cubicle type desk, sitting in a cold, hard chair, with bulletproof glass between prisoner and visitor, a handset connecting the two. No physical contact to offer a touch for support, or a comforting pat on the hand for either party.

Alan found an open seat and waited for Mitchell to be brought in. He had gotten used to seeing him escorted by the guards, shackled and cuffed. He watched as a new inmate was brought out for the first time to see his wife; the new ones always cried through the first visit. Mitch came through the door and shuffled to his seat. The guard removed the cuffs so he could pick up the handset.

"How's it going?" Alan asked.

"Good, great, couldn't be better. Every day is just like a summer camp, only without the hot chicks."

"Yeah, okay. Do you need anything?"

"Cut the small talk Alan. I can tell you're avoiding something, so just give it to me."

"I have some bad news, Mitch."

"Of course you do, what has Leo done now?"

"Actually, this doesn't have anything to do with Marissa. It has to do with Dad."

"Well the only bad news you could tell me about Dad is that he killed our mom."

"Not exactly. They did get in a fight though. Guess Mom had got tired of Dad going out drinking all the time and coming home drunk. This time she was ready for him. When he came home and started hitting on her, she pulled out his shotgun. He was pretty surprised. At first I think he was a little scared and he started to back off, but then he made a sudden move to grab it away from her and the gun went off. Mom blew a hole in his stomach the size of a baseball. He was dead before he hit the ground."

"I'm listening, but still not hearing the bad news."

Alan's voice started to crack as he continued. "Mom was so shocked at what she did. She fell apart. I've never heard someone make the sounds she made as she tried to revive him. I had to pull her off. When the authorities got there, they said she had to be taken to the mental hospital. She's been assigned a lawyer, they say she'll be charged but won't serve any time as it was self-defense. But she's bad off. She just stares out the window. She won't talk, she won't even look at me."

"The old man had it comin'. Mom just gave him what he deserved."

"There's more." Alan swallowed hard before continuing. "I had to pay to bury Dad and the hospital that Mom is in costs money, too. Mom doesn't have any money. I had to use the money I had in my account and the money you had sent to me to pay Leo."

"How much?"

"It costs a lot, Mitch. I didn't have a choice."

"How much?"

"All of it. I had to use all of it."

"All of it? You used all of my money to bury a man who hasn't seen me once in almost ten years and put our mom into a crazy farm? You're going to pay it back. Every penny."

"Mitch, it was my money too."

"Your money? Your money, how do you figure?"

"I had money from working at the cannery."

Mitch cursed under his breath.

"Listen Mitch, I did it all for Mom. She would have been heartbroken if I hadn't given Dad a decent burial. I did it for her. And I had to be sure she was taken care of didn't I? They are our parents, remember? So no, I'm not paying it back. I have always done everything you have ever asked of me, because we are family. Mom is our only other family. I knew this was going to upset you. I didn't want to tell you, but you had to know."

"It's okay, Alan. You did what you had to do. I wish I could be there for the funeral and to see mom."

"Yeah, I wish you could too."

"I think I need to go now. I think I need time alone."

"Okay Mitch, if that's what you want. Do you need anything?"

"No, I'll see you next week," Mitch motioned for the guard to come and take him back to his cell. "I'll get you more money, this time make sure it gets where it is supposed to go."

Alan watched Mitch walk out of the room with his head lowered. His reaction had been very strange, and Alan couldn't help but wonder what was really going on.

Mitch shuffled back to his room, with his guard escort in tow. "You okay?" he asked Mitch when they reached his cell.

"Yeah, I just found out my old man died."

"Sorry to hear that. You want me to send in the Chaplain?"

"That'd be great, thanks." Mitch sat down on the edge of his thin mattress. Thirty minutes passed, when he heard the footsteps coming. The guard opened the door, and the Chaplain stepped in.

"You can leave us, I'll be fine," the chaplain said to the guard.

"You asked to see me, Mitchell? The guard told me about your father. Death of a loved one is difficult to deal with, especially for inmates, who are not afforded the luxury of grieving with family."

Mitch who had stood to look out the small window into the hallway turned to the chaplain, "He's gone, you can cut the crap. I need to get some cash, fast. Since my old man died, my brother has emptied my stash. I'll be dealing with Alan later, but right now the cash is more important."

"I thought you might be in need. I have brought you the good book in which you will find all your answers. I think study will provide you with some enlightenment. I've taken the liberty of providing a selection of readings and making some study notes for you in the margins."

"Also, would you pray for our brother Leo, in Seattle? He has been missing for a few weeks now, and we can't find him. We are concerned that he may have been led astray."

"I'll check with the minister to see who in the congregation is available to pay him a visit. I'll let you know what I find out."

"I am feeling much better now. We can call the guard."

Chapter 36

Leo's pager log registered ten unanswered pages. Eight appeared to be from Alan Olsen, over the last few weeks, one yesterday from the Chaplain, and one today from a number he didn't recognize. He knew better than to ignore them, but he didn't want them to know he wasn't in Seattle. His cell pager beeped again, it was the number he didn't recognize, maybe it was just a wrong number, he'd go ahead an answer it. He went to the pay phone at the grocery store and placed the call.

"Hello?"

"Who's this?"

"Leo? It's your minister. The congregation has been concerned that you haven't been to church lately."

Leo could hear his own heartbeat hammering in his head. This was not good; he would need to think fast. "I know. I've been out of town on some business, but I'm back now, so I should be at the next service."

"I see. The Chaplain has expressed some apprehensions, saying that perhaps you've been led astray. The deacons feel that your work has been compromised and it's time for you to come in for an intervention."

"I assure you my field work is intact. Please let the Chaplain know that I appreciate his concern, but an intercession is hardly necessary."

"I don't have to remind you that the California donations are helping to fund our work here, and it is important that they get timely mission reports."

"Yes sir, I'll make sure I give them one shortly."

"See that you do. I'll check in with you at the end of the week, Leo. If things haven't changed by then, the deacons will make a house call. And Leo, never forget, our prayers are with you, even unto the ends of the earth."

Leo hung up the phone. Being on the prayer list was not good news. Alan or Mitch must have got nervous when he wasn't giving them regular reports on Marissa. He would have to move quickly to avoid getting them both killed.

He checked his watch, he had two hours.

Chapter 37

It was Saturday, April 7, 1990. Judge Linda Stone had graciously agreed to come in on her day off to marry Jack & Marissa. A small group had congregated at Wexby's waiting for the newly married couple to appear. Mr. and Mrs. Reed, preceded by their small wedding party were met by a welcoming group of co-workers and friends, waiting to wish them well when the limousine arrived.

Jim had closed the bar for the day. White linen table cloths and candlelit centerpieces of pale pink tulips and white roses elegantly topped the guest tables. Spring bouquets cascading with trails of gossamer bows, hung from the wooden pillars, softening the usual rustic decor. Their favorite band was already set up next to the hardwood dance floor, which Jim had polished to perfection. Waiters mingled through the small gathering, offering champagne and appetizers.

Marissa couldn't have been happier if she'd had a year to plan her wedding. It was beautiful. She smiled at Jack, who was being greeted by a group from Boeing, as she turned to greet a few more guests. Once everyone was seated, waiters began serving dinner to the guests, beginning with the wedding party.

Jack turned to his lovely bride, "Mrs. Reed, you look incredible. How are you doing? Has this been too much for you?"

Marissa smiled, "Absolutely not. It is perfection"

"I hope you'll be ready for the romantic night I have planned."

"Why Jack, I'm surprised at you, lusting at a woman wearing a pristine white dress."

"Don't you worry about my lusting, because when I carry out my plans, you won't be wearing that pristine, white dress!"

"Jack Reed, you are going to make me blush!"

He leaned in close to her ear, "I hope that's not all I'm going to make you do."

"I will deal with you later, when there aren't fifty extra sets of eyes watching us!"

"I will hold you to that."

Jack's boss came up to wish them well, and began making some idle conversation with him.

Marissa decided it was a good time to slip away for a few minutes. She turned to Betsy, "Be right back, I'm going to the ladies' room to freshen up."

"Do you need help with your dress?"

"No I'll be fine; I just wanted you to know where I was in case Jack is looking for me."

Marissa walked to the restroom off the hallway in the back of the restaurant. She searched through the small beaded handbag that Mrs. Gottsfrey had loaned her, looking for her lipstick. When she turned towards the mirror she saw him standing behind her. At first she tried to pretend she didn't notice him, thinking she could buy herself some time if she didn't panic. She carefully applied her lipstick, but her trembling hand didn't go unnoticed.

"Marissa," he said as he reached for her shaking hand, "it's okay. Everything will be okay if you come quietly and quickly with me. I have our car waiting just out in the back. No one else has to be hurt if you just cooperate."

"Please, Leo. Don't do this."

"If I don't do this, he will. Someone else is already on the way. They weren't happy with the job I was doing and now they are coming for you and for me."

"If you turn yourself in the police will keep you in protected custody. You know I work for the District Attorney; I'll make sure they take good care of you. Please Leo, if you won't turn yourself in, then at least leave now, and don't come back."

"Can't do that." He stepped closer and reached up with one hand and lightly brushed away a tear that started to slide down her cheek. "Don't cry. You look so beautiful today. I knew you would. We need to leave now."

Leo didn't miss the grimace as she jerked her head back and pulled away from him.

"Don't touch me!"

"Marissa, calm down, it's not good for the babies. I've got our house all ready. You're going to love it. It's like the Barbie dream house with a white picket fence and a pink nursery." He stepped towards her closing the gap between them.

Marissa tried to be brave. She wanted to hold her ground, and stand up to him, but every step he took towards her, she continued to step back until she felt the cold tile wall against her back. She was trying to concentrate on what he was saying, while looking around for a way out. Leo could see her eyes darting around.

"There is only one way out of here, and it is with me. Now, we can do this the easy way, or the hard way. I don't want to have to drug you, but I will if I have to." Leo pulled out a syringe from his pocket and removed a cover. A small squeeze produced a squirt of clear liquid as he readied the needle. 'What's it going to be?"

"HELP!!!" Marissa screamed. Leo took a swift step forward and plunged the needle into her neck.

Chapter 38

The wedding party was seated and the music continued to play while they waited for the toast from the best man. Jack was beginning to get concerned and leaned over to Betsy. "Betsy, would you mind going to check on Marissa. She's been gone quite awhile; I just want to be sure that she's okay in there."

"Sure Jack, be right back."

Betsy walked into an empty ladies' room. On the floor was Marissa's handbag, a few feet away from that was her opened tube of lipstick. "Mar, are you in here?" she called out as she began opening stall doors. Once back in the hallway she noticed the back door was standing ajar. She could hear a car engine idling. She carefully pushed it open, looking each way into the alley.

"Marissa, are you out here?"

Betsy heard the car's gears engage and the tires throwing gravel as it jolted forward. From the doorway her view of the vehicle was limited to the rear passenger side. She caught a glimpse of Marissa's white dress caught in the back door of the four door sedan. She ran out into the alley, met with a cloud of dust, as the car sped down the alley towards the street. She quickly ran back into the restaurant, plowing into Detective Cordova who had just come out of the men's room.

"Marissa's in trouble! I think she was kidnapped."

Betsy told the detective what had happened, giving him a description of the car and the only three letters of the Seattle plate she was able to make out in the dust. A few minutes later Jack and Ben were standing in the alley with them, as the police were putting out the word of a citywide search.

Mr. & Mrs. Van Horn stood on the pavement in disbelief, with an all too familiar feeling of helplessness. "What can we do?" Mr. Van Horn asked. "We can't just sit here doing nothing. We won't lose another daughter."

"I assure you we have our best men are working on it sir."

"Are these the same 'best men' that haven't even come close to finding this maniac?"

"I understand your frustration, Mr. Van Horn. We are frustrated, too. But we need to stay calm and focused so we can bring your daughter back safe and sound. Right now we are canvassing the immediate area on foot for witnesses and our patrol cars are watching for any vehicles matching the description Miss Emery provided for us. We've sent a team to her apartment. If you'd like to help, we could use a current photo of Marissa to circulate to our officers in the field. Also, we are bringing in search and rescue dogs, so we need something she has worn recently so they can get Marissa's scent."

"We'll go to her apartment and get you those things," Marianne offered.

"Yes Ma'am, I'll radio that to ahead to let them know you're coming. It might also help if you would address the guests before leaving, so they are aware that we are just doing our jobs and we need to question all of them to see what information they may know. They may not even realize they were standing next to him. Any information about a missing guest someone saw earlier could provide us with a potential lead."

"I'll take care of that before we go. Here is my cell number; I want a report on any progress within an hour. Are we clear?"

"Yes sir, I'll be sure Detective Cordova has your number and gives you a call."

The Van Horns returned to speak to the guests.

Mrs. Gottsfrey and Bill had started helping Jim refilling glasses of soft drinks and water. Judith was offering words of encouragement to guests who were worried about Marissa, but also frazzled from the situation.

Jack and Ben were seated at the back of the room with a police officer who was trying to keep Jack calm. His eyes were red, his un-tucked tuxedo shirt was unbuttoned, and his bow tie was hanging loose around his neck. William watched as Jack ran both hands through his hair along the side of his head; the young man was clearly worried to death. William wished he had reassuring words he could offer, but having been through this once before, he knew these things didn't always turn out well, it was best not to offer empty hope. As he approached, Jack stood to meet his father-in-law with teeming tears and a worried expression.

William gave him a fatherly hug, and then pulled back. "Jack, I know it's hard but we need to be strong for Marissa. Marianne and I are going back to the apartment to get a few things the police have requested. It would be helpful if you would stay here and keep the guests calm until the police have had a chance to interview each of them. We will get back here just as quick as we can. Once the police release everyone to go home, we will figure out what we should do from here."

"I know you're right, sir. I just can't help feeling responsible. I'll never forgive myself if anything…"

"Son, this isn't your fault. You had nothing to do with this. Self-blame won't help her, so let's each do what we need to do to get through this."

"Yes, sir."

The Van Horns left Wexby's by taxi. William took Marianne's hand, "She's going to be okay. We're going to find her," he said, thinking if he said the words out loud perhaps he might come to believe them. Marianne could only nod as she stared out the window silently watching as one building blurred into the next on the short drive to Marissa's apartment.

When they arrived, William asked the taxi driver to wait while they went up to grab a few things. They were met at the door by an officer in charge of the team inside. "Mr. and Mrs. Van Horn, please come in. We need to know if you notice anything different about the apartment."

"Something's not right," she said. "I know Marissa and Betsy were in a hurry when they got ready for the ceremony, but they didn't leave it this way. Someone has been here."

"That was our assumption as well. We are dusting for prints. I know you were sent to retrieve some things for the search team, so if you would, I'll walk with you and you can tell me what to open, so we can be sure not to disturb any possible evidence. We have laid down paper on the floor, please try to remain on it as much as possible while walking through the apartment."

Marianne found the photograph of Marissa she had taken last week, which was to be a wedding present for Jack. She pointed it out to the officer, "That is the most recent photo of my daughter. It is a wedding gift for her husband so we'd like to get it back, but I think it is the best one to use." The officer pointed to the framed photograph as one of his men confiscated it, placing it into an evidence bag. Mrs. Van Horn continued down the hall to Marissa's bedroom.

A police officer stepped aside to let her enter and pointed to the open closet. "We think that he may have brought her here to get some clothes, as there isn't much hanging in her closet."

Marianne peeked inside. She paused before speaking to steady her voice against the growing lump in her throat. "Many of her things have been packed into storage since the pregnancy, but she had purchased several maternity clothes for work. They are all missing. There's also the bag she had packed for their honeymoon that should have been right here. There should be a shirt and a pair of jeans she wore yesterday that are in the clothes hamper, you can use for the dogs."

"Thank you ma'am," he pointed again to a team member with gloves who retrieved the necessary items. "Could you speak with the officer in the living room please? He will have some questions for you, but mostly he wants to know anything out of the ordinary that you notice."

"I will be happy to help you anyway I can, but I think if you bring back her roommate, Betsy Emery, she was here getting ready with her, so she would know if anything was out of place."

"Do you know if she is still at the restaurant?"

"She was there when we left."

"I'll send a car to pick her up. Is there anything you need to take from here for tonight that belongs to you?"

"No, we're staying at a hotel."

"Please check with the officer before leaving. If you'd like to return to your hotel for some rest, we'll know where to find you when we have news."

Chapter 39

Jack was pacing the floor now; the police had finally finished with the last guest and were getting ready to release everyone to go home. The officer in charge came over to Jack.

"Mr. Reed, we have completed our interviews, we'll be returning to the precinct to put together our reports and to give a briefing to the department and the press. Perhaps you'd like to make a statement?"

"I'll meet you there, I have a few things to finish up. I'd like to see the guests off and then change clothes first if that's okay."

"The press conference is scheduled in ninety minutes. Is that enough time?"

"Should be. Did you find out anything useful?"

"We need to compile our information and then we'll sit down with you and the Van Horns before we go to press, to bring you up to date."

"Very well. I'll see you soon."

Jack walked to the stage and turned on the microphone. "I'm not sure what the appropriate etiquette for a situation such as this is, but on behalf of Marissa, myself and the Van Horns, I'd like to thank you all for your patience and cooperation with the police. I know this has been a difficult afternoon. We appreciate your support." Jack's voice was starting to crack, "Please keep us in your prayers, I know we are going to bring Marissa back home, where she belongs. The police have said you can all go home.

When Jack stepped down he was met by friends and family who offered their support and words of encouragement, as they filed out the door. As the last guest was leaving, Betsy returned from the apartment.

"Jack, they have a lead. Apparently, Leo must have gone to our apartment before coming here. He took Marissa's clothes and a few things from the nursery. The police think it's an indication he plans to keep her and the babies alive. They also found a pass key on the floor. In his rush to grab up her things, he must have dropped it."

"A pass key? For what?"

"They don't know yet. It had an emblem on it, and a magnetic strip. The police are taking it to their lab to see if they can pull information from the strip and match the emblem to any known logo for hotels and such."

"I'm going home to get changed and grab a few things. After that I'm going to the precinct, do you want to come?"

"Sure, let me get Ben. Do you want me to call the Van Horns?"

"Tell them we'll meet them there."

Chapter 40

The group arrived at the police station and were taken to a conference room where Detective Cordova was standing in front of a podium, with a collection of police officers were awaiting a briefing.

"Good evening, folks. Come on in, have a seat. Here's what we now know. Leo Fernandez went to Marissa's apartment around 4:00 p.m., just after the wedding had started. From what the victim's room mate was able to tell our people, it looks like he took Marissa's clothes, the bag she had packed for the honeymoon, and some nursery items, including two portable cribs. What we are gathering from this information is that Leo has some long term plans for Mrs. Reed and her unborn children. Although Leo Fernandez is considered unstable and dangerous, our profilers believe he will not harm her without provocation.

As you know, we recovered an unusual pass key that was found on the floor in Marissa's room. We have been able to determine the key's emblem matches a company logo issued by a private electronic gate company in Vancouver, Canada. The magnetic strip on the back of the card can be read by the company,

Two of our officers should be arriving there momentarily to see if they can trace the key card to an address.

Because the driving time is less than three hours, we believe he could've been in Vancouver before we were able to compile our information. We aren't holding out much hope to catch him at the border, but we have contacted officials at border patrol for ferries, trains, airports and all border crossing stations. The Canadian police have agreed to work with us to find Mrs. Reed and bring Leo Fernandez back to the U.S. for prosecution.

We're optimistic that we will have Leo Fernandez in custody within the next 24 to 48 hours. Do you have any questions?"

Detective Cordova searched the faces of Marissa's family and friends. As would be expected, her abduction was taking its toll on them. Her parents and her groom appeared to be holding it together by a thread. Jack was the first to speak.

"What is happening to Mitchell Olsen? Have we determined his role in all of this? If he is behind this, then he would know where Leo took her."

"We have contacted the warden at San Quentin. They are questioning him and we're still waiting to hear back."

"Waiting to hear back? That seems to be your standard answer. Isn't there something more that we can be doing? What if he hasn't left town? What if he is right here under our noses? He's great at hiding in plain sight!" Mrs. Van Horn snapped, then looked down at the wadded up tissue paper crumpled in her hands. Her husband reached over to place a comforting hand over hers.

"I assure you we are doing everything in our power to find her. If there is nothing else, I'll go and check on our progress. I'll be making a statement to the press within the next 30 minutes.

Mr. Van Horn, Mr. Reed would either of you like to make a statement? Sometimes this is effective in eliciting help from the public."

"I'll do it," Jack volunteered.

"We'll stand with you," Mrs. Van Horn offered. "We're family and we'll stand as together as one."

Chapter 41

Mitch welcomed the change of scenery. The interrogator had been at him for three hours. They were willing to do anything to get him to talk; they started off with threats, but quickly moved on to bargaining, since there really wasn't much you could threaten someone who was already in a cell twenty three hours a day. He was intrigued that they were actually giving him more information on Marissa Van Horn than he had been able to get from Leo Fernandez in the past few weeks. For example, he now knew Marissa was married to Jack Reed, Leo was acting on his own and Marissa was missing. They had asked him a lot of questions about Canada, so it would stand to reason they thought he had taken her there. The more questions they asked, the more answers they gave him. While he wasn't pleased that Leo had kidnapped Marissa, he was in no hurry to help them find her either. The more convinced they were that he might have vital information, the better chance Leo had of getting away from them. If they didn't find Leo, then he could send someone to find Leo and Marissa. If he got to them first, they would never find either of them. Leo had done him a very big favor.

He had already negotiated a deal with the warden, which allowed him 15 minutes extra outside each day in the yard, a pack of smokes now, and one for later. He knew he could have asked for just about anything, but if he kept it simple, it would be easier to convince them later that he had been reformed by the fine rehabilitation program here at San Quentin. He decided that he had given Leo enough of a lead, it was time to declare his innocence.

"Look, the fact is I don't know anything. I haven't had any contact with Leo since he was released."

"We know that isn't true, we know you are paying him to watch Ms. Van Horn."

"You can't prove anything. Check my file; I've been in a rehab program for several weeks now. My therapist and my spiritual counselor can confirm this. I was very young when I committed my grievous crimes against the Van Horn sisters. I wish them no ill will. I hope you find her safe and sound. She deserves happiness with her new husband. I just want to serve my time and possibly get an early parole so I can be reunited with my family. My brother and mother need me, now that my father has passed away."

"Yeah, you're a prince. We know you have sent her things; little pieces of mail that represent threats to her. It is in your best interest to cooperate with us Mitch. We can help you make that early parole if it turns out you had nothing to do with this."

"I haven't sent Marissa anything since entering the program. They have really helped me make peace with myself and my situation. I am a much calmer man, since I found God. He has made a difference in my life."

The officer opened Mitchell's file. "It says here that you meet with your religious advisor three times a week and your therapist twice a week."

"Yes, sir."

"The notations made by your therapist state that he feels you are making progress and that when you first came in a few months ago, you were very agitated and obsessed with Marissa."

"Yes sir, that's true. But both Dr. Ford and Miss Marshall have helped me realize the sickness that this has caused in my life and how I need to let this go. I have found strength in God. I only wish the new couple a well and happy life. If I knew anything of her whereabouts I would have told you immediately. I don't want anything to jeopardize with my rehabilitative progress or the possibility of my early parole."

"Mitchell, I don't know you like these guards do, so I'm not going to give you the benefit of the doubt. I don't buy for one minute that you have found God or that you hold any good wishes for the Reeds. I'm finished negotiating with you and I'm sending you back to your cell. I don't think you are either willing or capable of offering us any assistance. But know this. If I find out that you had information of any use to us, or that you have in anyway been a party to this, I will be sure that you are brought to justice through a swift process which may or may not involve a court room. Are we clear?"

"Crystal. I regret I haven't made a favorable impression. It sounds like you have repressed anger and hostility probably brought on by all the violence that you must see in your line of work. I'll say a prayer for your soul tonight."

"Get him out of my sight!" The officer shouted at the guard.

Chapter 42

By the time he pulled the car in front of the gate, it was dusk. He reached in his pocket to pull out his pass-key but it wasn't there. He looked in his other pocket, not there either. He searched the floorboard of the car. Nothing. He decided he must have left it in his other jacket. As luck would have it, another resident of "Bayshore Estates" pulled up behind him and using their remote access, opened the gate allowing him to pull through. He wound his way along the wooded road, catching glimpses of the shoreline beyond. How he wished Marissa was awake to enjoy the drive to their new home.

He pulled up in front of the cottage. He was reminded again at how perfect it was. He knew she would love the white picket fence around their property, the white clapboard siding on the Cape Cod style cottage, and the red geraniums hanging in baskets from the gables of the front porch. The neighbor across the way waved to him as he pulled into the drive way. Leo waved back.

He parked the car in the garage, immediately closing the door. He was dressed in a tuxedo and she was still in her wedding gown. He pulled her out of the back seat. She was still heavily sedated, but willingly wrapped her arms around his neck, "Jack, are we there yet?"

"Yes, honey. We're home. I'm going to carry you in, so hold on okay; I don't want to drop you."

"I can walk; you don't have to carry me."

"I'm going to carry you, it's tradition."

She obediently put her arms around his neck, he scooped her up to carry her into the house, much the way a groom would carry his new bride over the threshold of their new home. Once inside he carried her to the master bedroom and laid her on the bed.

"Here we are my love."

He had thought of everything. He had rose petals on the bed, and a vase of roses on the nightstand. The knotty pine paneling gave the room a warm and cozy feel. The view of the shore through the sheers was inviting and romantic. He had long white silk scarves hanging from each of the four posts of the brass bed. He wished he didn't have to tie her up, but he knew that in a few more hours when the medication wore off, she probably wouldn't think he was Jack anymore and he would have a hard time convincing her to stay. He would have to keep her restrained until he could trust her not to leave him. He wouldn't force himself on her. After all, he didn't want to harm the babies; it was close to her due date. By that time, he hoped she would accept him. And then once the twins were born they would consummate their relationship.

He hated duct taping her mouth, but he couldn't risk the neighbors hearing her if she were to call out for help. They knew he was bringing home a bride today, but of course they assumed she was his bride. Until he could persuade her of that, he would have to be very careful with her.

Marissa was unconscious again, when he cut the small strip of duct tape, and covered her mouth. She reached up as if batting away a fly to take it off, but he caught each of her hands, and put them up over her head. He leaned over to her ear brushing his lips against her cheek, "It's okay, it's just a dream honey. No worries, you're safe, go back to sleep." He waited for a minute or two, until she had relaxed back into a deeper sleep before continuing. He secured her hands and feet to the bed posts with the silk scarves, using a square knot his scoutmaster would have been proud of. He turned on some quiet romantic music that he had bought from a time-life series advertised on television. Then he continued with his work. He still had a lot to do before she woke up. That was when the doorbell rang.

Chapter 43

The desk sergeant was waiting by the door with the message when the press conference ended.

"Sir, Officer Jones called with word from the gate company. He said to tell you that the pass-key encryption was to the Bayshore Estates, in Vancouver."

"Excellent. Did he leave a number where I can reach him?"

"Yes sir," handing the pink slip to Cordova. "He also said to tell you there are over 300 homes in that subdivision. The Canadian police are canvassing the neighborhood to see what they can find out. They're contacting the homeowner's association, but since it is after hours they are having some trouble locating the director. He said you can reach him at that number if you have questions, but he'll call again when he has more information."

"Thank you, sergeant."

Cordova turned his attention to Marissa's family, who were standing within earshot. Jack looked at him and said, "I need to go."

"Jack, wait a minute. Where are you going?"

"Where do you think? I'm going to find my wife."

"Jack, you don't want to do that. Let the professionals handle it. You'll just get in the way."

"The professionals haven't been handling this so good so far. I'm going to Canada."

Ben and William looked at each other and then turned to Betsy and Marianne. "We're coming, too."

"But we aren't even sure she is there."

The group began taking turns, peppering Detective Cordova with questions.

"Did Mitchell Olsen have anything to say of substance?"

"No."

"Did your men find any other leads at the girls' apartment?"

"No."

"Have they found an abandoned car matching the description of the car I saw leaving the restaurant?

"No."

"So you don't have any other leads?"

"No."

"Come on, I am sure my boss will loan me a plane, we can be there in an hour."

The group followed Jack to the door, who held it open as each person when through it.

"Detective Cordova, you coming?" Jack asked.

He paused for about two seconds before grabbing his holster, his jacket, a small black bag and his notebook.

He stopped by the sergeant's desk before rushing out the door, "I'll be in Vancouver, you can reach me through the Vancouver Police or my pager. If you need to leave me a message, use the number Officer Jones left."

Leo looked through the peep hole in the front door. It was his neighbor lady from across the street. He opened the door.

"Mrs. Schumacher? It's really late is everything okay?"

"Nick, I don't want to bother you, but I couldn't help notice you pulling in, I made cookies earlier and thought maybe you and your lovely bride might want a little snack before turning in tonight, I remember you said you were coming in late," she said, handing him a plate of chocolate chip cookies.

"You are so sweet," taking the plate from her.

Mrs. Schumacher tried looking past him, into the house, "Any chance of meeting her?"

"You know, it has been an exhausting day, so my wife is lying down right now."

"Sure, I understand. By the way, you look so handsome in that tuxedo. If I were a few years younger…"

"Thanks again, I'll be sure to introduce you towards the end of the week, we have plans to just kind of keep to ourselves this week, so if you hear any… uh..noises..remember, it is our honeymoon you know! "

"Oh, Nick, you bad boy! If I was your wife I'd want you all to myself, don't you know! You young people enjoy yourselves, eh. I promise I won't bother you again," she said, flashing him a knowing smile.

"Good night, Mrs. Schumacher," he replied, closing the door. He sampled one of the cookies on the way to the kitchen.

Mmm, chocolate chip, his favorite. He hoped Mrs. Schumacher wouldn't become a nuisance, because he would miss her cookies. He deposited the cookie platter on the counter and pulled a frozen dinner out of the freezer. He popped it in the microwave, before checking on Marissa who was still sleeping soundly.

Leo went back to the garage makings several trips to bring in the suitcases and things from the car. He carried the baby items into the nursery, depositing the smaller items on the dresser. More than likely Marissa would want to organize this room herself, when she was feeling better.

He returned to the bedroom where he had left Marissa's suitcase. First, he unpacked her toiletry bag, neatly arranging the items into the bathroom's vanity drawers and dressing table. Then he placed her garment bag on the chair and carefully pulled out each item had been packed so thoughtfully for the honeymoon. He opened the drawers to the dresser, placing her delicate undergarments into the drawer and carefully hung her clothes in the cedar lined master bedroom closet. He opened up the last section of her suitcase; the sight of it caused his breath to catch and his pulse to race. Her night gown, intended for her honeymoon night, was a pale pink silk fabric with spaghetti straps carefully folded with a potpourri sachet placed on top of it. The fabric across the bodice was sheer enough to give a glimpse of the beauty beneath; he slid a finger along to top edge of it before lifting it to his face, slowly breathing in the heady lavender scent. He closed his eyes thinking about Marissa, longing to see her in it, waiting for him to take her. He took one last breath before hanging it over the door, so she would see it when she woke up.

When he turned around, her eyes were wide open and glaring at him. He walked over and sat on the bed. She immediately began fighting violently against the restraints, making noises through the duct tape. He reached over and ran the back of his hand down her cheek and neck. She pulled her head away from him.

"I know you're mad at me, but you'll soon see this is for the best. We will have a wonderful life here."

Marissa struggled again, but the knots were holding tight. "I was a boy scout, well not for long really, I never quite fit in with all that morally straight stuff, but I did master knot tying before I was booted out, so don't wear yourself out trying to get those knots to come loose. My dinner is ready in the kitchen so I'm going to go eat. I know you need to eat too, so I'll bring you back a tray but only if you are going to be good and not make any noise. Otherwise I'll have to go to plan B to make sure you are nourished. Let me assure you, plan A is much better."

He turned and left the room, with Marissa still struggling, hot angry tears rolling down her cheeks. She glanced around the room. It had a honey colored pine paneling, a Battenberg lace valance, with white window sheers. Under normal circumstances Marissa might have found this room inviting, even comforting. It was obvious that this was a place he had created to keep her for a long, long time. She wasn't getting anywhere with pulling on the scarves. She needed to do something to get him to untie her. That was her only hope at an escape any time soon.

Leo sat at the kitchen table thinking how in a few months they would be sitting there together in the morning pouring over a newspaper, sharing coffee and croissants. He still couldn't believe his luck in meeting up with Nick Iverson at the general store. They had hit it off right way. Nick had told him all about the sweet deal he had made on his new place in Bayshore Estates. He had bought the place from a retired couple who had decided to move back to the city to be close to their grandkids. When Leo said that he was interested in finding some property in the same area, Nick was more than willing to allow Leo to come by for a tour of his new place, even though he hadn't moved in yet. He explained that his furniture was arriving in a few days, and he hadn't even met his neighbors yet. Yes, Leo knew that it was a match made in heaven.

Nick followed Leo back to his hotel and picked him up to drive him out to the estates. They chatted about how they could improve their golf game, even though Leo had only watched golf on television, he kept up his end of the conversation like a pro. Nick had taken early retirement, when he had won the lottery. Now he traveled extensively, but that this place would be home. His furnishings were arriving the next day. He suggested that after the movers left perhaps they could get out on a course for a round of golf and have dinner together.

When they arrived at the house, Nick showed Leo his new golf clubs and was more than willing to allow Leo take some practice swings in the garage when he asked. Nick never saw the seven iron as it made contact with his head. Leo thought it was a good shot, considering he had never golfed a day in his life. It must have been Leo's lucky day, because the previous owners had also left behind a chest freezer in the garage. Nick fit inside perfectly. Leo found some bleach on one of the shelves and made quick work of the blood that had splattered on the garage floor. He cleaned up the clubs and put them back against the garage wall. Then he hopped into Nick's sports car and drive back to the hotel to pick up his things.

When the moving company arrived the next day, Leo signed for Nick's things. As he watched as the truck leave, he waved to his new neighbors. Mrs. Schumacher had been kind enough to invite him to dinner with her and the mister, so he wouldn't have to fix dinner. The elderly couple had been thrilled to hear that in a few months Nick was bringing home a bride. Leo had spent the rest of the week unpacking Nick's things, scattering around some family photos. He had found Nick's financial records and cancelled checks. He practiced Nick's signature until he was certain he had it mastered. Getting an I.D. wasn't a problem and it seemed money wouldn't be either.

Marissa had heard him coming back. She had to convince him to remove the duct tape and untie her. When he walked in, she tried to relax herself rather than struggle against the restraints.

"I made you some dinner. Are you hungry?"

Marissa nodded her head.

"Okay, here's the deal. If you promise not to yell, I'll remove the duct tape and feed you dinner, if you start to make any loud noises, I replace the duct tape and then we go to plan B." Leo produced an I.V. bag with fluid to further emphasize his point. "This is enough to keep you and the babies nourished until you either cooperate or deliver. You can have Plan A—the dinner I made, or Plan B, a needle and a bag. If you want Plan A, nod now."

Marissa nodded obediently.

He reached over and gently pulled the tape off. He held it there cautiously for a minute to be sure she wasn't going to scream.

"Leo," Marissa gasped. "I need to use the restroom, please. I haven't gone since this morning. The babies press against my bladder and I'm very uncomfortable. I promise I won't try anything, just let me use the bathroom."

He thought about this for a moment. "Okay, but I'm coming in too."

"I don't care, I just need to go."

Leo carefully untied her, never taking his eyes off her for a second. He tied her feet together leaving just enough slack that she could baby step her way into the restroom. It wasn't fool proof but would prevent her from kicking him or running away. He tied her hands together behind her back to prevent her from hitting him. Feeling that he had her relatively secure, he helped her into the bathroom.

"Leo, how am I supposed to lift my dress and lower my panties?"

"I'll do that for you."

"Leo, come on, let me have some dignity."

"Sorry, I can't trust you yet. Do you want to go or not?"

"Yes, I want to go."

Leo raised her wedding gown up around her waist revealing her white lace panties. He looked into her eyes, and pulled them down slowly from the sides. His breathing was ragged as he lowered them. Marissa tried to think of something else besides his sweaty hands touching her skin and the cheap thrill he was getting from this. He lowered her down onto the toilet, then he turned his back to her. "You have five minutes; I will be right outside this door, so don't get any ideas."

He left the door ajar. Marissa used the time to look around the small bathroom for an escape route. The bathroom window wasn't large enough for her to get through in her current state. It was up high over the shower and she immediately noticed that Leo had nailed the bathroom window shut. It felt good to sit upright and clear her head a little. She called to Leo, "Leo I'm finished, but I need to uh…clean up. Please untie my hands. I can't go anywhere. You know that because you nailed the window shut. Besides I'm too big right now to fit through it. Even if I could fit, I can't climb up there. You don't need to humiliate me this way."

Leo conceded her point, and went in to untie her hands. "Now, can you give me just a little privacy? Can I maybe change my clothes, please? This dress is very uncomfortable. I promise no tricks."

"Okay. What do you want to wear?"

"I think there is a sweat suit in my bag. I'm kind of cold, could I wear that?"

She heard him walk over to the closet, and within minutes he had produced the sweat suit and some clean underwear. "Everything you need should be in there. I am right outside. I will give you five minutes to get changed."

"Thank you, Leo." Marissa took the clothes and reached down to untie her feet, but Leo was already there. He quickly untied her feet and left her with the clothes.

"I'm keeping the door open."

She removed her sweats from the hanger and eased out of her wedding gown, carefully hanging it on the hanger, then handing it out the door to Leo. "Leo, can you hang this in the closet, please?" He took it from her, and hung it in the closet.

Five minutes later, when Marissa came out of the bathroom, Leo offered her the micro waved dinner he'd brought in earlier. "I made you dinner."

Marissa sat down on the edge of the bed and began eating the cold spaghetti and soggy cheese bread. It wasn't appetizing, but she was hungry and she needed to eat for the babies even if it was a TV dinner. "So how do you see this working?" she asked him.

"What do you mean?"

"I mean you have me here, what are your plans? Are you going to keep me captive until Mitchell Olsen gets out of prison and then hand me over? Have you been instructed to kill me now? Or are you to torture me first, the way he did my sister?"

"You have misunderstood my intentions here."

"Really, how could I have done that, you abducted me during my wedding, you drugged me, and brought me to wherever here is. What intentions could I have misunderstood?"

"My plans are simple. I am keeping you here until it is safe to do otherwise."

"Safe? Safe from what?"

"Safe for me to trust you. When you realize that I can keep you safe from him, you'll trust me, then you'll see that I will take care of you. You'll get used to being here. Maybe you'll fall in love with me, like you did Brian and Jack."

"Leo, I will never fall in love with you, NEVER! You are a cold blooded killer. You have spent years helping Mitchell Olsen mentally torture me; you killed the father of my unborn children less than seven months ago. You killed Mr. Sheldon, a man who had a wife and family, who meant no harm to you. You tried to kill the man I love, twice! How could I possibly fall in love with you?"

"I know I don't deserve it—"

"Deserve it? What you deserve is a cell right next door to Mitch. If I ever get out of here that is where I will be sure we put you!"

"I know it will take some time, but I'm sure you will learn that I'm not quite the evil monster you think I am."

"Leo, there isn't that much time left in universe for that to happen."

"Are you finished with your dinner?"

"I've lost what little appetite I had left."

"I will need to tie you up. I don't want to drug you again, so I am hoping you aren't going to try to pull anything while I'm doing it. I don't think it is good for the babies, so in their best interest perhaps you will consider cooperation. I am going to sleep in the next room, so if you need something you can call me."

Marissa thought about his words. She really wasn't in any condition for a heroic move. She was certain that unless he was unconscious she couldn't get away from him. It was better if he didn't drug her, not just for the babies, but so she could think clearly.

He walked over to her, "Lie down on the bed." Marissa did as she was told. He secured the scarves again, threw a blanket over her for the night, turned out the lights and went to sleep on the sofa.

By morning Marissa's back was killing her from being in the same position for too long. She needed to go to the bathroom again, which she had done two other times during the night, and the procedure had been the same each time. Leo came in, untied her, sat on the bed and waited. He had shown no signs of trying to hurt her, beyond keeping her against her will. She still hadn't come up with a way to overpower Leo, without hurting herself or jeopardizing the twins, so she continued to comply. She would just wait and see what today brought.

Leo had taken care of Marissa for the morning. He needed to get to the store to get some food so around 10:00 a.m. he told her he had to go to town for some supplies. He was leaving her for an hour or so. He would have to duct tape her mouth again, so she couldn't make any noise.

"Leo, you can't leave me here tied up like this! What if I need to go to the bathroom while you're gone? What if I go into labor? What if the house catches on fire and I can't get out?"

"I'll only be gone an hour. I'm sure none of those things will happen while I'm gone. By the way, I need you to stop calling me Leo. The name is Nick, Nick Iverson from now on."

"Leo—"

"Ah-ah-ah…Nick"

"Whatever! Where is the real Nick?"

"Never mind that. I need to go now, so I can get back. I won't be long." He pulled a strip of duct tape off the roll and reached over to put it across Marissa's mouth. She turned her head away from him. He tried again, this time holding her head steady with one hand, while fumbling around with his other.

Marissa couldn't help herself, she knew it would cost her, but she had to start fighting back. He needed to know she was never going to give in to him. When he tried to cover her mouth the second time, she managed to lock her teeth into the flesh of his hand and hold it for a second or two. Instinctively, Leo pulled away.

"Damn you, Marissa!" and slapped her hard across the face. "I've been nothing but nice to you, but that isn't getting me anywhere! He grabbed up the duct tape again, and roughly put it across her mouth. "I'll be back!" He left stomping out the door. Marissa heard the door to the garage slam shut and the car start.

She pulled against the scarves again, trying to see if by chance any of them were loose enough to slip free but they only seemed to cinch up more. She relaxed again, staring at the ceiling, trying to figure something else out. She finally came to the conclusion that the only way would be to go along with him, making him believe that she had changed her mind about him. That was when she heard the knock at the door.

Chapter 44

Leo wandered through the market, picking up the items he needed. He had driven off in a huff over the incident with Marissa. He actually felt bad he had hit her, but he needed to make her understand that he's in control. Perhaps he hadn't made that clear to her the night before. He knew she would come around eventually. He liked the idea of being her husband. He decided to make it up to her by picking up a bouquet of flowers at the cash register. He'd put them in her room to give her something pretty to look at. He also picked up a couple of magazines he thought she might like and some bubble bath. She needed to see that he would be a good provider and could take care of her.

At first she tried just a gentle tap, tap, tap. Outside on the porch, Mrs. Schumacher stood patiently waiting. She had seen Nick drive off alone, so she knew that Mrs. Iverson had to be home alone. She knocked a little harder, "Mrs. Iverson? It's just me, your neighbor from across the street," she called out. When knocking didn't produce any results, she went ahead and rang the bell. Still nothing. Then she thought she heard muffled sounds, but couldn't tell where they were coming from. She rang the bell again. Once more she heard muffled sounds. She wasn't sure what those noises were exactly, maybe just a TV on inside. Maybe Mrs. Iverson was around back on the deck. She would just walk around and check.

Carl couldn't believe his luck. He had been in the parking lot looking at a map to see where how best to access Bayshore Estates from the beach, when who should pull up but Leo Fernandez. He decided to follow him into the store and see what he was up to. He kept a safe distance pushing a cart around, randomly adding things here and there, as he followed Leo around the store. When he got up to the check-out stand, he made sure he was next in line behind him. He pulled a magazine off the rack, pretending to pass the time as the checker rang up Leo's order. Just as Leo was writing a check to pay for his purchase, Carl conveniently leaned in, "Excuse me, but can you tell me what time it is?"

Leo looked up from his check to glance at his watch, "11:30."

In that brief second, Carl was able to get a look at the address in the left corner of the check.

"Thanks."

Carl watched as Leo left the store, as he was dialing the chaplain from the payphone.

Marissa could hear the footsteps leaving the front porch. The room she was in was around the back of the house, so it was no surprise that whoever was there hadn't heard her. Then she heard footsteps on the wood deck out back, coming closer to her. Again she tried calling out, but was only able to produce a loud humming noise at best. She tried pulling on the scarves hoping that perhaps the brass bed would rattle or bang against the wall. Then she heard a light tapping noise against the glass patio door of the living room. She tried rocking the bed again and making as much noise as possible. She realized her efforts were in vain, when she heard the footsteps retreat moments later.

Leo parked in the garage, and began to unload a couple of bags of groceries. As Leo pulled up, he was alarmed to see Mrs. Schumacher coming around the side of the house. He stepped back out of the garage to greet her.

"Mrs. Schumacher?"

"Good morning, Nick. Did you have a good night?"

"Yes, thank you. Your cookies are awesome. The misses and I enjoyed them with some champagne and strawberries, by the fire. Did you, uh, need something?" pointing to the side of the house where she had come from.

"Oh, I just thought I'd come retrieve my platter, it was an anniversary gift. When no one came to the front door, I thought maybe your wife was around back on the deck."

"I'd be happy to get the plate for you. Mar said she was going for a run on the beach when I left, so she was probably out there when you rang the bell."

"Didn't you say she was six months pregnant?"

"Yes, I did," Leo answered, realizing this was a big mistake, "but she still wants to keep in shape. Perhaps 'run' was the wrong word. She's always been athletic, so even though she only takes brisk walks now, but we still jokingly call it her run."

"I see you have your hands full. Why don't I take something from you and help you inside?"

"Thank you, but my wife would kill me if I let you do that. I'll tell you what, as soon as I unload these, I'll bring your plate over myself. I'm sorry I didn't bring it back first thing, but Mar insisted we couldn't return it empty. She even sent me to the store to get ingredients to make something special to send back with it."

"Isn't that sweet?" Mrs. Schumacher replied. "You tell her, to take her time, no rush; she can bring it back whenever she wants."

"Are you sure? I can bring it over in a few minutes."

"Absolutely, I'll look forward to Mrs. Iverson bringing it over herself, so I can meet her."

"We'll do it, soon. She's still trying to settle things in the house. You know how women are, she wants to reorganize the kitchen. Apparently I have put some things in the wrong places, and she can't find anything."

Mrs. Schumacher laughed, "I don't doubt it, Nick. Mr. Schumacher wouldn't know the first thing about organizing a kitchen, don't you know. I'll meet her later."

"Have a good day." Leo watched her walk away thinking that was a close one.

Chapter 45

The Bayshore Estates was an upscale complex of private beachfront property along a two mile expanse of Vancouver's west coast. The homeowners were a mix of retired people and high profile executives who summered here. According to the home owner's association, they had strict policies regarding renting out property, but recognized that many families who only used their homes for recreational use, often allowed friends to borrow their home for vacations. If they chose to rent it out, it was mandated that it would be for long periods of time, to prevent a parade of vacation tenants coming through every week.

Officer Jones had teamed up with the Mounted Police to canvass the Bayshore Estates area and its surrounding areas. He knew they were losing precious time. As it was, they were unable to conduct a thorough search last night. The subdivision is considered private property to which they had to be granted access either by homeowner's association or the court. Mrs. Hodges, the HOA manager didn't open her office on Sundays until 1:00 p.m. or so the sign had stated on the door to the office. Officer Jones and

Officer Richardson were impatiently waiting when she arrived an hour late for work.

"We want to cooperate with you but we don't want you alarming our homeowners. Our back section is still under development. We can't have a reputation that we have criminals living here, what would that do to our sales?"

Officer Jones stopped himself from questioning the woman's personal integrity when she would put her annual sales figures ahead of a saving a life. He took a deep breath to compose himself before speaking, "Mrs. Hodges, if you are able to provide us with some information, it would prevent us from questioning all your residents. We will only resort to going door to door if we don't find what we are looking for any other way."

"I suppose if you were discreet that could work. What do you need?"

"We'd like a list of any new homeowners and a list of homes that are generally used as vacation homes, especially those that are currently unoccupied but furnished."

"Right now we have 300 residences that have been completed in this phase of development. Thirty of the homes are used as vacation homes. I will photo copy that list for you. Of the thirty there are fifteen have been rented out on a long term basis. Of those fifteen, five that have new tenants within the last couple of months. I will break down the lists for you by category. If you'd like to start with the new tenants, I can have it ready in fifteen minutes, so you can get some of your men started."

"Thank you. We'll be outside organizing our teams, until you get us the lists."

Jack, Ben, Betsy, the Van Horns and Detective Cordova arrived as Officers Jones and Richardson emerged from the office. Richardson brought them up to speed as Officer Jones organized the men in pairs to visit each of the five homes with new tenants, and instructing the mounted police to take to the shoreline. They were to look for anyone matching Leo or Marissa's description, circulate their photos and question residents as they went. They were to meet back to give reports in a couple of hours, at which time they would divide up the remaining lists as needed. With orders in hand, the men, including Jack, William and Ben dispersed.

Chapter 46

The Boeing jet landed at 3:00 p.m. at the Vancouver airport. They had received information on where the search was taking place from their contact at the Canadian police station. Carl met them at the airport and once everyone was inside they departed for the Bayshore Estates. It was a thirty minute drive to the coastal subdivision. Carl began giving Earl and Ray orders as they rode in the back.

"Your uniforms and supplies are in the back. You can get changed and ready while I drive. When we get to the drop off point, we can go over the maps and our plan."

Earl and Ray took turns struggling to get changed while bouncing around in the back of the work van, which only proved more difficult when Carl left the main highway, and began winding around on the access road. By the time they were dressed, Carl had pulled onto a dirt service road, heading to a canopy of trees in a densely wooded area. He parked and joined them in the back.

"As you can see on the map, this access road winds around and dead ends here at the beach," Carl explained, pointing to red 'x's on the map. If you walk south along the coast about half a mile, you should be behind the house that Leo is using. For now, all you need to do is act like you're part of the search team and see what you can do to gain access to the house tonight when it is dark. I'll wait for you here. Everything you'll need is in this satchel. Be back in two hours."

By 7:00 p.m. the search party had no more information than they had five hours earlier. They had met back at Mrs. Hodges office that they had commandeered for a base of operation. They had covered about half of the subdivision, but none of the residents had remembered seeing Leo or Marissa, and no one knew of any other new residents. Mounted police continued to patrol the coastal area, but still had no further leads.

Back in the van Ray and Earl gave Carl a logistics report. "We found the house, it is as you predicted about half a mile up the coastline. There is an outstretch of rocks between the sandy beach and the deck of the house, with a small path that meets up with the stairs to the balcony deck. There is a sliding door that accesses the living room," Ray explained.

"Leo is definitely in there. We saw him through the binoculars, but the girl wasn't visible. If she's with him, he must have her confined to another room. More than likely it's the bedroom that also faces out towards the back, because the shades are pulled in that room," Earl continued.

"Right now our plan is to wait until 9:00 so it will be dark, walk back up the beach to the path and go in through the slider. Even if it is locked, I don't think it'll be much trouble to jimmy the door open. Earl is going to go to the front door and distract him, so I can get in the door open. When I'm good to go, he'll come back around to the back. We'll go in together, when the timing is right."

"That sounds like a good plan. Remember, the minister was very clear in his instructions. We are to make sure she is unharmed and that he is dealt with quickly and quietly. We don't need to call any attention to ourselves."

"Got it. You have the pass-key?"

"Right here. I'll pick you up out front at 10:00 p.m. sharp."

"Radio contact only when necessary."

"Roger that. Okay, so let's eat, we'll get a little rest, and be ready to go in an hour."

Leo brought dinner into Marissa. He had put one of the roses from the bouquet on the tray, and had made her chicken, rice and a green salad. He sat in the chair while she ate on the bed.

"Leo, I mean, Nick, I was wondering if maybe you could let me take a bath tonight. I'd really like to use the bubble bath you bought me."

Feeling encouraged that she referred to his gift he agreed. He walked to the closet, pausing in front of her night gown hanging on the door. He ran his hand over the bodice.

"Don't even think about it."

He went into the closet and pulled out a pair of stretch pants and knit sweater. He opened the bureau, removed some undergarments and scrunch socks, then placed them on the bathroom counter.

He walked over to the bed and untied Marissa's feet. With a hand tightly gripping her elbow, guided her to the bathroom. "Thirty minutes and the door stays open."

Marissa walked into the bathroom, and removed her sweats, throwing them out onto the floor. She sat on the edge of the tub, turning her back to Leo while she ran the bath water. I know you want the door open, but it is creating a draft. Can you just close it a little?" He sighed. He knew she wasn't going anywhere. He wanted to please her so she would start to trust him. He walked over and closed the door, leaving it slightly ajar.

She quickly removed the rest of her clothes and slid into the bathwater. She could hear him sit down on the bed. Perhaps if she took long enough he would get bored and fall asleep.

Earl and Ray jumped out of the van. They cut through the woods, climbed over the rocky wall, and hit the sand within ten minutes. "We made it to the sand drift, over. Radio will be silenced until the job is complete."

The two men made their way down the beach, traveling quickly and quietly. They were dressed in police attire, carrying side arms and using their flashlights to illuminate their path. As they got closer to the house, they encountered a mounted police officer. "Find anything yet, they called to him."

"Nothing yet. Yourselves?"

"No luck. We just came about half a mile from down the coast, everything is quiet."

"I didn't expect we'd see anything out here at this time of the night."

"We're going to move up to the street before checking back in."

"Okay, since you both just came from that way, I'm going to turn around and make one more pass along the water."

"See you at check in."

The two men continued forward as the officer on horseback eased out of their range of sight.

"Okay, he's gone. You ready?"

"Let's do it."

The two men, made their way up to the house. They could see movement inside as they edged their way along the side of the house. They were close enough now to hear Leo talking inside. Call it luck or fate, but Leo had conveniently left the slider open. They would have no problem getting in.

Leo leaned back against the pillows. Through the meager crack, he could see her reflection in the dressing mirror. He could hear her sloshing around, even as the water was still filling the bath tub. Damn, she was beautiful! He imagined himself walking in and running a hand over her pregnant belly, as he would if he were the babies' father. He wanted her to want him. He closed his eyes for a few minutes, leaning back against the pillows. He envisioned her coming out of the bathroom in a towel. She was so cute with her hair wrapped up in the white terry towel. Like gentle ocean waves lapping against the side of a boat, the sounds of the water moving in the tub were hypnotic. He was being pulled farther into his dream state. He could feel her breath on his face as she leaned over the bed to kiss his forehead. He could almost feel her weight gently resting against him, as he anticipated hearing his name on her lips, her hand slowly moving to caress his—."

"Nice to see you, Leo." This was not the angelic voice he had imagined. He opened his eyes to see two men standing over him. He had seen them only once before, when he was introduced to them as the deacons. One of them turned on the television that was on the dresser.

"The minister sent us. He said to tell you that intervention was never an option," as Earl thrust one of the scarves down his throat. "Is this the duct tape you used on the girl? Stop trying to talk, I can't hear you," as he used it to hold the scarf in place. Ray stepped in with a pillow, "May the Lord your soul to take, Amen" as he held the pillow over Leo's face. Struggle as he may, he could not fight against the weight of the men holding him. Within minutes, he was gone.

Marissa could hear what she thought were voices when she shut off the water. She wondered what he was doing and what she needed to worry about after she got out. She heard the t.v. on, then the floor boards squeaking a little. She relaxed again, thinking if she waited long enough he might be asleep when she got out. That's when she would run to a neighbor's house for help. She heard footsteps coming towards the door, she thought he was coming in and she grabbed the towel to throw it over herself, not wanting him to see her. The footsteps stopped just short of the doorway. She heard what sounded like a knock at the front door. Suddenly, the bathroom door slammed shut and she heard it being locked from the outside. She noticed the knob on the inside of the door had been removed altogether. There was only a deadbolt and the thumb turn was on the outside of the door, nothing on her side. She stood to get out of the tub. She heard a scraping noise followed by a gunshot, then silence. She stood holding her breath, afraid to make any sound. Maybe whoever was out there didn't know she was there, and she wasn't sure she wanted them to. She felt vulnerable, standing there with just a towel for protection. As quietly as she could, she stepped out of the tub and onto the floor mat. She toweled off, slipped into her clothes and quickly towel dried her hair. She switched off the light, remaining in the darkness, while listening for any movement.

"Ray, over here!" she heard someone shout, then footsteps heading her way. She heard what sounded like walkie-talkies squawking, followed by a lot of talking but she couldn't make out anything. She finally decided that unless she yelled for help, she might be losing the only people within earshot of her.

"Hello? Hello! Can anybody hear me?"

No response, just more noise. Then she heard someone at the door, "Hello? Is anyone out there? Leo, let me out!"

The door to the bathroom was unlocked and opened slowly. Marissa was relieved to see the officer standing there. "Miss Van Horn?"

"Yes, is he gone?"

"Leo Fernandez?"

"Yes, Leo Fernandez. Where is he?"

"You're safe. My partner shot him while he was trying to escape. It is over. If you'll come with us, we will reunite you with your family just as soon as we can."

"I need to get on my shoes first."

"Yes ma'am. You go right ahead. I'll step out to the living room to call in that we found you." Earl left the room and went out to talk to Ray.

Marissa found her tennis shoes in the closet. She sat on the foot of the bed to put them on. She noticed some duct tape on the floor, the bed was disheveled, one pillow was on the floor and one of Leo's shoes was lying near the door. Where would Leo have gone without both his shoes on? The officer had called her Miss Van Horn. If he was a real police officer wouldn't he know she was married and call her Mrs. Reed?

Mrs. Schumacher opened the door wearing her house coat and slippers. From somewhere behind her a voice was shouting, "Who is it?"

"Excuse me a moment," turning her head, "It's the police, Lou, now will you shut up!" turning her attention back to the two men standing on her front porch.

"We're sorry to come by so late, but we are searching for a missing woman and we think she might be in your subdivision. Here is her photo, have you seen anyone who looks like this?"

"Hmmm..no, no I'd remember if I saw her."

"We believe her to be with a man named Leo Fernandez. Here's his photo, do you recognize him?"

Mrs. Schumacher stared at the photo and was slow to respond."

"Ma'am?"

"This looks kind of like Nick."

"Who is Nick?"

"Nick Iverson, he lives in that house across the street. He moved here ahead of his wife to get things ready. He's a handsome and charming man. I told him if I was just a few years younger… Well anyway, he brought home his new bride on

Saturday night. He said they were getting married that day and would be driving home afterwards from Seattle."

"Did you see his wife?"

"No, I've been over twice but she was busy with other things, so Nick said I should come back another time."

"Sounds like it could be our man, we'll check it out. Mrs. Schumacher, you have been very helpful. I'd like you and Mr. Schumacher to please make sure your doors and windows are locked. Please remain in your home. Leo Fernandez is a very dangerous man. If we make an arrest, we'll be back to take a full statement.

"Yes, sir, we will."

As the officer and Jack walked towards the house across the street, the officer turned to Jack and said, "Mr. Reed, I need you to stay back. We don't know what to expect, I'll call for back up before we make our move, but you will need to stay out."

"Time is wasting. I am your back up. If you think I'm waiting another minute to let that creep harm Marissa, you're wrong. Let's go."

Marissa started catching bits and pieces of the conversation in the living room.

"Does she suspect anything?" she heard the bald one say.

"Not a thing," the skinny guy said. "She thinks we're the police here to rescue her. She's putting on her shoes, then we'll take her to the van and meet up with Carl."

"The minister said we'd get a bonus if we do this without injury to the package."

"This is a home run, let's get her and get out."

Who were these two men? Who was the minister? What was the package and what did it have to do with her? Marissa stood there for another minute trying to figure out what she was going to do. The only way out of the house was past the two men. The windows were nailed shut. She knew she couldn't overpower one man, let alone two and in her condition she doubted she could outrun them.

Ray came back in the bedroom. "Are you ready Miss Van Horn? Miss Van Horn!" Marissa was lying on the floor, holding her stomach, groaning.

"You know I'm not feeling so well. I think you need to call me an ambulance. I think I'm in labor."

"Earl, we need to call for back up! Miss Van Horn thinks she's in labor!"

Earl came in the room. "Miss Van Horn, are you sure you can't make it to our car. We will drive you to the hospital."

"O-owe! Owe! Oh no! Oh No! I need an ambulance. Please!"

Then she heard sirens, followed by tires screeching. Earl looked out the window, then back at Ray. "No need to call for that backup they're already here." His eyes kept darting around. He kept nodding his head towards the back door, like he wanted Ray to follow him.

Ray knelt down next to Marissa. "Miss Van Horn, we're going to get you that ambulance. Are you okay if I leave you alone for a few minutes?"

Marissa grabbed her stomach, "Just hurry!" she yelled at him.

"Yes, ma'am, we will surely do that!" Ray ran from the room. She heard Earl and Ray running out the back door. When she was sure they had gone, she stood up and headed to the front door. She yanked it open ready to bolt, looking back over her shoulder as she ran through the door to be sure they hadn't come back in. She immediately plowed into a hard body, nearly knocking him down.

"Marissa?"

"Jack!"

He scooped her into his arms. "Thank God." He pulled away, giving her a once over, noticing the redness at her wrists and the bruise Leo had left on her face. He ran a gentle thumb down the side of her cheek. "Are you okay?" then looking down and touching her stomach, "Are the babies okay?"

"I'm absolutely fine, the babies are fine, but the police need to get around back, there are two men posing as police officers. They ran out the back door when you knocked. I think they killed Leo." The officer behind Jack motioned for his team to go around the back of the house.

From out back she heard someone say, "Police! Drop your weapon!" followed by gunfire.

Jack pulled Marissa down to the floor. "Stay down. We don't know where they are."

Moments later, Officer Jones walked through the door. "Mr. and Mrs. Reed, all clear, you can come out now."

Jack and Marissa were taken to the home owners' office, where Ben, Betsy and the Van Horns were waiting. Detective Cordova joined them, telling them how they found Leo's body on the patio and recovered a body from a freezer in the garage, they had identified as the real Nick Iverson. They had the two men who had posed as police officers in custody, but so far they weren't talking. Marissa told him what she had overheard and how she had faked labor pains to stall them. After the police were satisfied they had what they needed, the group went to a hotel to get some sleep before flying back to Seattle.

Chapter 47

"I was wrong about thinking I could keep you safe. I think we should talk to someone about helping us set up a new life, in a new place, with new identities," Jack said.

"I should have left months ago, and then you wouldn't be going through this," Marissa replied."

"Not this again! I told you when I proposed that I would go anywhere or do anything as long as we were together. I meant it then and I stand by that now. Tomorrow I want you to talk to your parents. They may want to stay here until the girls are born, we can wait a week or so after that, then we leave. That should give us enough time to tie up loose ends here, and give the authorities time to get a plan in place."

"Jack, I don't know. Leo is dead, they caught the other two guys, and Mitch is still in prison. Maybe we don't need to do that now. Think about your career, your family, my family. If we have to start over, and we won't see them again."

"I have thought about it. We are a family. Keeping my family safe is more important than anything else. If you are worried that you will miss your folks then of course I will reconsider, but as far as my career goes, I can find a new one. As far as my family goes, I've already made peace with that too. You and the girls are my family now."

"I'll talk to my parents, then I'll talk to Rosenthal, he can help make the necessary arrangements."

Marissa's parents weren't happy about the kids having to go into hiding, but understood that it was necessary to keep them safe. They promised they would work out some way to be in touch after everything had settled. But the meeting with Mr. Rosenthal quickly changed that.

"Jack, Marissa, this is Ed Carson of Retread, Inc. He's an expert in relocation for individuals in situations such as yourselves. He will give you the pros and cons of their program."

"Jack and Marissa, I'd like to explain how my company works. We are an independent company; we are not affiliated with any government entity. I started this company fifteen years ago, after working for the FBI witness protection program. There was a woman who needed protection; she didn't qualify to be in the program because of the criteria outlined in the program guidelines. Before we could find another way to protect her, she was killed. I knew then that there was a group of people, with unique sets of circumstances that could benefit from similar services the witness protection program provided, but they were unable to access them. There are resources available if you seek them out, but for the most part they require going through illegal means, which often prove to be unreliable and untrustworthy.

My company uses legal channels to operate. When the FBI cannot accommodate an individual's needs, they refer them to us. Mr. Rosenthal has explained your situation. We believe we can help you make a fresh start. We have to have a full commitment from you before we can proceed. You will have to agree to completely severing all ties to your current lives, including family. That means no secret visits with the grandparents of your children, no birthday or Christmas cards, no returning for a visit, even if it is an emergency. No taking in your mom or dad when they become elderly, no returning for a funeral, there is no going back. If you violate our agreement, we cannot guarantee your safety or that of your family members. It puts our people at risk who are trained to take a bullet for you. You also will not be eligible for relocation again.

The lives you have had before now are over. Jack and Marissa Reed and their twin daughters are dead. It is a point of no return. Even if you are able to keep up your end of the deal, I have to tell you nothing is 100% foolproof. It is difficult setting up people in a new place with new names. You have to be able to tell lies about yourselves and be convincing. It is a daunting task even when we are dealing with an individual, who has few connections to family and friends. When a whole family is involved it can prove nearly impossible. Retread is good at what it does, but I would be less than honest if I didn't tell you we have had leaks in our system. On rare occasions, even when we do our best, our system can be compromised and then we have to start over again. No system is perfect, but we have the highest success rate in the business. My question for you is: are you sure this is the kind of life you want for you and your family?"

"No it isn't the kind of life we want, but what are our options?" Jack asked.

"You can continue as you are, we can help you with home security, self defense training, that sort of thing. But that isn't what I would recommend. Marissa's already had too many close calls. Let me explain how the rest of this works. We keep your first names or at least a variation of them; we find this helps our clients' transition into their new lives better if we can keep some familiarity. We relocate you to a new place, usually a larger metropolitan area, set you up in new jobs in related fields to what you do now. We can create a slightly different past for you, altering all your critical information. We give you new social security numbers, new birth certificates, new passports. You keep your new address and phone numbers unlisted. We use private post boxes to get you mail. We set up a dummy corporation that owns your home, all the utilities, phones etc… are in that name, same with your vehicles, insurance, banking, credit cards; all your basic needs will be handled through the corporation. All your other needs you pay cash for. That way there is no paper trail whatsoever.

We recreate your work history, which is supported by references that will be verified should anyone check. Provided you don't make national news with some scientific breakthrough that plasters your picture all over the papers, it works fairly well.

You will start your new life with the history we create for you. Using the security measures we can discuss later on, you go about your life as you normally would. You register your kids for school, you get involved in your community, and you make new friends. Appearance of a having normal family is crucial to reduce suspicion. People who keep too much to themselves, end up calling attention to themselves since they are mysterious. Rather than have people trying to figure out who you are, you show them. You live like people with nothing to hide."

"So what would be our next step, if we decide to do this?"

"The next thing we need to do is fake your deaths. Jack Reed and Marissa Van Horn-Reed, married in Seattle, are killed in a car accident, on a trip to California to visit Marissa's parents before the birth of their twins. We run it in all the papers in both states; we have eye witnesses and everything. Again, this makes it less likely they will look for you. Even if someone comes across your name, it will look like a coincidence. Only crash photos and old high school photos will be run with the story."

"Since you are an independent organization, I assume this isn't a free service, so how much does this cost us?" Jack asked.

"We don't charge our clients directly. At the point where the dollar determines the quality of service our clients receive it becomes compromised by what they can afford rather than what they need. We have two divisions of our company. One is offering basic security to wealthy clients and corporations which is the side that generates our income; the other is our relocation service, which essentially operates as a non-profit organization. We fund the program through donations and endowments. Some of our families are quite wealthy, upon entering into the program they sign over properties, trust funds, and investments. Other people, who are satisfied clients, make bequests to us in their wills. Many of our assets and safe houses have been acquired this way. If you are able to do this, we are most appreciative, but Retread prides itself on helping people; we don't feel comfortable putting a price tag on someone's life. So far this method has worked out well for us and our clients."

"You have given us a lot to think about. When do we need to let you know our decision?"

"We know that Leo Fernandez was a member of the Sangre Brotherhood. They are a well connected prison gang, with members both in and out of the system. They are ruthless men, known for racketeering, drug running, pornography and murder for hire, just to name a few. If they are involved in what is going on here, then we need to move quickly in order to stay ahead of the people who Mitch Olsen has engaged to help him. It is believed that their current operators are either in custody or dead, so moving swiftly before they have a chance to regroup and put someone else in place would be prudent. You'll be taken to our safe house training facility, where we train you while we are recreating your histories. It will feel like boot camp."

"Our people will work behind the scenes to legitimize your existence in a new community before you are placed. When we are through, you will step into your new lives, appearing as a typical American family, relocating for a new job opportunity. For the best outcome we would encourage you to reach a decision within the next day or two."

"What about my pregnancy? I'm due to deliver in a few weeks."

"Not to worry, we have access to excellent medical care facilities and specialists. Do you have any other immediate questions or concerns?"

"It's certainly a lot to consider," Marissa commented.

"Thank you for your time. We'll be in touch," Jack said, shaking hands with Ed.

"Marissa, I will miss you terribly, you have been such a wonderful asset to our office," Mr. Rosenthal said, "but I hope you will give this serious consideration. I think you deserve some time without constantly looking over your shoulder."

"Thank you, sir. We appreciate all you have done for us. Jack and I will let you know tomorrow."

Chapter 48

April 2006

Jackson and Marissa Deerfield had found Alexandria, VA a pleasant place to make a home for their family. They enjoyed the rich history of the town, and its easy access to Washington, D.C. was a bonus. Retread, Inc. had placed them in a beautiful home with a spectacular waterfront view of the Potomac River. The colonial style home was large enough for their growing family to make happy memories together. Its cherry stained hardwoods and traditional paint color scheme offered warmth and charm.

Retread had also found Jack a position with a private engineering firm in Washington, D.C. Marissa was working for an attorney dealing in family law. The twins, Cassandra and Samantha were almost sixteen now. They attended a private school, were at the top of their class academically, and considered to be well-rounded teenagers. Sam was the captain of the girls' rowing team, and Cassandra was class president. The girls gave Jack a run for his money when it came to dating boys, and had nicknamed him 'Colonel Klink' after watching repeats of Hogan's Heroes on Nick at Nite. Marissa loved spending time with them, shopping for clothes, taking in a chick flick, or just having a girls' day out.

Their younger brother, Cody had just turned thirteen. He was the star soccer player on his team; able to play nearly any position, but his favorite was goalie. He had a passion for building model airplanes, which was a hobby he and his father shared. He was inquisitive by nature, making him an avid reader, spending hours at the library. Being the youngest, Cody could nearly do no wrong. He was relentless when it came to bullying the family into a game of scrabble, which they all knew he would win, but would indulge him just the same.

Life had moved on for the Deerfields, but Marissa still missed the life she had left behind. She wished that her folks could meet their grandchildren. She hated that they couldn't have family vacations to visit Jack's sisters and their families. She missed Ben and Betsy, often wondering how their family was doing. Retread's private detectives had kept them informed on their parents. Jack's parents who had been older than Marissa's folks had both passed away a few years ago, Marissa's father had retired. Her parents still lived in the same house she grew up in, but now took time to travel, a dream her mother always had. They frequently met up with Mrs. Gottsfrey, and included her in their plans when they went on cruises or abroad. Marissa took comfort in the fact that they had stayed close to her.

Retread also kept tabs on Mitchell. The last sixteen years had thankfully gone without incident, but a week ago, Marissa was informed Mitchell's prison sentence had been served and his release had been granted. Mitchell Olsen was a free man.

Chapter 49

Mitchell had been devastated by the news of Marissa's death. His obsession with her had become the fabric of his existence. Losing her was like losing part of his identity. For years the thought of one day reuniting with her had motivated him through each day, thoughts of her running through his head making plans of how he would find her and remind her of what she meant to him, and what he should mean to her. It was only Cynthia Marshall's frequent visits that kept him encouraged as to the state of his future.

Cynthia, or Cyn as he now called her, had visited two to three times a week for the past sixteen years. At first she was doing 'God's work' for the First Baptist Church, helping sinners to repent their sin and find new hope in the future and redemption. As time went on, Cyn was drawn to Mitchell for other reasons. She saw the raw pain that afflicted him and his need to be nurtured. She felt a calling within herself to provide that for him. He had confessed his darkest secrets to her, how in love he had been with the woman he had been accused of attacking. He had told her how it was the girls' idea to have a threesome. Although it wasn't what he had wanted, his desire to make her happy won out and he complied. Afterwards, the woman had asked him to kill her sister, because she couldn't stand being reminded of having shared him with her. When the authorities had come, she turned on him, so he ended up here. She could see how conflicted he was over what had happened. She felt an undeniable outpouring of emotion for him. How confusing that must have been for a young man, struggling with his convictions of morality, yet tempted by the intensity of lust.

Eventually Cyn's visits became less about dealing with Mitchell's sin and more about Mitch getting to know Cyn. They managed to steal secret glances, or 'accidental' touches under the table when the guards weren't looking. She promised him she would wait for him to be released. She knew that with God's help they could have a glorious future. Mitchell told her he would look forward to the day when together they would find the way to heaven.

Today, Alan made what he hoped would be his very last visit to San Quentin State Prison. This time there was no security check to go through, no log book to sign, no table to sit at or handset to speak into. He took a pull on his cigarette as he waited in the parking lot for Mitch to walk out of the gates. Although they had hoped for an early parole for Mitch, after the fiasco in Canada and Leo Fernandez being killed, the parole board had considered Mitchell a flight risk and refused to accept his so-called rehabilitation. Since he had served his full sentence they had approved it with probation and required he registered with the state as a sex offender.

Mitch came out through the gates. He saw Alan leaning against the side of his Jeep Wrangler, putting out his cigarette as Mitch approached.

"Look at you," Alan said, hugging his brother's neck. "You clean up pretty good when you don't have to wear an orange jumpsuit."

"How 'bout that. Who knew?"

"How's it feel?"

"Very strange, kind of scary in fact. I've been in there so long; the world isn't the same as it was when I went in."

"It's changed a bit, that's for sure, but we'll get you acclimated in no time. Are you ready to go?"

Mitch took one look back from where he had just come. Although he had dreamed of this day for a long, long time, it was a little overwhelming to be leaving it. He turned back around, to get into the car, "Ready." The brothers got into the jeep. As they drove away, Mitch took one last look back, with somewhat mixed emotions, knowing he was leaving the only home he had known as an adult.

They hit the freeway with Alan talking about his homecoming. His mom was cooking his favorites for him and they had given his room a fresh coat of paint. But Mitchell found himself spellbound at his new surroundings, looking at the cities they were passing through, amazed at the growth and changes that had occurred in the last twenty five years. They made small talk for most of the two-hour drive home to Modesto, interrupted with awkward spans of silence.

They finally arrived at the Olsen home. He got out and slammed the car door, standing fixed to the driveway for a moment. If he had stepped out onto the moon, it couldn't have felt more alien to him. The trees were larger, the homes were older, and the house was much smaller than the one he held in his memory. He was nervous about going inside. He hadn't seen his mom for the past several years; making him anxious about seeing her now. He had felt guilt about his past when looking into his mother's face, seeing her disappointment reflected in her eyes. So much time had passed, he wondered if it would still be there.

"Mitch...Mitch?" Startled from his thoughts, Mitch turned his attention to the sound of Alan's voice, now coming from the front porch. "Hey, Mitch, you comin' in?"

"Yeah, just getting a good look at the house. When did you paint it yellow?"

"Mom did that right after dad died. She said it was time for some cheer around here."

"I like it, looks good."

The house was different than he remembered it. Instead of nicotine stained walls, they had clean, crisp paint. Family photos in silver frames were displayed on the fireplace mantle, including his senior picture they had taken at the beginning of his last year of high school. The furniture looked fairly new, and the tile floor gleamed. The dining room table had been set for four, a vase of daisies in the center. The aroma coming from the kitchen smelled like Sunday pot roast and mashed potatoes. Mitch couldn't propel himself past the entry hall, drinking it all in.

"Mom…Mom, we're here," Alan called out.

Vivian Olsen had spent the sixteen years, since her husband's death in therapy. She had finally come to believe she deserved better. She had often thought about going to see Mitchell, but the fact was he was so much like his father, she was afraid of the feelings that would surface if she saw him. Feelings she had finally been able to set aside. Knowing he was coming back home was difficult. But she was stronger now and felt that she owed Mitchell the possibility of a fresh start like she had been given. After all, he too had been a victim in this house.

Vivian heard the boys come in the door. She came to the kitchen door wearing denim Capri pants, a teal blue knit shirt and sandals. She had on makeup, earrings and a necklace. Her short hair was styled and her nails were neatly manicured. Vivacious was the first word that popped into Mitchell's head. Had he met her on the street he wouldn't have recognized her. He couldn't remember a single day he had seen his mom wear lipstick or any jewelry other than the simple wedding band her father had given her the day they married. She actually looked younger as a woman in her late sixties than she had twenty five years ago.

She stood in the doorway, getting a look at her son. With tears in her eyes, she walked directly to him, opening her arms to him, then wrapping them around him, "Welcome home, son."

All the years of secretly being angry with her for not visiting melted away when he heard those magic words, "Welcome home, Son." Mitch couldn't hold back the flood of his own tears. "Thank you, Mom. It's good to be home. I missed you." He held her embrace for a couple of minutes before letting go. He heard the bathroom door down the hall open, then footsteps behind him.

"Hello Mitch, your mom and Alan invited me for your homecoming, I hope that's okay?"

"Cynthia!"

"Welcome home, Mitchell."

Mitchell pulled her into an embrace, "It's good to see you."

"Good to be seen," turning to Vivian, "He looks pretty good don't you think?"

"Yes, he does. Are you hungry? I've made your favorite, pot roast, and everything is ready."

"That sounds terrific, I'm starving."

"Can I help you with anything, Mrs. Olsen?" Cyn offered.

"No thanks, I think I have it all on the table, shall we?" she said pointing to the dining room.

"Mom, I don't think I remember ever eating in this room before."

"That was because your daddy always said it was for company, but we never had any. What's the use of having a dining room if you aren't going to dine in it? Cynthia would you ask the blessing before we start passing the food around?"

"Yes ma'am. Shall we join hands?" she asked taking Mitch's in her own, giving it a slight squeeze before bowing her head. "Dear Lord, thank you for bringing Mitch home safely and for the food we are about to eat….."

The family reunion continued for several hours. When it was time for Cynthia to leave, Mitch walked her to her car.

"You know I have to register as a sex offender, right?"

"Yes, I know."

"And that doesn't bother you?"

"Why should it, you told me the truth. Besides that was a long time ago. You aren't going to go after young girls are you?"

"No young girls. But there is one girl who I wouldn't mind going after."

"Oh yeah? Who's that?"

"You know who," and he pulled her to him, and kissed her with the urgency that had been building within him.

"What are you doing tomorrow?" she asked.

"Hmm, after I meet with the Mayor to get the keys to the city, I have my book signing… what do you mean what am I doing? I don't have any plans."

"Okay, well how about I pick you up, and we go out to lunch."

"That's a long drive back for you isn't it?"

"I don't mind, I'll see you at noon, okay?"

"It's a date."

After she drove off Mitch went back inside. Vivian had already gone to bed, but Alan was waiting for him to come back in. "Have a seat, we need to talk," he said.

Mitch sat across from him on the couch. "Okay, what's up?"

"The chaplain called. Seems you asked him to do something for you. He said to tell you that the dove brought back an olive branch. Does this mean something to you? Mitch, you just got out. What are you up to?"

"I need to make a call. Is there a pay phone close by?"

"No Mitch, there isn't and I'm not letting you make that call until you tell me what's going on."

"Fine. A few months ago, one of the chaplain's associates was doing some work in Alexandria, Virginia. Carl, that's the guy's name, ended up having to meet with a lawyer that deals in family business. He ran into this woman who worked there that looked familiar. He was introduced to her has Marissa Deerfield. At first he couldn't place her, but then he remembered her from sixteen years ago when he was in Canada. He never met her but had seen pictures in her portfolio and the press coverage that followed when she went missing. He wasn't positive that was her, but something in her face struck a familiar cord."

"It can't be. You know she's dead. We've seen the pictures, her family buried both her and Jack together at Lakewood Memorial Park. I've seen the headstone myself."

"They are running a background check on her, if the chaplain came up with an olive branch that means they found her for sure."

"Mitch, let it go. Listen, Mom has let you come home to stay, Cynthia seems like she is in love with you. Can't you just let it go? You can make a good life for yourself."

"I would already have a great life if I hadn't spent the last twenty five in prison. So, no Alan, I cannot just let it go. If she is still alive, when I'm through with her she will wish she wasn't."

The walls in the house were paper thin. Vivian lay awake listening to her sons argue. She could only hear tones so she tip-toed to the door. Quietly, she opened it just a crack so she could make out their words. Could it be true about Marissa still being alive? She remembered when they ran the story of her death. The article in the paper had described the heartache she had endured in Seattle. Had her boys been responsible for all the awful things that had happened to her since the trial? She had wanted so badly to believe that Mitch had been reformed and that Alan had avoided his influence. Listening to them now brought back those feelings she had on her last visit with Mitch at the prison. The anxiety rising in her chest was causing a churning in the pit of her stomach. She was fearful of what harm would come to Marissa Van Horn. She was terrified of what he would do to her if she went to the authorities. She had heard enough; she closed and locked the door.

She sat down on the edge of her bed, praying for the strength to do what needed to be done.

Chapter 50

Vivian sat in her car with the engine running for several minutes, summoning the courage to get out and walk to the door. She doubted they would welcome her into their home, but she knew this was the right thing to do. She needed to somehow right some of the wrongs her family had done. Perhaps she could prevent more pain and suffering. Before she could ring the bell, the door opened. The two women stared at each other for a moment.

"Mrs. Olsen, won't you come in?"

"Yes, thank you, Mrs. Van Horn."

"How could he have found us?" Marissa asked Ed Carson. The call from Retread had come less than an hour ago for Marissa and Jack to meet Ed at a division office in Arlington.

"We haven't confirmed who is behind it, but someone is definitely checking out the history we created for Marissa. We're concerned since there wouldn't be any reason for anyone to be doing this kind of a background check. We have put traces on the information requests. They are being generated from of a

California location. The Sangre Brotherhood is now nationwide, with connections that fly under the radar, using an untraceable system. The FBI has been after them for years, but they are very good at covering their tracks. We believe they may be repaying favors Mitch did for them while in San Quentin. Based on the information that Mrs. Olsen gave your mother it sounds as if he is coming after you."

"What do we do? I don't want to uproot the kids unless we have to."

"At this point I think we set up extra security detail for your family. We keep you home and out of sight for a week or two. We let them dig as deep as they want, letting your history stand for itself. With any luck, they'll believe what they find and let it go. But if he has really found you the only solution is an emergency extraction. That means a radical change for you and your family."

"Our children have no idea about the past. They are living normal lives right now and I want to keep it that way."

"I understand, we'll do our best, but you need to prepare yourself for the possibility. We have every reason to believe that we are still in good shape, so let's just hang in there folks. In the meantime if anything starts to feel odd, even if you think you are imagining it, you need to let me know right away. I'm going to go back to the office now and get my men working on this. I'll be in touch."

Mitch hung up the phone. The chaplain said they were unable to conclusively determine whether the woman Carl had seen in Virginia was Marissa Van Horn. Marissa Deerfield's past checked out on paper, but that didn't always mean anything. They would keep her under surveillance for the next few weeks to see if they could find anything else out.

He met with his parole officer as prescribed by the terms of his release. That went fairly well. His parole officer had given him a list of employers who participate in the rehab program from San Quentin who would be most likely to hire him. He promised to check in with a few from the list this week.

Things with Cynthia were going better than he had hoped. Alan had been right. She was head over heels for him. As much as he enjoyed the sex, it didn't stop him from thinking about Marissa. Once he accidentally called her Marissa. Although she was upset at first, after he explained that she had been on his mind because he had a strong conviction that he needed to forgive Marissa, as God had forgiven him, Cynthia apologized to him for her jealous thoughts. Mitch was finding it increasingly difficult to keep up the ruse of being a reformed Christian man. She was starting to drive him a little nuts with all the bible study, prayer and pressing him to attend weekly services with her. He was becoming bored with her, and she had more than served her usefulness to him. He was thinking maybe it was time to help Cynthia have a face to face with the man upstairs.

Chapter 51

Mitch didn't have a car yet, so he was using the city bus. He got off at a stop near Downey High School. He walked up Coffee Road just as school was letting out. Within minutes a throng of students were flooding the parking lot and turning the street into a raceway of teen drivers. Girls were hanging out of cars, yelling to boys in the one in the next lane. Other drivers were honking horns and squealing tires as they hit the gas when the light changed. It was reminiscent of his high school days; he could almost picture himself standing in its halls watching the cheerleaders in the morning, walking through the main hallway.

He kept walking, turning at the end of the block, near the park. He was getting close now. Within a few minutes he had found his way onto her lane. He found a shade tree across the street from the Van Horn home. Suddenly the garage door rolled open. Mrs. Van Horn appeared with a basket of gardening tools and went to work puttering around her yard. So, they still lived there. This could really work in his favor. A few minutes later, Mr. Van Horn joined her and they worked peacefully side by side. He felt a jealousy creep up within him. His own parents should be having moments like these. For that matter, so should he. He wondered again, not for the first time today, if she really was dead or just in hiding. If she was hiding he needed something to flush her out. He knew just the thing.

Ed Carson had called Jack at work and asked him to meet him at their house. He had some news to give Marissa and felt it was best if he was there. Jack found Ed waiting a block away as he drove home. Ed followed him to the house and they went in together.

"Hi honey," Jack said planting a light kiss on Marissa's head. "Ed called and asked if I would come home to meet with him. He has some news."

"Okay. Before we start, Ed, can I get you a drink?"

"No thanks. Can we sit down?"

"Sure, let's go into the family room."

"Marissa, I'm afraid I have some bad news. Your father was killed this morning in a single car automobile accident."

"Are you sure?"

"His car went off the road and rammed a power pole. It looks like he had a blow out on his tire, causing him to lose control of the car."

"How did you find out?"

"Your mom called the emergency line. She said she didn't want you to come home, but wanted you to know. She made it clear that your safety was a concern to her. She wanted you to stay where you were, even though she knew you'd be tempted to come home. Apparently Vivian Olsen stopped in for a visit a couple of days ago. She had overheard Mitch talking about looking for someone. Although she didn't catch any names, she suspected he was looking for you. Vivian went to your mother to warn her. Of course your mother assured her that his suspicions were unfounded and she had nothing to worry about."

"Ed, I have to go. I need her to know I'm okay."

"No you don't. We've discussed this before. You can't do it. You'll jeopardize everything we have in place if you do. They'll be watching for it."

"But Ed, I'm all she has left. When Jack's mom died, at least his father still had Jack's sisters and their family. My mom has no one. Please, Ed, can't you figure something out?"

Ed looked to Jack for back-up. "This is Marissa's decision. If she wants to go, I'll support her. She's had hard enough time keeping away all these years."

"Maybe it's time to come out of hiding. My mom is going to need help. I've been a prisoner in my own home for two weeks now. If he is going to find me anyway, what's the point?"

"Okay, okay. I'll get you out to California. We'll set you up with a makeup artist and see what we can do to give you a disguise of sorts. Your visit will be very short and you'll have to have a body guard the whole time."

Chapter 52

William Van Horn's service had been set for 2:00 on Friday at the Lakewood Memorial Funeral Home. Mitch had arranged for someone to be watching Marianne Van Horn 24/7 in case Marissa made an appearance. He would know soon enough if she was still alive. In the meantime he had work to do. He had bargained with the Chaplain for some extra help, in return Mitch would pay a visit on a brother who had found himself in need of confessing his sins to the police. The brotherhood frowned on soul cleansing, but since he had, he must be ready to meet his maker. Mitch was making sure he kept his appointment.

Marissa's makeover was so convincing that Jack hadn't recognized her when he met her at the airport to say goodbye. They had given her a dark tan, a blonde wig with a very stylish cut, a new wardrobe that was far less conservative than Marissa's usual business or soccer mom attire.

"I don't know if you're busy later on, but my wife will be out of town for a few days, if you want to meet at my place," Jack said trying to make light of the situation at hand, folding his arms around her waist.

"Tempting, but what do you plan to do to get rid of your three children at home?"

"They're teenagers. We can dump them off at a mall, throw some money at them. We won't see them for days."

"Keep that in mind, maybe we can use it when I get back."

"Don't think I won't hold you to that Mrs. Deerfield. All joking aside, Marissa, please be careful. I don't want to lose you."

"I promise. Thank you for understanding."

"Say hello to your mother for me. Tell her how sorry I am."

"I will." She reached up and kissed him. "I better get going, the pilot is waiting for me."

"I love you."

"I love you, too."

Marissa flew into the Oakland Executive Airport on one of Retread's private jets. Ed had arranged a company car and sent Jake along to be sure there weren't any problems. She checked in to the Double Tree hotel in downtown Modesto. Ed had arranged to have her registered with an Optometrist convention, so the room wasn't in her name.

Once checked in, Jake drove Marissa to her mother's house. He dropped her off in the front of the house, then found a place to park where he could watch the house. He would have preferred to accompany her, but she insisted on doing this alone. He watched as she rang the doorbell.

"Mrs. Van Horn?"

"Yes."

"I'm Marilyn Hartford, your attorney's office sent me to make sure you didn't need any help with the arrangements for your husband's funeral," Marissa said, handing her a business card.

Marianne stared at the woman before her. The arrangements had already been finalized, and she had already met with their lawyer, so she was confused by the visit. She read the business card in her hand, "Hi Mom, it's me. Please don't react until we are in the house." Marissa lowered the dark sun glasses for a moment, meeting Marianne's eyes and watched as recognition crept across her mother's face.

"Oh yes, of course. I'm so sorry, where are my manners, won't you come in?"

Marissa stepped into the house. As soon as the door was safely closed and locked, the two women dropped pretenses, falling into an embrace of warmth and tears. "Mom, I'm so sorry I wasn't here."

"Sh-sh, don't even start. I wish you hadn't come now. I'm so worried about your safety."

"Mom, it'll be fine. I had to come. I needed to come."

"Let's sit down. I don't want to waste a minute. I know you can't stay long."

"I'm here until Saturday that only gives us about three days together. Not all of those will be just you and I. No one else can know I am here, so you have to pretend I'm your estate advisor that you've hired to help you with the arrangements. Can you do that?"

"I think so."

"You can introduce me as Marilyn Hartford. The funeral home thinks I am a representative from your family lawyer's office. So, how are things, what do we need to do?"

"Nothing, everything is arranged. Your father and I had everything planned and written out years ago, we didn't want anyone to have to deal with anything. We didn't want you coming out of hiding to take care of us.." Marissa's mom broke down.

Marissa reached out and took her mom's hand. "I've missed you so much. I would give anything to just be able to see Dad one more time."

"He loved you so. He was so proud of you."

"He was a good father and a good man."

"The viewing is tonight, did you want to go?"

"Yes, but it will have to be as your advisor. I will be in the room with you, but will appear to be in a professional capacity."

"I just can't believe you're here."

"Mom, I brought you something." Marissa pulled out a photo album. She sat next to her mom and for the next few hours they poured over photos of Marianne Van Horn's grandchildren. She was thrilled to find out that Jack and Marissa had a son. Cody looked a lot like William. The girls looked like Marissa. The kids seemed to be doing well; she wished she could see them in person.

They drove separately to the funeral home. Marissa watched her mom go inside. She couldn't believe she had to leave her alone to go through all of this. She wondered how her mom would do by herself when she left. She knew her mom was a strong woman, but her father had always been her anchor. Without him there she knew her mom would give in to her fears. She would need help. Marissa would need to find a way to help her.

After thirty minutes, Marilyn Hartford went into the viewing. She was the only person in the room at that moment. She approached the casket, looking down at the man who had been her loving father. She reached out a hand to touch his, as her tears spilled onto his jacket lapels. "I love you, Daddy." She didn't think it would be so hard, but she found herself unable to control the intense emotion she was experiencing. Her mom came in, just as she regained her composure. Her mom had obviously been crying as well. She resisted the urge to go to her and throw her arms around her.

One of the neighbors came in at that moment. "Marianne, Enid and I were so sorry to hear about William."

"Thank you Charles. It certainly wasn't the way he had expected to go. He had so much life left in him."

More neighbors and friends came in and out. Marissa mingled with the crowd, making small talk, listening to stories about her father. While it was comforting to see the outpouring of love and friendship in her father's honor, it was also bittersweet. As she stood listening to these people sharing experiences they had had with her parents, it was also a painful reminder of the years she had lost with them—important milestones in her children's lives they had not been able to share, memories that were never created. She was grieving not only for the loss of her father, but the loss of what should have been.

The next morning, she went back to her mom's for breakfast before they left for the service. To her happy surprise there was another guest. Mrs. Gottsfrey had flown in and was seated in the dining room when Marissa got there. They hugged for a long time, and once again poured over the photo album Marissa had made for Marianne.

"Judith, can you believe I have a grandson?

"Isn't he handsome?"

"I think he is the spitting image of his grandfather. William would have been so excited."

"Mrs. Gottsfrey, you have to tell me, how are Ben and Betsy? Do you hear from them?"

"Yes, I do. They got married right after your accident. The accident made them realize that life was short and they shouldn't waste it. They have two kids, a boy who is fifteen and a daughter who is twelve. They still live out on Whidbey Island. They visit me from time to time. The kids think of me as a third grandma."

"How's Bill? Are you two still together?"

"Well, no. Bill had a heart attack a few years ago. I'll spare you the details of what we were doing when it happened if you don't mind, but let's just say he died a happy man."

"Oh, Judith!" Marissa laughed, "As my kids would say too much information!"

Marissa watched them gawk at the photos for the next hour. They had missed out on so much, not being able to share in their grandkids lives. Her mom would have loved to see the girls singing in the chorus, or Cody playing soccer. Going back to her secret life would not be easy, but she knew she had to do it to keep them safe. Sad as it was, the photo album would have to be enough for now.

They had a quiet graveside service with just the three of them. After dinner, Marissa said her goodbyes. Mrs. Gottsfrey said she had nothing she had to hurry back for. She said would stay with Marianne for as long as she was needed.

Carl called Mitch later that night to confirm that Marissa was in attendance with a body guard. He had tracked the rental car back to Oakland and watched them board a corporate jet belonging to an outfit called Retread, Inc. They are a security company, but that is really a cover for the relocation service they provide. They had an operator at the tower, who confirmed their flight back to Alexandria. A ground crew is waiting to tail her when they make their landing.

Chapter 53

Marissa had been home two weeks, when an envelope arrived addressed to her. Inside was a copy of her father's obituary and a note that said "One down, one to go." Marissa's hand was shaking when she dialed Ed Carson's number. "He knows where we are and he's going to go after my mother."

"Okay, slow down. How do you know he knows where you are?"

"He sent me a note, in the mail addressed to Marissa Deerfield, at this address. Ed, we don't use this address for anything. The only mail we get are letters addressed to 'resident' or 'current owner'. I was so careful, how could he know?"

"Marissa, what did the note say?" She read it to him and told him about her father's obit.

"If he's responsible for your father's death, then it stands to reason he did it to flush you out. He expected you to come. If he expected you to show up, then he had someone in place to follow you home. This is bad. We have to do an extraction, today!"

"No, we need to make sure my mom is safe. Can your people go get her?"

"Yes, let me take care of that and I'll call you right back."

"Okay, but I'm going to go get my kids from school. I'll call Jack and get him home right away."

"Do you see Jake parked out front?"

"Yes."

"I want you to go out and get in his Hummer. He will drive you to pick up the kids and bring you back home until we can make other arrangements. I'll send someone to get Jack as well. Let's all meet back at your house in say an hour?"

"Fine, but Ed, when you get here, you better be able to tell me my mom is safe."

Marissa walked out and got in the front seat of the SUV next to Jake.

"Mrs. Deerfield, where do you want to go first?"

"Let's pick up Cody first; the girls have a prom meeting after school, so they will be getting out a little late."

"We'll do."

When they arrived at the junior high, Cody was sitting on the bench talking to his friends. Marissa watched for a minute before walking over to get him. He was so happy. His tousled blonde locks blowing in the breeze, as he and his buddies bounced around a hacky sack. He was oblivious to the danger he was about to find out he was in. She wanted to spare him that agony. His young life was about to change for good; his innocence about to be robbed from him.

"Dude, isn't that your mom?"

Cody looked up to see his mom walking towards him. "What's she doing with the FBI looking guy?"

"Ooooh, you're busted!" the kids were teasing him.

"Hey Cody, we need to go."

"Is anything wrong Mom? What's with the bald dude in the shades and the black SUV? Are we being arrested?"

"Nothing like that, let's go Cody. Tell the guys good-bye."

Cody grabbed up his backpack and threw the hacky sack back to one of the boys. "Later, dude."

"Later, Cody! Don't forget to write from prison!"

"Funny, c'ya."

"C'ya."

Marissa couldn't help but smile at their short sentences. A product of technology, text messaging had created a short hand that had carried over into day to day conversation. English teachers across the country should be cringing.

The pair got into the Hummer and Jake continued his drive to the high school.

"So are you gonna tell me about Morpheus here or do I have to wait until we enter the Matrix?"

Jake got a chuckle from that one. "I'm Jake. I'm your driver for the day."

"Cool, nice to meet you. But Mom, why do we need a driver?"

"I'd like to explain everything just once, it's a long story and your sisters need to hear it as well."

"Whatever." Cody pulled out his iPod and stuck the head phones in his ears. He reached in his back pack and produced a book, settling back in his seat for the rest of the ride.

They arrived at the high school a few minutes later. The girls were out front. Marissa was taken aback by the vision of her beautiful daughters, flirting with a couple of boys she recognized from their elementary school days. Cassandra twisted a tendril of her auburn hair around her finger, smiling at the boy who was completely mesmerized by her. Sam threw a teasing punch in the arm to the guy standing next to her. When did they grow up to be young women? More to the point, when did those boys grow into men? Now she was thinking like Jack.

She knew the change would be hardest on the girls. They were both so social. Leaving their friends would crush them. She also worried about the effect the news itself would have on them, when they found out they had been lied to their whole lives. The man they had come to know as their father wasn't. They had grandparents they had never had the chance to meet and a story about their mother that they had never been told. Trust was such a fragile thing when it came to teenagers. Jack and Marissa had worked so hard to maintain this with their children. Kids didn't always accept that some things were done for their own good. Marissa worried that this would shatter their trust beyond repair.

As Marissa got out of the Hummer, her cell phone rang.

"Hello?"

"Beautiful aren't they?"

"Sorry? Who is this?"

"What's the matter, don't you recognize my voice?"

Marissa felt ice run through her veins. She looked around, trying to see if she could see him somewhere, but her mind was racing so fast she just couldn't focus. She looked back at the girls, they were still there.

"Where are you?"

"You don't need to concern yourself with that. You'll see me soon enough. The girls are gorgeous though. They look just like you. In fact so much so that I see us all together very soon."

"Mitch, you leave them out of this."

"So you haven't forgotten me. Well I guess that's something."

"What do you want?"

"We'll get to that in a minute. Have you heard from mommy dearest lately?"

"Mitch what have you done?"

Chapter 54

"Mitch what have you done?'" he mimicked. "Did you know she had no idea you were living in Virginia? Is that any way to treat your mom? I tried to get it out of her, but I guess she really didn't know, because she wouldn't give you up. It's too bad she didn't know because it could've been much easier on her if she could have just told me what I wanted to know."

"Mitch, if you hurt her I'll—"

"You'll what Marissa? You didn't care enough about her to let her know where you live. You know my mom has always known where I was for the last twenty five years. What do you think that did to her? What do you think that did to my dad? It killed him you know. An eye for an eye, that's what I say."

"Look Mitch, I don't know what game you're playing but I want you to leave my family out of it."

"I don't think you're in a position to call the shots. Keep your phone on, I'll be in touch."

"Mitch!...Mitch!" He had hung up. Marissa was visibly shaken by the call, panic written on her face. Cassandra had been watching her mom, wondering what had her so upset. She tapped Samantha on the shoulder, directing her attention towards Marissa. The two girls said good bye to the boys and walked over to their mom.

"You okay Mom?"

"We have to go. We have to get out of here, now."

"Okay, where's the car?"

"It's the black Hummer parked at the curb."

"Mom, what's going on?"

"Girls, don't question me right now, you will be told soon enough. Just get in the car, now."

Marissa had hoped she would be able to calmly tell the kids what was going on and why their world was being turned upside down. She kept scanning the parking lot and the school grounds to see if she could spot him. She opened the back door to the SUV and the girls climbed in. They looked in the driver's seat and saw Jake.

"He's here somewhere, he just called me," Marissa blurted out when she opened the passenger door, "and he has my mom."

"What do you mean he just called you?" Jake asked.

"As soon as I got out of the car, he called my cell."

"Okay, tell me what he said."

"Mom, what's going on? Who is Jake?"

"Girls, I need you to be quiet right now. We are on our way home, when you dad gets home we will sit down together and explain everything."

"Mom, you said you mother was dead."

"Girls, please, you have to trust me right now."

"What did he say?" Jake asked again.

"First he said my daughters were beautiful, like he was watching me and knew I was here picking them up, then he asked if I had heard from my mom lately and made it sound like he had talked to her and tortured her to find out where I was."

"Okay, I'm calling Ed." Jake barked an order into his head set and within minutes had Ed on the phone and had explained the situation. "Uh-huh....uh-huh...yeah...got it...will do." He clicked off, "Ed said he has a crew on the ground at your mom's. They were just getting ready to go in when I called. He'll call back when he knows more. In the meantime, I'm to take you to headquarters; Jack is on route and will meet you there."

"Mom, I thought we were going home! What is going on? You're scaring us!," Cassandra pleaded.

"I can't explain right now. Please I need you to be patient a little longer."

About that time a black SUV pulled out in front of them from a side street, tires squealing as it forced its way into traffic. Jake instinctively hit the brakes to avoid hitting it, just as white work van pulled out to flank their rear. He ordered a code into his headset again, telling someone his location and giving description of the two vehicles. When he finished he looked at Marissa, "Here we go. Everybody needs to have their seat belts on, hang on we are going for a ride."

About that time Jake hit the gas, purposely rear ending the car in front, sending him careening into a parked car on the side of the road. Jake swiftly moved around the collision and put the pedal to the floor. The van following them, kept pace. They came up to an intersection and Jake stopped for a red light. Before the light turned green, he watched for just the right opportunity. When there was a brief break in cross traffic, he hit the gas and screeched through the intersection. Once through, he hit his brakes, waiting for the white van to follow his lead. When traffic cleared as second time, the van flew through the intersection, only to make an abrupt stop, in order not to run into Jake. As luck would have it, a large truck coming from the side street came barreling through the intersection on a yellow light. He collided with the van in pursuit. The van rolled onto one side, scraping pavement as it slid into oncoming traffic. Jake hit the gas again, never looking back. He called someone again, and reported, "Object destroyed."

"I don't think we're being followed anymore, so it's safe to take you to headquarters now."

They wound around the back country roads of Braddock County for another forty-five minutes until they came to what looked like an old fashioned country church, complete with white clapboard siding and a steeple. "We're here. You can go through the front doors. Jack and Ed should be inside. I need to go park around back so it can't be seen from the street. As instructed, Marissa and the kids bailed out of the Hummer, and walked through the door.

The interior of the building looked like NASA mission control. Operators on headsets sitting in front of computer monitors were cloistered in cubbies around the perimeter of the room. In the middle of the room was a main station that seemed to double as a reception area. Cody looked around, "Cool, this looks like CTU on '24'! Mom, are you a secret agent?"

"No Cody, do you see your dad anywhere?"

"There he is," Cassandra shouted, pointing to a glassed in office off to the left.

"Okay, let's go."

Before they could move a receptionist came over, "Mrs. Deerfield?"

"Yes."

"Right this way please," she instructed, leading them to Ed's office. She opened the door for them, "Go on in, I'll be right back with some snacks and cold soft drinks."

Jack jumped up and walked out to meet them. He swept Marissa into a hug. "Are you okay?"

"Yeah, it got a little hairy, but Jake is a good driver, so we are all here in one piece."

"Dad it was so cool, you should have seen him driving in and out of traffic like it was 'Too Fast and Furious!"

"I'm sure it was Cody. How about you girls? Are you doing okay?"

"Sure, the X-men routine is getting kind of old though. Are you going to tell us what's going on?"

"That's our Sam, cut to the chaise."

"Why don't you all come in and have a seat," Ed invited them into his office, motioning to the sofa and chairs. "I'm Ed Carson. You don't know me, but I go way back with your parents. Before we move forward, I'm going to give you about thirty minutes or so, to talk as a family. Afterwards, we can all talk together."

"First, what did you find out about my mother?"

"She is doing fine now, but I won't lie to you, Mitch was pretty rough with her. He had hit her a few times, so she has some bruising; he had left her duct taped to one of her kitchen chairs, where she had been for twenty-four hours before we found her. She was severely dehydrated. It was good we found her when we did."

"Is she going to be okay?"

"We have her at our medical facility. The doctor's have said that she has been through a great ordeal, but overall she is fine. They are giving her intravenous fluids and treating some minor injuries. They expect her to make a full recovery in very short time."

"Thank you so much."

"Just doing my job, here's Sophia with some refreshments. I'll be back."

Once they had both left the room, Jack took Marissa's hand. They looked at each other, taking in a deep breath of resolve. "Cassie, Sam, Cody, we have some things to tell you about; things that happened before you were born. These things are affecting our lives now and are about to change your lives forever."

They spent the next thirty minutes briefly filling in the major details of the situation. The kids asked few questions, seeming to just let all the facts absorb.

"It's like waking up in the middle of a good dream and finding out that's all it was," Cassandra said.

"Why didn't you tell us before now?" Samantha asked.

"It was for your own safety. We had to work so hard to keep it a secret and we didn't want you to ever feel like you were living a lie" Marissa explained. "I know this is a lot to take in and things are moving way too fast. We're sorry it came to this."

"Will we get our stuff form our house before we move?"

"We'll have to ask Mr. Carson that when he comes back. I'm just not sure how this works, or what we are doing this time, Cody," Jack answered.

Cody moved over to sit on the couch next to his mom. He took her hand and squeezed it, "I'm sorry about your sister mom. I bet that was really hard."

Marissa kissed the top of his head. "Thank you for that Cody. Yes it was, but that was a long time ago."

Ed came back in the room. "Okay folks, here's what we know. Mitchell Olsen has not made his last two appointments with his parole officer. As of right now, he's considered a fugitive. The police are actively searching for him. He is believed to be with his brother Alan and another man named Carl, who incidentally had been working with the two men who were apprehended in Canada when Leo Fernandez abducted Marissa."

"You were abducted too?" Samantha asked.

"We haven't told you everything yet, but that isn't important right now, we'll fill you in on the rest of the details later. We need to hear what Mr. Carson needs to tell us right now."

"Here's what we know. First of all, the black SUV that Jake called in from the chase was identified as one that was stolen from Mitchell Olsen's neighbor just a little over a week ago. We now believe he and his brother Alan stole the vehicle and used it to drive across country. They're a dime a dozen so even with police on the lookout for it, they were probably already across state lines by the time it was reported missing and no one gets too excited over a stolen car these days. Now that we know they're in the area we've put out a bulletin on the make and model, but more than likely they've already disposed of it.

Knowing they're at large doesn't leave us with many options. We have a safe house fifty miles from here. It's up and ready to go. Our recommendation is that we move your family there immediately. Give us time to apprehend Mitch and his gang.

If we do, you might be able to move back into your house very soon. We'll bring your mother to the new safe house, where she can stay with you."

"Is there any other way?"

"This is the best way we can keep you safe."

"Okay, when do we leave?"

"Right away. Jake is waiting out back. He can arrange for anything you need when you get there."

"Mitch, you okay?"

"Yeah, I wonder if Carl lost them."

The car alarm on the vehicle they hit was going off, drawing attention. The SUV was still drivable, so Mitch put the car in reverse, pulling away from the car Jake had pushed them into. A group of spectators had come out from a nearby deli to see what was going on. Mitch threw the car into drive, and took off down the road. He could see Carl about a half a mile ahead of them in traffic. Then all of a sudden there was a loud crash. They could see a huge truck pushing what looked like Carl's van into oncoming traffic. Smoke billowed above the flaming van. All lanes of traffic came to a rapid halt, blocking Mitch and Alan in so they couldn't move.

When traffic finally resumed moving forward, it was in small increments. By the time they made it to the intersection, emergency road crews were already there, and they had Carl on a gurney, a blanket pulled up over his head, loading him into the back of a EMS vehicle. Mitch kept going, not wanting to risk being asked any questions.

"Now what do we do?" Alan asked.

"We'll call the minister and see what he can do to help us out."

"Mitch, how we paying for all this help you're getting?"

"Don't worry little bro, I have friends in high places that owe me favors. As a bonus, I offered them a sweet deal for a trade on some teenage girls. Internet Porn is big business these days, so I promised them a set of hot teenage twins. They were thrilled."

"You don't mean Marissa's girls? Mitch—"

"You're not going soft on me are you Al?"

"Course not, but Mitch, those girls didn't hurt you, why involve them? You're just complicating things."

"They are the price of doing business, besides don't you want to have a little fun. One for me, one for you. We have to check out the product to make sure it's good before we deliver don't we?"

"I don't know Mitch. I'll have to think about it."

"You'll have to think about it?" Mitch chuckled a little, "Yeah, you do that Al, you think about it. It's a good thing I'm out. We need to teach you a thing or two about being a man. You hungry? Let's get something to eat."

"Whatever you want Mitch."

"Don't sound so down. It'll be fun, you'll see!"

Chapter 55

An hour later Jake pulled into a gated community. Rows of town houses lined each side of the street. "This entire complex is owned by Retread. The people living here are a combination of Retread employees and others like you are housed here temporarily while waiting on a more permanent home. Everyone is instructed to be polite, but ask no questions and give no answers. If anyone starts asking you any questions besides me or someone who I introduce to you with specific instructions to do so, you are to tell me right away. Here we are, home, sweet, home."

They all got out of the car and walked up a steep stoop of a three story town house. "It's bigger than it looks. The bottom floor will be my quarters, the main floor is shared by all of us, and your family can divide up the four bedrooms upstairs. There is a supply closet in the hall that should be stocked with toiletries. There are towels hanging in the bathrooms. We have a housekeeping service that will come in daily to tidy up and do laundry. Meals will be brought in; they are prepared at the safe house up the street. All the employees are highly trained security guards; they are armed and live on site.

On the main floor we have a small kitchen stocked with convenience foods, feel free to help yourself, if there is something you would like but don't see, write it on the list on the fridge and housekeeping will pick it up for you. There is a small selection of books, DVDs and games on the shelves, again, if there is something specific you would like put it on the list and it will be here the next day."

"Cool, can we just stay here?" Cody asked.

"No, we cannot!" Cassie blurted, "We are going home as soon as possible."

"That is the idea," Jake replied. "Okay, a few rules."

"Ugh, are we in jail or something?" Samantha asked.

"These rules are to protect you and every member of your family. Compliance is mandatory," Jake continued. "Number one, no telephone calls in or out."

"No phones? Kill me now!" Cassandra, who could sometimes be a bit of a drama queen, flopped onto the couch and folded her arms.

"As I said, compliance is mandatory. Number two, no one goes outside without me. Think of me as your shadow."

"A very large shadow," muttered Samantha under her breath to Cassandra, who snickered.

"What was that? Did you have a question?"

"Yes, what about our smoke breaks, our conjugal visits and our prison issued jump suits?

"Cassie, Jake is just doing his job, trying to keep us alive. Maybe we could spare him the drama?"

"It's okay Mrs. Deerfield, I don't blame them for being pissed off they have to be here. I'd be mad too. Anyway, that's it. Look around; let me know if you have any questions. I'm going to be downstairs. There is a guard at the gate 24/7, and we have an entire detail that will work in rotation around the outside. They will stay in the unit next door. There are panic buttons in every room," pointing to a bright red button on the wall. "Be sure you know where they are. Don't hesitate to use them if you sense there is something wrong."

After Jake had left, Cassandra turned to her parents, "What about the prom? We were supposed to double date with Matt and Amanda. What about our dates? Are they just going to think we died or something?"

"We just don't know all those answers yet. We hope it won't come to that."

"I was kidding; you mean that could really happen?"

"Believe it or not, it already has once before you were born. The only people who knew you were alive were Grandpa and Grandma Van Horn. They were never told where we were and we weren't allowed to have any contact."

"No way, we can't let our friend think we are dead. That's so 'not cool'."

"Would it be cooler to have you really be dead?" Jack inserted himself into the confrontation Marissa was getting from the girls.

"No, I guess not."

"That's right, let's be patient. Why don't you go upstairs and pick out your rooms? Remember we need to leave one open for your grandmother."

They spent that night getting settled in. The kids continued to ask questions which Marissa and Jack patiently answered all of them. The one question that never came up was if Jack was their father or not. That was a discussion that would eventually take place, but they hoped to put it off for now. There was enough to take in for one day.

Mitch hung up the phone. "That was the minister. They were able to persuade a Retread employee to share information. Apparently the whole family has been taken into protective custody at one of Retread's compounds, with a 24/7 body guard detail."

"So this means we're giving up and going home right?"

"No! What's the matter with you? We aren't giving up. I've come too far, waited too long."

"But Mitch, be reasonable. We can't possibly take on a compound with an army of guards. How are we going to get to them?"

"We don't. I have a plan to get them to come out on their own."

"Whatever you say, Mitch." Alan was tired; he didn't like the sound of this. He had promised his mom that if she let Mitch move home he would keep him in line. So far that wasn't working for him so well.

Chapter 56

Marianne Van Horn arrived by helicopter out on the open landing field next to the complex. She wasn't thrilled at the choice of transportation, but understood it was the best way to insure they weren't followed. A guard met her at the landing pad, then drove her to the Deerfield's townhouse. She walked up to the door and rang the bell.

Jake opened the door, "Mrs. Van Horn? I'm Jake; it's a pleasure to meet you."

"Likewise," she replied, shaking his huge hand.

"Your family is in the living room. Can I take your bags and jacket?"

"Thank you that would be lovely." Marianne made her way through the opening and was met by Marissa.

"Mom! It's so good to see you." Seeing the bruising on her mother's face brought tears to her eyes. "I'm so sorry that he did this to you."

"I'm fine, let's not talk about this now. I have more important things to do."

Jack walked up to her, “Marianne, I have missed you,” he scooped her into a bear hug. “I’m sorry I couldn’t come out with Marissa.”

“It’s okay, I wish she hadn’t come either, perhaps all this wouldn’t be happening now.”

“Don’t even think that. I needed to be there. It wouldn’t have changed a thing. He was determined to find me. I was foolish to think he wouldn’t.”

“Well, don’t you think it’s time I met my grandchildren?” looking past Marissa and Jack to the teens standing behind them.

“Oh my goodness, yes, of course! Mom, this is Cody, Cassandra and Samantha.”

“Nice to meet you,” Marianne said. “I have wanted to meet you your whole lives.”

“What do you want us to call you?” Cody asked.

“What would you like to call me?”

“How about Gran?” Samantha suggested.

“Is that okay with the rest of you?”

“Yeah.”

“Sure.”

“Okay, then Gran it is, now get over here and give your Gran a hug!”

As each of the kids took turns hugging Marianne, she couldn’t help but smile while tears were streaming down her face.

“Mom, we were just getting ready to eat some lunch. Are you hungry?”

“Famished. I’d just like to get freshened up a bit first.”

“The powder room is through there.”

“Thanks, I won’t be long.”

After lunch Ed called to say that Carl, the guy in the car behind them during the chase, hadn't survived the crash, so they weren't able to question him to get any information that he might have been able to provide. Mitch and his brother Alan were fine. They drove off before the Retread unit could get in place. They would have to stay put for two to three more days while a permanent solution could be found. The family was very quiet that night, each lost in their own thoughts, contemplating an uncertain future.

Mitch was anxious to have what had possessed his thoughts for the majority of his life. He was not pleased about these new developments, but waiting was something he had become accustomed to. He was certain if they failed again, Marissa would disappear for good, so he understood the need to make arrangements that would be carried out with precision and produce the desired results. Alan and Mitch were discussing his plan that would bring the girls to them rather than having to go in after them when the minister called.

"Looks like you need to move fast. Our sources tell us they are going to relocate in a few days. Everything you have asked for is ready."

"Thanks for the information."

"Mitch, don't forget our deal. The DA is getting close to making an arrest. We can't have our man locked up. You need to take care of business."

"I'm on it, it'll be done tonight. I'll be in touch when it's finished. You make sure you have my supplies and equipment ready."

"One more thing, Mitch. I have orders to tell you that after we get you set up, we're out. The brotherhood doesn't usually involve ourselves in these types of things, but you have been a faithful member, so we are making this one time exception. Know this, if anything goes wrong, you and your brother will be put on the prayer list."

"Understood."

Mitch hung up the phone. "Okay, stay here until you hear from me. You know what you need to do."

"Mitch, I don't like this. Let's just go home."

Mitch headed for the door. Before he left he turned and said, "Too late to go home. I have to take care of some loose ends. Game on, Bro. You be ready."

Chapter 57

The local police found the black SUV behind an abandoned warehouse in Fairfax county. The vehicle had been burnt, creating challenges for authorities to identify the body encapsulated in the wreckage. The license plates of the vehicle matched one of the vehicles that had been reported as part of the chase that resulted in yesterday's fatal accident. The coroner's office was already on scene and had pulled the charred body from the torched vehicle, ready to transport it to the lab.

"Hey Paul, any ideas on how long it will take to I.D. the vic?" the officer asked the coroner.

"Depends. I'm told the victim might be a parolee from California. I've already called the prison there to request the dental records. It's the best way to I.D a burn victim. They should be there when I get back. If they're a match it won't be long, a couple of days maybe. If not…you're guess is as good as mine.

Alan was sitting in the cheap motel room waiting for Mitch to return. He had gone out only once in the last two days to the minimart across the street to grab some food. When Mitch didn't come back the first night, Alan assumed he was just getting rid of the SUV. He had spent the last forty-eight hours looking out the window, pacing the floor or waiting for his cell phone to ring. It was nightfall again and still no word from Mitch. Alan was starting to get nervous, but it wasn't like he could go to the police. What would he say? "I'd like to report my brother missing—and oh by the way, you're already looking for him?"

He checked the window again before settling on the bed with the remote. He started flipping channels looking for something to take his mind off his current situation. The local news was on. A reporter was standing in front of what looked like a bombed out SUV.

"…found last night. It is now believed that the body recovered from the wreckage is none other than Mitchell Olsen of California. He was recently released from San Quentin after serving twenty five years for the brutal murder of a teen. His parole officer issued a warrant for his arrest when he didn't report for his weekly check-in last week. Authorities have confirmed that the vehicle behind me was stolen from Olsen's neighbor just days before he was reported missing. According to inside sources from San Quentin, Olsen was rumored by inmates to have been a member of the deadly Sangre Brotherhood. Police are still collecting information in the investigation but suspect the murder may be linked to the notorious gang. A coroner's report confirming the victim's identity to expected to be released sometime tomorrow. Still at large is Olsen's brother, Alan, who fled with him. He is wanted for harboring a fugitive and accessory to grand theft. If you have seen this man, or know his whereabouts," Alan's picture filled the screen, "please call the FBI tip line. Back to you, John…."

Alan couldn't believe what he just heard. The police were now looking for him! He quickly jumped up to look out the window again. He shut the drapes, bolted the door and began to pace the floor. He started thinking about who could identify him. The motel manager, the mini-mart check cashier although she seemed more interested in her soap than him. He didn't think he had made eye contact with anyone else. He'd have to leave tonight before the police found him. He was throwing his things into a bag when someone was pounding on the door. Then the words he had dreaded, "Police! Open Up!"

Jake was listening to the briefing he was getting from Ed Carson. "…I understand…..yes, sir." Jake hung up the phone. Jack and Marissa were anxiously waiting for him to share the news. "The coroner has made a positive match of dental records to those provided to them by San Quentin. It would seem that Mitchell Olsen is dead."

Relief washed over Jack and Marissa. "So how soon can we go home?" Marissa asked.

"Ed wants you to stay a few days. He wants to be certain there's no further threat from either Sangre or Alan Olsen."

"But the threats have always been generated by Mitch. Surely they will leave us alone now."

"Perhaps, but we want to play it safe. Ed has suggested that we can leave here tomorrow, return to your home with a full security team to cover you for the next few weeks. Once they have apprehended Alan Olsen and we're sure there's no further threat of danger we'll back out and your family can resume you regular routines."

"I guess we can live with that," Jack said, smiling down at Marissa, "what do you say?"

"Let's get packed!"

The pounding at the door continued. "Police! Open up!" Alan looked around the room as if wishing would make and escape hatch magically appear. The only window overlooked the corridor where the police were standing. "Alan, we know you're in there." The closet was an option of course, but Alan was pretty sure they'd look there. Reluctantly he opened the door. It was not the police but Alan wasn't entirely relieved.

Chapter 58

Three weeks had passed since the Deerfeilds had returned to their home. Gran had made herself at home in the guest room, and enjoyed getting to know her new family. Everyone was back on schedule.

The girls' had both gone to their prom held at the Gadsby Tavern, an historic building in Alexandria. They had made it a 1920's themed party, with couples coming in era appropriate costume. Jake had rented a limousine to drive them in, so no one had to know they were actually under guard so to speak. Cody was back on the field, kicking around the soccer ball with the kids.

Marissa had decided to stay home with her mom, and catch up on life. Jack was back on the job but had refused the body guard that Ed had assigned to him.

It was a Friday afternoon; Marissa was finishing her grocery list. They had planned to have a family barbeque this weekend, so she needed to get to the market. Included on the list were the kids' friends from school, and some neighbors. The kids were planning some backyard tournament games, like bocce ball and lawn darts. Jack was in charge of tending bar for the grown-ups, and Marianne was making her potato salad and pies. They would still have the security detail around, but everyone was looking forward to the weekend. It wouldn't be much longer and they'd be living completely on their own for the first time in years. Marissa couldn't be happier. It was hard to imagine what life would be like without looking over her shoulder, security checks, and lies.

Cassandra was sitting in her last class before lunch break, when she got the text message from Jared asking her to meet him behind the gym after class. She had been hoping he was going to ask her out, since they had been talking since prom night. She didn't want her body guard watching. She knew she was safe at school, so after class let out, she walked in the hall and told him she had to make up a test and would be staying in the classroom for lunch period. She asked him to wait outside because it would just be too weird having him watch her take a test.

As soon as Ms. Harper had left the room, she opened the window and climbed out, walking along the path between the two buildings then cutting over to the gym. When she rounded the corner she could see Jared waiting for her, but looking in the opposite direction. She snuck up behind him, and was about to say, "Guess who," when she was grabbed from behind. Another man with a gun, came out from a nearby bush, and turned Jared around to face her. He had duct tape over his mouth, and his hands had been handcuffed and secured to his jeans using plastic trash ties that had been attached to his belt. Within minutes the two kids where gagged, bound together stuffed in the back of a school district work van.

"One down, two to go," Mitch said, giving Alan a high five. Alan was less than enthusiastic, but returned the high five just the same. As much as he hated this whole thing, he had now committed a crime. There was no turning back.

Samantha had just finished rowing practice. She was on her way back to the gym when she got a text message from her sister. "Meet me behind the gym, alone!" was all it said. It seemed a little cryptic, but Cassandra did have a flare for drama. She followed her teammates into the locker room and then slipped out the back door, escaping her body guard would be waiting in the front. She had no sooner taken a step out the back door; when she found herself face down on the dirt. She tried to struggle and fight them off, but the element of surprise was in their favor. Before she knew what was happening two men gagged her, bound her and threw her into the back of a yellow van. Once inside she could see she was not alone. Cassandra and Jared where tied together, struggling against their restraints without success.

Marissa's grocery cart was nearly full and becoming quite heavy as she wheeled up and down the aisles adding the items from her list. Her cell rang, she looked at the caller ID, it was Samantha.

"Hi Sweetie, is everything okay?"

"Everything is hunky dory," Mitch replied.

This was not the voice she was expecting to hear. Marissa's first impulse was to grab her body guard, but Mitch continued.

"Don't even think about alerting your guard. I have two very lovely girls in my company. I want you to say sure honey if you understand what I'm saying."

Marissa looked around trying to see where he could be, "Sure honey," walking away from Jake. She cupped the mouth piece, "I thought you were dead."

"I have friends in high places, too, Marissa. It wasn't hard to change the name on some dental records to fake my death. But we can discuss these details in length later on. Right now, you're going to lose the guard, then walk out through the store's back room. A car will be waiting for you. Get in. He will bring you to me, so we can have a happy family reunion. Are we clear? If so, say 'I can't wait to see you."

"Don't you lay a hand on them, do you hear me!"

"Oops, wrong answer, do I need to make my point clearer for you?"

"No!" she said a little too loudly, then softer, "I mean, no. I can't wait to see you."

"Good, we'll see you in a few."

Marissa clicked off, "Jake, I really need to go use the ladies' room, it will only take a minute and I'll be right back. Can you just hang on to the cart for me?"

"Maybe I should accompany you, Mrs. Deerfield. I don't think it's a good idea for you to leave my sight."

"Jake, I'll be fine."

Marissa took her purse and left for the back room. Before walking out the door, she dialed Jack's cell number. Leaving the line open, she stuck the cell phone into the back of her waistband under her shirt. She carefully walked out the door, immediately spotting a white Suburban with its motor running. She opened the back door and got in, quickly setting her purse on the floor board, hoping the driver hadn't noticed.

"Throw your purse out and shut the door." She did as she was told, knowing that it worked in her favor. When Jake found it, he would know something was wrong. She heard the doors automatically lock. The handles which operated the rear passenger doors had been removed.

Jack answered his cell phone, he could hear Marissa talking, but obviously it wasn't to him.

"Where are you taking me?"

"To your family reunion."

"You're Alan aren't you?"

Alan didn't like that she had recognized him. He tried to ignore her.

"Alan, why are you doing this? You don't have to be like him you know. You can help us."

Alan didn't like her talking to him, reminding him of right and wrong. "I can't help you, so don't ask."

"Sure you can Alan. It's not too late. I know Mitch has my girls. Please, we can stop right now and get help. They would cut a deal with you if you help us get them back."

"You ruined our lives. You put him in jail. I didn't have a brother because of you. My father started drinking because of you. Do you know what it was like visiting him every weekend for twenty five years? I haven't had a life of my own. Why should I help you?"

"Alan, think about it. I was only sixteen, the same age my girls are right now. Do you really think I was to blame? Even if you believe that, what are my girls guilty of?"

Her words were sending pangs of guilt and doubt through his mind. He also knew what Mitch was capable of. Mitch wouldn't hesitate to kill him for even thinking of helping them. He needed to keep his head clear.

"Alan, please, I'm begging you. If not for my family, do it for yours. Think about what this will do to your mom."

"Shut up, bitch! I can't think with you talking like that."

Marissa knew she was striking a cord. She sat silent for awhile, letting her words steep for awhile. Jack listened in, realizing that she was with Alan Olsen. Not wanting to lose the connection, he quickly picked up the handset of his desk phone and dialed Jake.

Marissa sat in the back seat, commenting on things along the way. "Alan, there's a 7-11 coming up at Bradenlock and Third, do you think we could stop. I need to use the bathroom."

Alan didn't want to engage her, so he tried to ignore her requests and kept driving.

"Alan, I really need a restroom, there was a Shell station back where you turned onto Lake Road, can we go back, I promise I'll be good."

Jack was relaying the information to Jake who was working with a tech team to locate Marissa using her cell phone's GPS chip.

"Jack, they picked up her signal, we have her location. Unless he finds the phone, we can track them. We have a unit on route now. Keep the line open as long as you can, so we know what is going on as long as we can."

"Okay, I'll do my best—wait a minute. The line just went dead. It's not my cell phone, I have plenty of bars, what's going on?"

"Her cell phone must have gone dead. Jack I'm on my way to pick you up. Stay where you are, we'll meet up with Ed and the team."

They turned onto an unmarked dirt road. A few yards down, Alan made a left onto a long, heavily wooded driveway. Eventually they reached a clearing; in the middle was what appeared to be a small, deserted farmhouse. The yard which had seen better days, was overgrown with weeds, remains of dead roses in the beds, and mud puddles where grass had once grown. The wood siding on the house was in desperate need of paint, revealing termite infested graying wood. Several of the windows appeared to have been broken, the victims of rock throwing target practice. The dilapidated front porch listed on one side, its wooden framework eaten away by dry rot and years of neglect. Marissa could only imagine what the inside looked like.

Alan parked behind what looked like a school district work van. He came around to her door to pull her out of the car. He grabbed her arm.

"You don't have to worry. My girls are in there, I'm not going anywhere without them."

"This way," was all he said, pushing her towards the front door.

Once inside, it took Marissa's eyes a few seconds to adjust to the dark room after coming in from outside. There was a battered sofa, an overturned table, and two chairs in a corner.

Broken glass from the shattered windows was scattered on the floor. Cobwebs clung to the decaying paneling, and a constant drip could be heard from a bathroom down the hall. A mouse skittered across the floor, as Mitch stepped out of the door to the basement.

"About time Alan, what took so long?"

"Mitch, I got here—"

"You didn't tie her up?" Mitch backhanded Alan hard across the face. "What were you thinking?"

Alan reached up to touch his lip, when he pulled it away, he could see blood on his fingers, "You busted my lip!"

"Be glad that's all I busted! Here, use this to tie her hands behind her back. Tie her feet together, too," he ordered, throwing a piece of rope to Alan. "Make sure it's nice and tight, we have things to do before we deal with her and we don't' need her making a nuisance of herself. No need to cover her mouth though, because there isn't anyone around for miles." Alan followed his instructions, binding Marissa's hands and feet with the rope, pushing her onto the couch when he had finished. Mitch started to walk away, but Marissa stopped him.

"Mitch where are my girls. I need to know they are safe."

"Don't worry, they're fine. I plan to be real gentle with them like I was with your sister."

Those words were enough for Marissa to throw herself at Mitch, who was just out of her reach. She stumbled and he grabbed her, by both her arms, forcing her back onto the couch. His face was inches away from hers now. "Don't be so anxious, your turn will come. We have unfinished business," as he ran his hand down her body, his breath hot on her face.

Marissa pulled back, repulsed by his touch, "You make me sick," she said as she spat at him.

He pulled his hand back, getting ready to slap her, but then he stopped himself. "Not yet baby, it's too soon. But I'll be back. I still remember you wanted it rough. I wonder how your girls will want it. Alan and me are gonna find out, we'll let you know. Better yet, maybe you'd like to watch? We aren't quite ready yet, so you can wait here, while we get all set up." With that Mitch turned around to leave the room. She could see a revolver in the back of his pants. She would have to be careful from here on out, if she pushed him too far he might shoot them, and she didn't want that. She could hear muffled sounds coming from beyond the door. So far she hadn't heard any screams and she hoped Jack had been able to get help.

She reached into the back of her pants and pulled out her cell phone, hoping that Jack had been able to stay connected. She dropped it onto the couch next to her, but it fell face down. She strained her arms so she could flip it over. When she looked down the LCD screen was completely black. She realized that somewhere along the way the battery had died. Rather than let Mitch see it, she shoved it into the crack in the back of the sofa, it was better that he didn't know she had ever had it in case by some stroke of luck Jack had been able to get anything from it. In the meantime, it would be up to her to get them out of here.

Marissa looked around the room for anything she thought could be used as a weapon against one of them. With her hands tied behind her back she could hardly hit them over the head with a chair. She doubted that would really work anyway, since she'd only seen that done in the movies. She had been trained in self-defense, but she needed either the element of surprise or the use of either her hands or her feet. Then she noticed the shards of glass lying by the window. She dropped down on the floor and inch-wormed her way across the room on her stomach. When she was within reach she rolled her body so her hands could pick up a couple of pieces. Then she scooted back over to the sofa. It took every bit of energy she had to push herself back up onto the couch, but she finally managed it. She managed to put one piece of the broken glass into her jeans pocket. She crammed the others into the cushions, except for one, that she began to use on the ropes around her hands. It wasn't easy and she knew she had very little time before he'd be back for her, but it was her only chance.

Chapter 59

Ed Carson and his security convoy rendezvoused with Jack and Jake on Lake Road at the point where they had picked up the last signal from Marissa's cell phone. They were looking at a map of the area spread out on the hood of Ed's car. He quickly highlighted any artery that branched off of Lake Road. Fortunately it was a country road, mostly open farmland, with fenced barriers to keep trespassers out. There weren't too many turn offs before the road came to a dead end at the Lake. Ed split his men up into eight groups, who immediately began canvassing the area. Jack stayed behind with Ed, wanting to be near where the information would be coming in.

Alan came back in the room. "It's party time. Mitch says I need to bring you in for a front row seat."

Marissa closed her hand around the glass piece and pulled the rope taunt, hiding the frayed pieces in her fisted hands. Alan untied the rope at her feet, grabbed her arm and led her into the basement, depositing her on a chair in the corner. She could see her daughters lying on a bed at the room's center both stripped down to their underwear. She could read a mixture of fear and relief when she was brought in. Trepidation came over her as she took in her surroundings. There was a familiar eeriness about this place. It was dark, the walls were unfinished, a single light bulb hung from the beams overhead. A tool bench was along one wall containing wood working tools and some rope.

Cassandra called out to her, "Mom!"

"Shut up!" Mitch shouted. "Did I say you could talk?"

Cassandra shrunk back. Marissa felt so helpless.

"It's movie time. You get to play the part of Jeannette Van Horn," he said to Cassandra, then to Samantha he said, "And you get to play the part of Marissa Van Horn. And lucky Jared here, gets to play the part of sweet little ole me. Jared you are going to be a star, before this night is through and you are going to be so thankful you will want to write me into your will. Now Alan here is our camera man, I'm the director and Marissa let's see, what can you be? Hmm…I know you can be the acting coach; it'll be your job to be sure that Jared here is creating the right mood. Now since I didn't like the first take on this twenty five years ago, I've taken the liberty of rewriting the script to play out more like I had in mind. I think you girls will get the idea as we go along, if Jared is doing his job right."

Alan took up his position, standing behind the video camera perched on a tripod in the opposite corner. Jared who was standing off to one side, had been stripped down to his boxers, and had his arms across his chest, his shoulders were slightly hunched over. He was clearly uncomfortable and kept averting his eyes.

"Okay Jared you're up. Now the first thing we need to do is get our Marissa Van Horn restrained. So you're going to have to use some of this rope and tie up her hands and feet.

Jared looked at Samantha. He refused to take the rope from Mitch. "What's the matter Jared, don't you want to be the star?"

"Not really," Jared mumbled slightly under his breath.

"What was that?"

"Not really," Jared said loud enough to be heard this time.

"You don't want to do this? Jared, Jared, what are we going to do with you? I get it, actors need motivation. How about this, you either tape up Samantha here, or I put a bullet through your brain. Is that enough motivation to get you going?"

"Yes sir," Jared reluctantly took the tape and approached Samantha. "I'm sorry, Sam, I don't want to do this."

"I know, it's okay Jared, do what he tells you so we can get out of here."

"How touching, get on with it!" Mitch ordered. When Jared had finished, Mitch turned to Marissa, "Now here is where you come in. Anytime that Jared isn't acting his part to his fullest ability, you need to correct him. If you don't, I will shoot him. Am I clear?"

"Yes," Marissa replied.

"Good. Now, Jared, my man, you get to climb on top of Jeannette. She's not like her sister over there that likes things fast and rough, Jeannette is sweet and tender, so you need to draw it out more. Make it slow and memorable, but still show her what you're made of. Alan are we ready to roll tape?"

"Yep."

"Action!"

Jared walked over and timidly crawled on top of Cassandra. He couldn't bear to look at her, feeling as humiliated as she did. "Stop it Mitch, don't put them through this. Can't you see they are just kids? They don't deserve this. Just let them go!" Marissa shouted.

"Cut, cut, cut!" Mitch called out, "Alan rewind tape, Jared, get up," He walked over to Marissa and grabbed her throat; "One more outburst like that and you will lose your job and will have to go back into the other room!" He relaxed his grip leaving Marissa gasping for air.

"Places, and....action!"

Jared again reluctantly climbed onto Cassandra, this time meeting her eyes. She turned her head away squeezing back the tears. Jared lay there, not quite knowing what was expected of him next.

"Cut, cut, cut! Jared, what's wrong now? Haven't you ever made it with a girl?"

"No."

"No! You mean you're a virgin? How old are you?"

"Sixteen"

"I thought all you kids had sex by the time you were fourteen. Okay, I'm gonna have to take you out and explain some things." He grabbed Jared pulling him up the stairs and out into the living room, slamming the door behind him.

Marissa had been working the glass against the rope. Each time she had cut through a section of braiding it was giving away a little more. Finally, she was able to get through the last one. She was careful to keep her hands behind her, keeping the rope from falling to the floor.

"Alan, you know you never did let me stop and use the bathroom, do you think it'd be okay if I used that one?"

"I guess. I'm only gonna untie your feet though and you got to keep the door open where I can see you and the girls at the same time."

He knelt down on the floor to untie her feet, so she could walk across the room. That's when she made her move. She waited until her feet were free. With Alan still bent over her, she brought her knee up as fast as she could, at the same time she held her two hands clasped together and brought them down hard on the top of his head, driving her knee into his nose. She grabbed a handful of his hair. Pulling his head up with one hand, she used the butt of her palm to ram his nose into his brain. Alan's eyes rolled back into his head before he slumped over onto a heap on the floor.

Marissa called out to Cassandra, who was already frazzled from the day's events. Now she was more than just a little shocked at watching her mom take down Alan using karate moves she'd only seen in the movies. "Cassie, come help me move him, quick, before Mitch gets back."

Cassandra was still a little dazed, and didn't respond at first. "Cassandra, please we don't have much time."

Marissa grabbed Alan from under the armpits and instructed Cassandra to pick up his feet. They could still hear Mitch outside the door, getting louder, obviously growing impatient with Jared.

"Let's get him into the bathroom." Cassandra followed her mom into the bathroom, where they dumped Alan in the shower. "Okay, you go lay back down as you were. Marissa turned on the water in the sink and the exhaust fan, then shut and locked the door behind her. She resumed her spot on the chair, wrapping the rope around her ankles and holding her hands behind her back. She looked at her daughters, “We’re going to get out of this, don’t worry. Help is on the way.” Both girls nodded in acknowledgement. Then they heard a gunshot.

Chapter 60

Ed's men checked in at what they had now set up as home base on the side of the road.

"Team two to base, over."

"Base to team two what have you got? Over."

"Ed, we've found what looks like an abandoned house about a mile north of your location. Its driveway is off a dirt road, about three quarters mile on the left from your present location. The driveway is somewhat hidden by the overgrowth. We went down to the end of it, and there looks like there are two vehicles; one white SUV and one work van. Requesting back up to check it out, over."

"Base to team three, you copy?"

"Roger that, we are en route. Over"

"We will wait at the drive way for team three. Damn it! What was that?....Base, we just heard a gunshot, over."

"All units to team two's location. Team two are you able to see anything, over?"

"Negative base, over."

"Team two wait for back up before entering the building. Over."

"Roger, Base."

Mitch came waltzing through the door, "Okay, we had some artistic differences and could not reach a compromise. Jared's contract was terminated with our studio. Anyone want to join him? No? Okay, let's get back to work. Alan will now be taking over for Jared, and I will be director and camera man. Alan, you ready?" Just now noticing that Alan wasn't behind the camera, he looked around. "Where's Alan?"

Cassandra pointed to the bathroom. Mitch tried the door, but it was locked. He could hear the water running from inside. He banged on the door, "Alan, hurry it up, we have work to do!"

Marissa could see the gun in the back of Mitch's waistband. If she could somehow get him close enough to her she could grab it.

"Mitch please, let the girls go. You have me, you don't need them."

"To the contrary, they are a rare commodity. Just look at them, all those years I lost. It's as if time has stood still and here I am, right back where I started. Who says you can't go home?" He walked over to Cassandra and ran a sweaty hand up her leg. Instinctively, she pulled her legs together. "See, now that's acting! That's what I'm looking for. Raw, unbridled talent." He reached up to touch her face, again she turned away. "They really do look just like you, how fortunate for me. It really gives a more realistic reenactment don't you think?"

"Did you know that your mom and I go way back? Long before she met your dad. Good times, good times. That's what gave me the idea to do a movie about the whole thing. I already have investors lining up to buy it when I'm done. Men just can't get enough of young, innocent girls. They especially love twins, so you two will be famous."

He looked over at Samantha, "Don't worry honey, plenty of ole Mitch here to go around. I'm really counting on you to make a real man out of Alan. He won't be as good as me though, I'm saving the best for last," reaching out with his hand to touch her breast. Samantha shrugged her shoulders trying to knock his hand way.

"Mitch, stop it! Stop it! Don't you lay a hand on them!"

Mitch looked over at Marissa, "What's the matter mom? Don't like your daughter getting all the attention?"

Marissa was trying to draw Mitch over to her, so she could get him away from the girls, but so far the plan wasn't working. Cassie looked over at her mom, holding her gaze for a moment. Marissa read something in her daughter's eyes, and shook her head 'No'.

Cassandra looked at Samantha. The two of them nodded. Mitch was still standing over her. Cassie used her feet to push Mitch away, Sam rolled sideways off the bed. Mitch regained his balance and went to the foot of the bed, bending down to pick Samantha back up off the floor. Marissa used the opportunity to make her move. She got up and jerked the gun from Mitch's waistband. Mitch dropped Samantha back to the floor, and spun around to face Marissa.

Mitch stopped cold, when he realized the barrel of his colt .45 was pointed at him.

Chapter 61

Ed passed out assignments to each of his men. While the teams were getting in position, team two had moved in on the house, looking in windows to further assess the situation. They could see into the living room, and beyond it into the kitchen, where there appeared to be a body lying on the floor. The doors off the living room were closed. They could hear muffled voices and were working their way around to the back of the house. They could hear sounds of running water coming from the basement. As they rounded the building muffled voices were becoming louder. They found a second basement window that had been boarded up with plywood. They could hear Marissa pleading with Mitch not to harm her daughters. They were unable to ascertain how many men there were, how they were armed, or where the girls were. They would be going in blind, with just one way in and one way out. That put them at a real disadvantage when it came to keeping the girls safe. They crept back to the edge of the yard, where they wouldn't be seen or heard before relaying their findings.

Marissa backed away, trying to get Mitch to step further away from her daughters. "Marissa, I think you need to hand that back to me. You know you're not going to use it. I'm going to get it eventually. You're not even holding it right."

She had to use both hands to hold the gun. Although Retread had taught her how to shoot a weapon, it had been years since she had held one in her hand. It felt cold, heavy and awkward.

"Cass, help your sister get the ropes off okay? Mitch, you need to make your way to the bathroom door, nice and slow. I'm not real steady and it'd be a shame if this went off accidentally."

Marissa's pulse was racing, holding a gun on Mitch was empowering. For the first time since she was sixteen she was in control of him. She slid the safety off, as she pointed Mitch to the door. She stole a look at the girls who were now on the floor in the corner together. Putting herself between Mitch and the girls, she stood in the passageway to the stairs.

"Okay girls, go get in the SUV out front. Alan left the keys in it. If I'm not out in five minutes I want you to drive away from here. No matter what happens, or what you hear, you are not to come back in here."

The girls did as they were told, easing behind their Mom. "Mom, what are you going to do? We don't want to leave you in here with him," Samantha said.

"Sam, I'll be right there, you go, right now. Get the car started."

Marissa waited until she heard the car idling out front. "It's just you and me now Mitch. I think I've known all along this day would come. I've always known it would come down to either you or me."

Mitch was desperately trying to figure out how to regain control of the situation. This wasn't the way he had seen this playing out. He knew he could take her. He lunged towards her, just missing the gun, but knocking them both to the floor. The gun flew from Marissa's hands, sliding across the floor. He was on top of her now, reaching over and past her to retrieve the weapon. His weight fully supported by her body now, she could feel something piercing her skin at the top of her hip. She fumbled around a bit, reaching into her pocket finding the jagged piece of glass she had put there earlier. She pulled it out and used it to tear into Mitch's face. He jerked his head back in surprise, bringing the gun up with him. He now had the gun pointing at Marissa's head.

"I'm ready to end this right now, Bitch!"

Marissa heard the car pulling away. She was ready, for whatever he did next. The barrel of the gun felt cool against her forehead. Mitch was still sitting on top of her, and she was certain this was the end. At least she had been able to get the girls out of there. Beads of sweat were forming on his brow as Mitch cocked the gun.

Everything seemed like it was moving in slow motion now. The sound of metal on metal, the clicking noise it made as it the mechanisms slid into place; the sound of the bullet tumbling into the chamber; Marissa couldn't hear anything else. The sounds so loud in her head, a freight train could be passing by and she wouldn't have heard it.

She could feel herself trembling and she hated herself for giving him the satisfaction. She squeezed her eyes shut, not wanting the last image in her head to be of Mitch Olsen's face.

She pictured her family, happily sitting around a picnic table. She didn't want to think of herself not there with them. She braced herself, preparing for the last sound she would hear in her life, waiting for it to come.

Ed's men intercepted the girls as soon as they made the dirt road. They quickly pulled them to safety, throwing jackets and shirts over them. Ed wasted no time in trying to get answers about what was going on inside. They told them that when they left Marissa had the gun, but they weren't sure what had happened after that.

"Good job, girls" Jack said to his daughters. "I'm so glad you're safe. Are you okay here for a few minutes, I want to make sure your mom gets out safely, too?" The girls both nodded, and Jack disappeared into a group of men hovering in the bushes.

Ed instructed his men, to go in through the front and back doors, quietly as they didn't want to distract Marissa, giving Mitch a chance to take the gun, if she still had it. Once in place they would all go in together. They crept along the sides and front of the house, keeping low as to avoid being seen through a window. Then they waited for Ed to give the order.

Once he saw they were in place, another gunshot went off. "Move in! All teams go! Go! Go!" Ed yelled into the walkie-talkies. The team rushed the house, running towards the basement, and down the stairs.

Jack heard one of the agents yelling, "Mr. Olsen, we have you surrounded. Put your weapon down and place your hands on your head." He ran in the house, trying to get to his wife. An agent stopped him at the top of the stairs. "Mr. Deerfield, hold on for just a minute please." Jack could see past him, his wife lying on the floor, a puddle of blood pooling around her.

Chapter 62

Alan Olsen lowered his weapon and placed it on the floor; he put his hands on his head and waited for the agent to restrain him. Two men, picked Mitch up pulling him off of Marissa, before reaching down to help her up. "Are you okay Mrs. Deerfield?"

"Yes, I think so."

Jack rushed in to her, pulling her to him. "I thought I had lost you."

"I thought you had too. It took me a few seconds to realize it wasn't me that was shot!"

The police had Alan in custody. They were getting ready to walk him out to a squad car. Marissa stopped them, "Just a minute guys..Alan, I'm not sure how or why you did what you did, but thank you."

"I woke up in the bathroom, I heard him out there, saying things, doing things, I knew were wrong. All the things he had told me all these years were a lie. I couldn't let him do it to you again. I couldn't let him do it to me again. It's over. You have nothing to fear from me. I am not my brother."

Retread agents pushed him forward and took him out to a waiting van. They would turn him over to the FBI for prosecution.

Marissa looked down at Mitch's body, in a heap on the floor. She turned to Jack, "You heard him, it's over. It's finally over."

Jack threw an arm around his wife and steered her towards the door, just as the paramedics pulled a gurney past the hallway. Marissa pulled away and rushed towards the opening. "Is Jared okay?" She asked as she kept pace with the EMTs.

"He has a gunshot wound to his abdomen, a head nasty head trauma and he's lost a lot of blood. He's unconscious, but he seems to be holding his own right now. We already have the hospital on alert with a surgeon on standby. I'd say he has a good chance."

"You hang in there Jared!" she said giving his hand a squeeze before they loaded him into the ambulance.

Jack pulled Marissa out of the way and turned her towards their waiting family. The girls rushed to her side, folding their arms around her. "Let's get you checked out so we can go home," he said as he led the group to the waiting medic team. The scene was filled with emergency vehicles, police officers, FBI and Retread employees. But that all blurred into the background as Marissa was finally able to let the events of the day sink in. It was finally over, this time for good.

Two men dressed in FBI uniforms stood away from the group watching.

"Chaplain, do you think we need to finish this thing?"

"No, she was only a threat to Mitchell's peace of mind."

"What about Alan? Are we going to take him out?"

"He doesn't know enough about us. Carl, I say we leave well enough alone. Let's get out of here."

Chapter 63

Vivian Olsen had been interviewed by Oprah, for a series on "Violence In the Family." Alan Olsen had made bail; his attorney had presented an argument based on diminished responsibility, saying he had been under duress. Cynthia Marshall found that she didn't miss Mitchell. Alan was really more her type. She would stand by him through the trial, saying they'd figure it out together.

Ed Carson had exposed a mole in his office, the same one who sold information on the Deerfield family's location. This finding initiated a full scale audit of their facility's hiring practices and procedures. It also required the relocation a few clients that they felt were at risk as a result of the breech in their security. Fortunately the damage was minimal compared to what could have been catastrophic.

Jared had made a full recovery and had been able to return to school before breaking for the summer. The girls made sure he was well taken care of. The three of them were inseparable. No matter what happened between him and Cassie, he would always be part of their family.

When the story, inclusive of Marissa's history, broke, it made national headlines. For the following weeks, the media followed her relentlessly, camping on her front lawn. Friends and their community rallied around the Deerfields, refusing to comment when approached by the reporters, so the buzz quickly died down.

Two months later, when life had finally returned to normal, the Deerfield family was finally having their backyard cook out. They had extended their invitation list to include the people at Retread, not as body guards but as guests. Mrs. Gottsfrey had flown in, and so had Ben and Betsy and their two kids. It was a sunny day, flowers were in bloom.

Ed was sitting at a table with Jack and Marissa as they watched the families socializing, laughing and enjoying themselves. "So, have you thought about your futures? I have something I'd like you to think about. I am getting ready to open an office in Houston. Marissa, you have the experience that we need to head up the office there. The pay will be great; I hear home prices are reasonable. Jack, they are holding a spot open for you at NASA as part of the engineering team."

"I think it's time to start those burgers, don't you?" Jack said to Marissa.

"They're in the fridge. Ed, how about a beer, would you like a beer?" Marissa asked.

"Aren't you even going to think about it?" Ed asked

Marissa got up, and waited for Ed to do the same. She leaned down and kissed him on the cheek.

"Ed, we couldn't have made it without you. We appreciate everything you have done for us and you are welcome in our home any time. It's a very nice offer, but we have everything we need right here."

"If you change your mind…"

"Ed, you're looking kind of tired, have you considered early retirement? Come on, let's go join the others. I don't think you've met Mrs. Gottsfrey yet, have you?"